Milton
in
America

BY PETER ACKROYD

Milton
in
America

PETER ACKROYD

Nan A. Talese

DOUBLEDAY

NEW YORK   LONDON

TORONTO   SYDNEY   AUCKLAND

PUBLISHED BY NAN A. TALESE
an imprint of Doubleday
a division of Bantam Doubleday Dell Publishing Group, Inc.
1540 Broadway, New York, New York 10036

DOUBLEDAY is a trademark of Doubleday, a division of
Bantam Doubleday Dell Publishing Group, Inc.

Book design by Claire Naylon Vaccaro

Library of Congress Cataloging-in-Publication Data
Ackroyd, Peter, 1949–
Milton in America / Peter Ackroyd. — 1st ed.
p.   cm.
1. Milton, John, 1608–1674—Journeys—America—Fiction.
I. Title.
PR6051.C64M55   1997
823'.914—DC20   96-22234
CIP

First published in the United Kingdom by Sinclair-Stevenson, London.

ISBN 0-385-47708-2
Printed in the United States of America
April 1997
First Edition in the United States of America

1   3   5   7   9   10   8   6   4   2

FOR CARL DENNISON

John Milton, the poet of Comus *and of "Il Penseroso," was also Latin Secretary for Foreign Tongues to the Council of Oliver Cromwell. His sympathies had been with the regicides, therefore, and he had even written a tract justifying the execution of Charles I. So by the early months of 1660, when it became clear that the Commonwealth was about to fall and Charles II return to England, Milton believed himself to be a man forsaken. He would be hunted down, imprisoned and no doubt executed for his collusion with the new king's enemies. He had been struck by blindness eight years before, and could scarcely remain unknown or unrecognized in London. He had no choice but to escape, while there was still opportunity to do so. And where better to flee than New England, where he would be assured of a joyful welcome from the Puritans who had already settled there?*

PART ONE

Eden

ONE

Come on board, friend Menippus, and float in the Tartarean air. The sparkling waves do smoke again, and there is sorrow on the sea. From the face of the deep, I call to thee. Sirens. Leviathan. The white-headed waters will not be quiet. Fair blow the winds, now strike your happy sails. Port after stormy seas is best. Spice, and ivory, and apes. The unmeasured ocean of my mind is forever beating.

Mr. Milton, sir.

To bed, John. The candle is dwindling. You punish your eyes with too much study. The dawn comes, and the sun strikes the rooftops of Bread Street, but you brood over fables and histories. What book is this, lying open on your elbow chair? *Nel mezzo del camin di nostra vita.* The poetry of Italy, in which I once wandered. Lycidas. Wandering down East Cheap. Odes. Heroes. I see blind Samson, snared and taken in the darkness. The fruit of lechery is woe, yet I am tempted still. Ah, Samson, in the eternity of East Cheap. In my youth I was handsome and beardless. In my youth I was desirous of great things. Come away, sir, come away. You must involve yourself in the affairs of men. Here are letters for the Council. The envoy waits.

Mr. Milton, wake up.

The voyage of Palinurus was not more blessed than this. I have sailed upon the rivers of London, the Walbrook and the Fleet, and I have crossed the lakes of Italy. The storm within your head, Aeneas, is known to me. Your journey is mine. And when the goddess Diana prophesied of Britain, he awoke and found the vision to be holy. He sailed away to that blessed isle, that isle of angels, as I am sailing now. England, new England. Will the towers of Elysium rise in the land? Or will this vision be dimmed? Oh yes, the stars move. We drift across the sky as well as the sea. Arthur. Arcturus. Pleiades. Sevenfold. When I was born, the wind was north. When the morning stars sang together, I started my journey.

Awake, Mr. Milton. Sir. Please.

Then the sun shone between the clouds as a blessing, lighting my face, and I could hear the mariners. Store away. Make safe. A storm. A tempest upon the waters. We are hard-pressed upon the rocks of Attica, and the flames on the headland presage our fate. Oh, you spirits of the deep, restore us. Revive my hopes, for I am blind. I am drifting down, and with Odysseus I walk among the drowned men with imploring eyes. Dark and deep. Oh, Lord, deliver us from the dream. And after this our exile.

Please rouse yourself, Mr. Milton.

What? What is it?

We have caught sight of the new land!

T W O

Is this our ending? Is this the long-wished-for shore?" His ebony chair was tied to a barrel of pickled herring on the deck, and a thick rope bound his waist securely. He was wearing a canvas coat, with long sleeves which billowed in the wind he had felt upon his face. His eyes were very wide. "Tell me, Goosequill. What do you see?"

"Grey stones like a marble. Great pebbles. Tall grass. It might be Hackney marshes on a wet morning."

"Fool. Look again."

The boy stood by his master, with his hand resting lightly upon his shoulder. "I can see little bays and sandy places. I see bushes." He began to whistle an old refrain, until his master asked him to be quiet. "The sea is calm enough now, sir. Shall I untie you?"

"No. Wait a little. I sense a movement through the water."

Goosequill was familiar with the blind man's unexpected but accurate impressions, and he remained quite still beside him; as he looked out toward Massachusetts Bay, the ship did indeed begin to toss and sway. "Oh, Lord. There is something else. Something on the foreshore."

"Speak."

"There is some kind of fire, and there are figures dancing around it. They might be foxes."

"Foxes never dance, except in masques. They frisk and gambol, but they have no flowing motions. These things may be natives, or devils. Do you believe in devils, Goosequill?" John Milton smiled, but then shivered in the strengthening wind. "Lead me within."

The boy untied him from the barrel, and helped him rise from his chair before guiding him through a narrow door and passage which led to the interior of the ship. There was always the same odor of corn and camphor, of orange peel and pepper, of vermin and gunpowder, of beef, and oatmeal, and beer, and cheese, all mingled but not mixed. After the sea breezes and the fresh wind of New England, they might have been entering the stale air of their London past. Some other passengers, hastening eagerly to the deck, waited reverently for John Milton to pass them. They bowed to him as he walked slowly towards his cabin, and then rushed out for their first sight of the new land. "It is truly the Lord's country," one of them called out. "It is an Eden in the wilderness." Milton stopped and smiled, as another traveler took up the refrain. "So proud a people will take root here, that a tree will grow towards heaven. We will be the cedars of the promised land!"

"I wish to God," Milton whispered, "that they would talk more sense and less simile."

The wind had strengthened, but someone called back into the ship. "Mr. Milton, we will soon have our port within sight! Freedom and glory, sir!" The blind man muttered a word or two, and Goosequill laughed out loud. "What was that, sir?"

"I was glossing the sacred text, Mr. Jackson, that God loveth a cheerful speaker."

Goosequill took his arm again, and led him down the passageway; Milton was so accustomed to this short journey to his cabin that he instinctively bowed his head as he passed under two great beams. His quarters were next to those of the captain of the *Gabriel,* Daniel Farrel; he was the most honored of the travelers upon this vessel, and had been given the greatest room. They had been eight weeks at sea but Milton's "lodgings," as he insisted upon calling them, were as clean and orderly as if they had left England only the day before. "Will you open the chest," he asked the boy as soon as they entered. "I yearn for ginger."

"I see conserve of roses, sir. Very good for the bowels. No? Wormwood for the stomach? Oh, here are some cinnamon and sugar, which sit nicely with good wine. I see no ginger, Mr. Milton."

"I was sucking upon a stick yesterday. Pass me the leather bag." It contained only dried herbs and the juice of lemons, which could not cure the sickness of the sea. "We are reduced to cinnamon, Goose." He sighed, and lay back against his canvas bedding stuffed with straw. "So is this the region? Is this the soil and clime?"

"I hope it is, sir. Otherwise we have made a long voyage to Blankshire in the realm of Nothing."

"Not a realm, you worm, a land. We will be free of all kingly follies here."

"I am glad to hear it. I never liked a ruler."

There was a loud knock upon the door, and they heard the voice of Captain Farrel. "Good morning, sir! May I?"

"It is the captain of brandy and barley sugar, Goose. Please to open the door." He waited until he knew that the captain was standing in front of him. "What news?"

"We are riding by Cape Ann. If we are not becalmed, we are only a few hours from Boston Harbor."

"So in the darkness of the night we have passed Winicowett and the mouth of the Merrimack?"

"I trust so."

"And our precise point now?" John Milton had, in his blindness, visualized the entire map of this region so that it had assumed full shape and volume in his mind; he could touch each bay or coast, and New England lay before him like a sleeper ready to awake.

The captain already knew his skill. "We are forty-four degrees and thirty minutes of north latitude, sir."

"So we have passed half of our New Albion. But the wind is stirring from the southwest, is it not?"

"So it is."

"Then surely we must stand about west-northwest in order to make our way?"

"Beautiful!" Goosequill pressed his knees together with pure pleasure at Milton's sagacity; there were times when he was almost convinced that his companion could still see.

"I have given those precise orders. You have a maritime humor, Mr. Milton."

After the captain had left them and returned to the deck, Milton rubbed his eyes savagely. "Maritime," he murmured to himself. "Merry time. Mary's time."

"Sir?"

"I was ringing the bells of our language. If I am not mistaken, there will be many a carillon issuing from this land. Better by far than our own sad and cracked notes. Yet will it still be our language after we have traveled so far?''

"I can still understand it, sir, except when you talk in rhymes or riddles.''

"But think of that dreadful waste we have crossed. Nine hundred leagues.''

"Dark and deep.''

"Those black-browed waves. Vaulted high and yawning wide to devour us.''

"We must have been very bitter. We were spewed out fast enough.''

"The mind has its oceans, too, Goosequill. It has its gulfs and currents. You have often told me that the sea is mild and temperate, but I have my own inward sight that reaches the highest altitudes and the furthest depths—''

Goosequill mouthed at the blind man, "Ordure of the highest altitudes.''

"—to bring angels or devils back into the thoughts of men.''

They sat in silence for a few moments, sucking companionably upon the cinnamon. "I am told,'' Milton said, "that Boston is a very fair town.''

"They say that the streets are paved with pebble stone.''

"Who are *they?*'' He did not wait for an answer. "It has no parishes, but there are three fine churches where we will be welcomed. Do you think I should present them with my new translations of the psalms?''

"It would be a charitable offering, sir.''

"Not that I need introduction or recommendation.''

"Of course not."

"I do not flatter myself. And it is better to be great here, Goosequill, than to serve evil men in London."

The *Gabriel* had kept its course, and to the starboard side the crowd of voyagers observed a lowland of cliffs, sand hills and rough vegetation; in this last week of June a mist had settled upon the sea, and the new land sometimes seemed to shiver and disappear into the haze. They had known only England: when the coast appeared again it was as if their own country had emerged from the waves, newborn, as empty and as pure as it had been before the Druids subdued it with their magic.

"The bay ahead!" One of the crew was crying out, and his voice could be heard even in Milton's quarters. "We sound ninety-three fathoms!"

Goosequill took Milton's arm and, putting the cinnamon in the pocket of his master's coat, led him back to the deck. "That yonker on the mast has an eye as good as Cyclops," he said.

"Do not employ classical allusions. What do you see?"

"White cliffs."

"Like those at Dover. No wonder that our fathers knew it to be home."

"It is in the shape of a half-moon, with two arms out-stretched towards us." As the ship was driven closer to the coastline, Goosequill leaned over the rail of the deck. "There is a high shore, sir, but many places of lowland. I see three rivers, or streams, running down into the low places."

"It is the bay of our hopes." John Milton held out his arms. "All hail, you happy fields!" Then a shadow passed across his face, and he put his finger up to his cheek. "What was that?"

"A little cloud. A little cloud coming to greet us."

"It is from the northwest?"

"I think it may be."

"Is it black?"

"An ash color. No. Grey like a pickled herring, with spots of a darker hue."

"Then I am sure that our good captain will soon have something to tell us. Do you sense the wind once more?"

"You sense it before I feel it, sir. Oh yes. Here it comes."

"A wind from that quarter is an evil omen, Goosequill. It is a harbinger of storm."

"A harbinger?"

"Messenger. Herald. Forerunner in the race. Do I have to be your primer as well as your provider?"

"If I am your eyes, sir, then surely you can be my words."

"Enough. Do you feel the air growing colder? This is an envious wind, Goose, frustrated, vagabond."

Already Captain Farrel was calling to his men; there was a general activity around Milton which caused him to turn his head eagerly, trying to catch every shouted word and hurried footfall. The other travelers were still huddled by the rail; the men held on to their hats, while the women tightened the pigskin threads of their hoods, as the deck shifted beneath them and the rigging began to beat against the wood. One of the sailors began to sing an old-fashioned rhyme about the curling sea, and all those who heard him knew that a storm approached. But it came more quickly than even the captain anticipated; the dark clouds bore down from the northwest, and with them came a cold wind so strong that the *Gabriel* was driven out to sea again. Milton clung to the rail, and shouted to his boy in the face of the encroaching gale, "Once more we are forced to commit ourselves to the troubled ocean!" Yet he loved a tempest. "Tie me to the rail. God plays with us like a boy with cherry stones. He is always the gamester!" Goosequill knotted the cord around Milton's waist, and then fastened it to the wooden rail. His master's fear seemed to have turned to exaltation and, as the wind and the rain whipped about him, he began to sing very loudly:

"So with thy whirlwind them pursue
And with thy tempest chase
And till they yield the honor due
Lord fill with shame their face."

"You are soaked to the bone, sir . . ."

"Ashamed and troubled let them be,
Troubled and shamed for ever,
Ever confounded, and so then die
With shame and evil weather."

He had a strong clear voice which could easily be heard between the blasts of the storm; he was singing death to his enemies, but this was in fact his translation of the Eighty-third Psalm which he had completed before leaving London and had committed to memory. The rain beat upon his upturned face and open eyes, as the *Gabriel* was drawn out to the open sea. His canvas coat was thoroughly sodden, and his long hair clung upon the skin of his neck and lay flat upon his damp collar. Goosequill stood behind with his hands firmly grasping Milton's shoulders, in case his master should be pitched upon the heaving deck or into the troubled waters, and still Milton sang.

Captain Farrel advanced unsteadily towards him, and shouted in his face. "Go below, sir! Now! A stiff gale has come upon us, and an overgrown sea!"

"I trust in my providence, Captain. I shall not go out like some candle in a snuff."

But he was speaking to the air: the captain had already hurried away, and was at once shouting commands to his crew. "Bear up the helm! Bring the ship to right and fetch the loglines to try what way she makes. Turn up the minute glass, and observe the height!" His words were like swarms and wings around Milton, but even then he could also hear the topsail being taken in and the foresail lowered in homage to the tempest. Then there was the sound of something breached or broken—he thought it was the ship itself but, from the cries of the mariners, he realized that the mainsail was being torn to pieces in the gale. Something rolled past him on the deck, and Goosequill let out a cry which might have been a laugh or a scream. "There goes our tub," he said. "That's where the fish were salting!"

A small party of the other travelers were now lamenting and praying loudly, while three of their number tried to make their way against the wind with their cloaks covering each other from the rain. One of them carried two horseshoes and, in the old-country custom, tried to nail them upon the deck as a charm against the violent sea. Goosequill watched, delighted, and described the scene to his master. "They slide like children at Frost Fair, sir!"

Milton kept his face up to the roaring sky as he spoke.

"They have become like the Indians in preparation for our landing!" Another barrel rolled past him. "The sea has turned more than their stomachs. It has turned their wits."

"We will soon be turning in very watery graves if we do not go within. Come, sir, for your safety's sake."

Milton laughed out loud, and his laughter was mingled with the elements. "Are you ready to be pinched and tossed in the reeling cabin?"

"I am."

"Then untie me. This storm has beaten us under the hatches."

The crosswinds drove the *Gabriel* from its appointed course but, after they had passed Cape Cod, the wind dropped and the rain abated. They had lost sight of land, but throughout that night Captain Farrel consulted the charts and the stars; he guessed, correctly, that they had passed the large island known variously on his maps as Nope, Capawock, Martha's Vineyard and Martin's Vineyard. But were they now to be driven upon the grey rocks and small islands that were so marked and treacherous a feature of this New England coast? At first light he found his bearings: the *Gabriel,* pitching on the still-restless sea, was less than half a league from a large island of hills and brushwood known to the captain as Munisses or Block Island.

"He plans to chart our course past Block Island," Goosequill was explaining to his master, "and make landfall at Petty something in the country of the Narrow—"

"Pettaquamscutt. Narragansett. Barbarous names. But not an alien shore."

They were walking upon the upper deck, past the broken tackle and the mainmast which hung in the shrouds with its sails rent in pieces. Only the spread-sail remained intact, to spoon before the wind and take them slowly towards the shore. "Like a rotten rag," Goosequill said. "Our little house has collapsed around us, sir, with all its beams showing their wrong side. We might have come from the world's end."

"Be less poetical, Goose. It does not suit you." Suddenly he was still. "What is that rustling near me?"

"A rat?"

"No. Quite different. Look behind you." Milton gazed, sightless, over the boy's shoulder.

Goosequill turned towards the wooden rail, and then touched his master's arm. "It is a bird," he whispered. "A pigeon. Like our pigeons from the woods, but more strongly colored."

"Does it move?"

"He chews his breast with his beak."

"It is our first greeting from the new land. This bird of calm has flown over the charmed waves towards us. I wish it had something in its mouth. A twig. A flower. Anything." He paused. "Now it is flying away?"

"He is going towards the land. Oh, yes, he is joined by another."

"They represent our hopes, Goosequill. As we follow them towards the destined shore."

The boy watched the birds until they were out of sight, and then with a sigh turned to his master. "Do you wish me to describe the little islands on our starboard side?"

"Are they highly delightful?"

"Oh no. Very barren and forlorn."

"Good. Continue."

"Very great black cliffs." He always took pleasure in his more doleful pictures, as Milton did also. "Much clay and dark sand. Sharp rocks. Hills with no shrubs." He put his hand up to shield his eyes from the sun. "There is one coming near us which has diverse colored rocks. There are mulberries or some such growing upon them. I wonder how trees could grow on such hard foundation."

"This is as God made it, Goosequill, when He created the world."

"Well, sir, it is desolate enough."

"Sacred, not desolate. If there is no rock so barren that a tree cannot grow upon it, then there is no land so forlorn that it cannot be nourished." He believed that he could still hear the beating of the wings of the birds.

The boatswain was calling the men to prayers, even as Milton spoke. At that moment, too, a fresh wind sprang up and caught the sail of the spread-mast; the ship shuddered and started to veer northeastward towards the small islands which Goosequill had described. Its tackle creaked so loudly that the prayers of the mariners could hardly be heard. "O eternal Lord God who alone spreadest out the heavens, and rulest the raging of the seas. Who hast compassed the waters with bounds until day and night come to an end—"

"Listen," Milton said. "Do you hear the movement of the wood? The boat is singing. It is singing to the angels who guide us."

It seemed, indeed, to be a fortunate wind; although the *Gabriel* could not keep the course that the captain had anticipated, it was driven past Block Island without running upon any of the foul ground and shoals which lay among these waters. Captain Farrel had come to Milton's side after the prayers were over. "God be thanked," he said. "We will land safely near Sakonnet Point without much trimming or steering among the rocks. You will then have the honor, sir, of being the first to set foot from this ship upon dry land."

So they made their way towards the shore, with the other travelers giving loud praise to the Lord as if they were in a conventicle. Milton stood with Goosequill at the stern, since he had said that he wished to face England at the moment of their deliverance from the sea and their arrival in the new land. The others were crowded upon the half-deck at the helm, where they felt the power of the restless and boisterous wind which again changed direction: the ship veered northwestward away from Sakonnet Point and drifted towards a more desolate part of the shore. The pilot and captain saw the danger. The full force of this wind was driving them close to a rock which lay, half submerged, in the water. Farrel called for the starboard tacks to be turned about, and for the anchor to be cast. But the ship could get no purchase upon the seabed. "The anchor comes home," one of the yonkers shouted. "The ship is adrift!"

"Veer out more cable!"

"There is none!"

The *Gabriel* plunged forward, and those who saw the rock approaching called out to their God to save them before the ship was thoroughly crushed and broken. Milton heard their prayers and laments, but his sightless eyes were still turned towards England. "I believe," he said calmly, "that we are in doleful hazard. I sense that we are in danger of oversetting." He could hear the cries of the goats and cattle in the hold, mingled with the screams of the children and the rush of the turbulent waters. He closed his eyelids for a moment, and seemed to experience a more intense shade of darkness. He reached out for Goosequill's arm, in order to steady himself upon the shifting deck, but grasped only the air. He fell, unbalanced by a sudden tipping of the ship and by his own sense of abandonment. A moment later he felt Goosequill's arm trying to lift him. "I looked out towards the shore," Goosequill shouted to him in the desperate gale. "We are being hurled upon some great rock!"

"Recommend yourself to God!" Milton shouted in return, but his words were lost in the noise of a great tearing and splitting asunder. The *Gabriel* was being lifted by the waves between two great rocks; it seemed to hang there suspended above the waters for a moment, but then with a great sigh it settled down upon the sharp stone and was beaten by the encroaching waves. The water rushed into the pinnace and overwhelmed the crew and the voyagers, while Milton and Goosequill were suddenly washed through an open scuttle hole into the ocean. The blind man gasped as he entered the white foam of the waters, although he was for a blessed moment free from all the noises of terror and confusion around him. He rose to the surface for an instant, his mouth open to the sky, but once more he went down. He was struck a glancing blow on the arm by a plank which had split from the ship's sinking timbers, and was hit in the side by a barrel which had rolled from the deck; but he felt no pain. In this extremity, so much like a dream of terror, he was surrounded by words as well as water; phrases beat within his head even as he began to sink, and he could hear "the fiery surge," "rolling in the fiery gulf" and "forever sunk under this boiling ocean." Why were fire and water so strangely mingled? He could not have shouted out loud, since he was beneath the raging sea, but he could distinctly hear that question spoken as he drowned.

He was being carried upwards by some great wave and was dashed against one of the rocks; he was lifted into a hole or crevice and felt the pressure of the hard stone against his bruised body. He flung out his arms in exhaustion, and found that his fingers were within some fissure to which he might cling; but then he began to slide down the wet rock. He clung on with all his fierceness, but he started to fall back into the sea. He was under the water when he felt Goosequill's arms lifting him up. The boy was straddled across a piece of the broken mast, some five feet in length, and he managed to haul his master upon it. He tried desperately to maneuver the mast towards land, but it was tossed upon the billows of the ocean; once more they were overwhelmed by water and, for John Milton hanging upon the wood, there was now no time and no motion. He was suspended between two worlds, and a general quietness gathered about him.

"God in heaven!" Goosequill shouted as a large wave lifted the mast higher than before: still they clung on, and suddenly the boy felt ground with his left foot. They had been driven towards the shore but, as he tried to rise, the waves beat him down. But he was lying in shallow water: he turned back for Milton and dragged him by his arms from the mast. They were both now lying in the shallows and, before another wave could reach them, Goosequill hauled the blind man onto dry land.

"Crawl or walk, sir!" he screamed. "This is no place to stay!" Somehow they pulled themselves from the shore, and came to rest against the trunk of a pine tree which had been thrown down in the storm. Cold, and weary, and sorely bruised, they wept.

THREE

That was the worst of it, of course. But our adventures started long before. Did you ever hear of Acton, Kate? The sweetest little place you could find. Well, that was the beginning.

Is that not in London, too? You mentioned it once as a good place for pigmeat.

They grow there, Kate. They are not eaten there. So I had plodded all the way from the city, in the spring of the year, when I saw an old wagon mumbling and grumbling ahead of me. All the shine had long gone from my shoes, as you can imagine, so I took it into my head to ride at the cart's arse. Do you know our London proverb, sit awhile and run a mile? Well, those were my thoughts exactly. So I got aboard her with a single leap—

Will you pass me that linen cloth, Goose? There. Now I am listening again. I will not stir.

So I leaped aboard and, never letting the driver see me, settled down as snugly as I might on her canvas cover. We had jogged along a few yards like old friends when I heard a munching and a crunching. Someone yawned, and there was a most aromatical savor of old cheese in the air. So I put my ear to the canvas, and I could plainly hear the sound of a lovely meal being consumed. Do you know the story of Dame Alice's pantry, all bare and nothing there? That was the sorry condition of my stomach, so I pinched myself to take courage and then whispered, "Any to spare?" There was a little low sigh from within, just like air coming out of a leather bladder, so I whispered again. "Not even a little piece of that good cheese?"

"Who are you?" It was a man's voice, but he must have been trembling like a gentlewoman trying to sell pickles.

Mr. Milton sometimes does tremble. I hold his hand until he is calm again.

Will you hold my hand now, Kate? Like this?

Go back to your seat, Goose, or I will never finish sowing this cloth. Be a good boy. Please.

So he asks me who I am. "Who am I, sir? A poor boy indeed. Please to refrain from sticking any sword or knife through the canvas."

He was silent for a moment. "What do you want with me, poor boy?"

"As I said. A little bit of that good old cheese. It would travel well down gutter lane."

"A London poor boy, then." He had a very mild and even voice, now that he had become calm. Like someone who was used to singing.

Oh I know his songs, Goose. He calls them his divagations. But what is a divagation? I have never dared to ask him.

It is some kind of food. Like a trifle. So I told him truthfully that I came from a long line of sausage makers. "In Tallboy

Rents by Smithfield, sir. I left my mother's womb like a piece of Andover pork.''

He laughed, and I liked him then. ''You are a spark, I see.''

''Forgive me, sir, but I do not think you can see.'' I do not know why I said it, Kate. I just said it. Do you remember how I told you about my sister? There was the same forlornness in his own voice. What is the word for it? It had no echo.

''How do you know that?'' He was sharper with me this time.

''My sister is a little blind thing, sir. I used to be her guide through the streets by the market.''

I wonder how she is, Goose. You have been away from her for two years now. Oh, I do pity her without you to lead her.

Cowcross Street. Turnmill Lane. Saffron Hill. I could pity myself too, Kate, if I am never to see them again. May I have your gracious permission to return to my story? Mr. Milton was quiet again under the canvas. I thought to myself, this gentleman is more silent than my dead cat. ''Is it dark yet?'' he said at last.

''Amost as dark as a blackamoor's arse.''

''You had better come within, then, poor boy. I have bread as well as cheese.''

So I slipped the knot from the edge of the canvas, and slid down into this bale of warm straw. He was propped up in a corner of the wagon, with a piece of cheese in one hand and a silver penknife in the other. He had long curled hair, like that of a king, and his face looked as finely made as a girl's. Not as fine as yours, of course. He did not have dark lustrous eyes, or a pretty, slim nose, or lips as yielding as a bed of down. May I?

No, Goosequill, not now. You'll wake the babe, and then you'll have to do some more fine talking to soothe her.

I know it. Mr. Milton had a friendly sort of smell, too. Almond milk and raisins mixed. "Here," he said. "Catch and eat." He cut off a piece of cheese, and threw it in my precise direction. It was down my stomach as fast as an eel in a culvert, and then he threw me some more.

"Excuse me, sir, but I can fetch my food if you wish. I am not yet a bear in Paris Gardens."

He laughed at that, and I liked him again. "Tell me more of your sister. Was she born without her sight?"

"Oh no indeed. She could see as well as anyone while she was a squab, but then she was scalded by a pan of hot grease. It was said to have cooked her eyeballs."

"Poor girl."

"But she recovered her spirits, being young."

"Indeed." He said no more for a moment, and I was about to ask for a piece of the promised crust, when he started up again. "I have been blind these past eight years."

"I am sorry to hear of it, sir. Was it hot grease, or an arrow, or some such?"

"Yes. An arrow from God." He leaned back against the side of the wagon, and I could see his fingers restlessly touching the straw around him. "The great evangelist was ordered to eat the book of revelation so that he might possess the gift of prophecy, but it was still bitter in his mouth."

I understood not a word of this but, as they say, better to talk than to fart. "I know all about books, sir," I said. "I used to read to my sister."

"You can read?"

"Oh yes. I conned my horn books as fast as any boy in Smithfield."

"Do you write?"

"With a very neat hand. I was apprenticed to a scrivener in Leadenhall."

"My father was a scrivener." I must have coughed, or hesitated, because he turned his head towards me. "I can tell, from your voice, that you did not serve out your term."

"I sound too young?"

"Too young by far. But a young boy is not permitted to leave his master or forsake his mystery. A young boy, in such a case, will find himself before the City fathers." He still seemed to be looking at me. "Is that why you are riding away from London?"

"Well, sir, I will tell you in two words—"

"No. Say nothing. Come and sit by me." So I slipped over to his side, and at once he put his hands upon my face. "Snub nose. Wide mouth. A Smithfield boy."

"My ears are my best feature, sir. They flap in the breeze."

"But you have an honest face. A face like a blessing. Now what shall we call you?" He was still fingering me like a potter, and I thought to myself that a new dish should have a new name. He was touching my head. "What is this? It is like a quill."

"It is called hair, sir. One piece of mine always stands up straight, however hard I brush it down."

"Goosequill."

"Which is to say?"

"Your name. You have a quill upon your head, and you can

use one in your hand. You mentioned that you could write, did you not?"

"I can wield a pen like a sword, sir."

"And I tell you this, Goosequill. A pen can make men bleed as easily. Do you know who I am?"

"No, sir. I do not." I was so pleased by my new name that I had no time to consider his.

"I am John Milton."

"Are you a scrivener like your father? There was a Sarah Milton on Saffron Hill, who boiled skin for tallow." His eyes were as wide as a hare's. "But no doubt she is too low for you. Terrible creature."

"So I am truly a stranger to you?"

"I beg to agree sir. I know no more of you than of the old man of Antwerp who ate his own feet. Did you ever hear of the case?"

"So will you do me the honor of a salutation now?" He was smiling. "Your hand, please, Goosequill."

"Here it is," I said. "Do with it what you will."

Have you noticed the slimness of Mr. Milton's hands, Kate? Of course you have. But he shook mine heartily enough. "I cannot offer you another piece of cheese," he said. "We are down to the rind. Why are you laughing, Goosequill?"

"I was considering that it is an odd way of meeting. Under the cover of an old wagon." I did not need to add, "Why is a blind man, and a gentleman, fleeing from London in such guise?"—because he already sensed my thoughts.

"There is a history I might tell you, Goosequill, as doleful as any tale of knight errantry—" Do you know if I look into the fire, Kate, I can see it all again before me. Look at the burning logs with me, and watch it. Hear it in the whispers of the wood. The darkness of the wagon, the sound of the wheels upon the road, Mr. Milton's blind eyes, and the gentle motion. When suddenly there was a terrific great jolt!

Goose, you scared me!

Pardon, pardon. But I wanted to interest you. There was so much pitching and tossing that we were rolled over one another in the straw. I could hear the carter swearing like a gay lady of Southwark, but Mr. Milton managed to preserve a very severe countenance. "I believe, sir," I said to him, "that we are over-turned."

"Very likely. Please be so good as to look outside and confirm our sad case." But I had no need: at that minute the carter came around and unfastened the cover while calling wildly on the Virgin and all the saints. "Close your ears, Goosequill. He is very profane. What can be the matter, Mr. Welkin, that you invoke the old idols?"

Now this Welkin was as fat and as blubbery as an old porker. "We have fallen into a hole as big as a pit, Mr. Milton. The horses are unharmed, thanks be to God, but one of the wheels is snapped like a biscuit. By God's Mother, who are you?" I was crouched in the straw as small as an egg, but he had noticed me.

"He is my new companion, Mr. Welkin. He travels with us."

"None of us will travel an inch further, sir, unless we are raised from this pit and a new wheel fastened."

It was a great still night of moonshine, and I helped Mr. Milton from the wagon so that he might savor the air. He

snuffed it up like a seeker after truffles. "There is a scent of
beasts and humankind somewhere to the west." This astounded
me, since there was nothing to be seen at all.

"That will be the village of Kingclere. A mile away." The
carter had taken off his hat, and was measuring it against the
moon. "We were heading towards it."

"You count the holes in your hat, Mr. Welkin," I said,
"and wait for me here." I had devised a plan even as I stood
there, and I ran off as fast as ever I could. Kingclere was only a
little place, and I soon made myself heard. "Help, good citizens
and villagers!" I shouted. "Help, good swains!"

Do sit down, Goosequill. You will fall over that footstool.

Then I added, more loudly, "In God's name help others and
so help yourselves!" They came out at my call, smelling of dung
and dust, and I explained to them that I was carrying a surgeon
from London, a wonder worker, a man of miracles. He was
traveling to Bristol to cool an attack of the sweating sickness
there before, as I told them, "it creeps through the night into
your beds." Of course they feared the advance of a contagion
more than their geese feared a fox, and they brought me cartwheels before I had time to drink off their ale. "Take your drink
with you," they said, "if it please Your Worship." It did please
his worship, and so I led them back merrily to the upturned
cart. "Say nothing," I whispered to Mr. Milton. "All is done."
Soon we were well clad again, but it was too late to travel
further. We sat around a fire which Welkin had kindled from
some dry timber, eating the bread and ale that the villagers had
left for us. I told Mr. Milton about his new fame as a surgeon,
and he muttered something. "What was that, sir?"

"Your wit is as quick as your step, I see."

"I am as subtle as a philosopher, sir. And I also know the art of standing still and whistling."

"Then whistle me an air."

I knew the refrain of "London Violets," and he nodded his head in time to its music. Do you know it, Kate? Well, I will sing it for you tonight in our bed.

None of your nonsense, Goose.

The next morning I awoke at first light, just as Welkin was harnessing the horses. Mr. Milton was already cleaning his face with a linen cloth. "Come, Piers Welkin," he called after he had finished. "To your prayers, if you please." He looked over towards me. "Goosequill may join us if he so wishes." So I knelt with them on the soft ground, as he began to gabble. " 'And I will bring you into the wilderness of the people, and these will I plead with you face to face.' Ezekiel, chapter twenty, verse thirty-five, Mr. Welkin." He stopped, and, just as suddenly, started up again. " 'And we in all humbleness prepare for the great and bloody battles of Gog and Magog, rivers of blood up to the horse bridles, yea, even the blood of those who have drunk blood for so long.' " You know how he can sound, when he is elevated? "What wondrous works are now to be performed!"

He sounds like my uncle in Barnstaple, Goose, who sells his poultry in the market. "Chicks and fowls! Delightful chicks and deserving fowls!"

He stopped his prayers abruptly, so I shouted out "Amen!" Welkin looked at me as if I had farted, so I added "Praise be!"

"From the mouths of your innocents, Dear Lord," Milton said, "come most godly words."

It was all very satisfactory, and we were soon on our way

once more. He asked Welkin if he had observed anyone following us, but there was not even an ant on the road behind us. So we sat up in the cart and jogged along easily enough. Of course I was curious, Kate, about this blind man's strange journey, and eventually I blurted it out. "Why did you seek cover, sir—"

"Why did I seek the cover of night and darkness, Goosequill?"

"No, sir. Why did you cover the cart?"

"Sufficient for you to know that I leave England in order to save England."

"That is good news."

"I leave England in order to pray for England. I leave England in order to be a witness for England. I leave England in order to *be* England."

"That would be a task to baffle Merlin, sir."

"We need no wizards or fairy, Goosequill. Providence is my guide."

"I am told that Providence is a paltry giver." I knew what I wanted to say, Kate, so I came out with it at once. "You need a companion with more flesh and blood."

"You mean?"

"Me, sir."

"You would guide me, as you once guided your sister?"

"If I can manage Smithfield on market day, sir, I can manage Asia and Africa and all combined."

"Do you write as easily as you speak?"

"I am proud to say that I can do it without thinking, sir."

"You will write to my dictate, then. Letters. Histories. Proclamations."

"And prayers, I hope?"

"Prayers will be very frequent, too. And in return I can promise you this, Goosequill. I will recompense you with immortality." I like fine words, as you know, but they cannot be cooked and eaten.

I think you might live off your words, Goose, you prepare and garnish them so lovingly.

Thank you, Kate. You have taken those same words out of my mouth. "That is very kind of you," I said to him. "But how am I supposed to live in the meantime?"

"God will provide."

"Then I hope God knows of me. Otherwise I shall grow rather thin."

"No impiety, please. We live in sacred times. He watches and protects us always." Then, with a smile, he took out a leather purse and shook it. "You will not starve like the followers of faithless Abyıon." Something with an "on" at the end. Could it have been Babylon? Or London? "I have coin enough to take us to the other side."

"And what side may that be, sir? Heaven or hell?"

"Your tongue is sharp enough to cut your own teeth, Goose. We are going far to the west, on the wide ocean, where we shall find a lasting seat." The cart rolled over a pothole, and we both jumped. "We are traveling to a land of refuge and a mansion house of liberty. We will find a nation of sages, of prophets, and of worthies. I am impatient to kiss that pregnant soil."

"It sounds a rather damp place. Does it have a name as yet?"

"Sion. Christ's Vineyard." There was a bead of sweat on his forehead, and I wiped it away. "The new Canaan. The Promised Land."

"Now I am completely lost. I cannot find my north and south in your world."

"It is the New World, Goosequill. It is New England. Our last and latest land! Mr. Welkin, lash the horses!"

Our destination was not to be Bristol, after all, but Barnstaple. Close by your own old home, Kate.

I don't want to think of it, Goose. I miss Hannaford so. I still dream of it. Our life in New Milton is changed from anything I knew before. And now that Mr. Milton has vanished—

Calm yourself, Kate. All will be well. Just look into the fire while I tell my story. So I asked him why we were traveling into the West Country. He said that there were friends there who would protect him. Protect you from what? I asked him. Wicked men, he said. An evil race of idolaters. Oh dear, I said, how shall we know them? Worms, he said. They resemble slugs all bedecked in finery. An easy task then, master. I must look for a worm with oiled hair and an emerald cloak pin. We reached your old neighborhood two days later, but he decided to remain outside Barnstaple in case, he said, of spies or paid informants. Of course, I was beginning to learn something of his history, and of the risks he ran. He has told you about Cromwell and the rest of those he served, Kate, but he may not have mentioned that he was being hunted down. The new restored king would be more friendly towards Beelzebub than John Milton. So we waited until dark before walking into town.

You came by way of Swimbridge, did you?

That was the very spot.

That is where my mother died of the fever. Did you take the path by the great barn or try the little track by the river?

Oh, Kate, it was all one to me. I know East Cheap from Golden Lane, but grass is grass. Old porker Welkin had gone before us to enlist the aid of the brethren, as he called them. So, when we came up to that church in the middle of the town, we were met by two rustic gentlemen who kissed us on both cheeks in the way of country folk. Will you show me again how it is done, Kate? No? "God be praised," one of them whispered. He was a foolish-looking fellow, with side-whiskers so long they might have tangled with his shoelaces. "This is still an age of saints!"

"I trust so," Mr. Milton whispered back. "Lead on." They took us to that row of almshouses close by and, when we entered a room full of your Devonians, he perked up considerably. I took his arm by habit, ever since he had started to complain of stiffness and aches and agues, but he courteously moved me aside. "I am now with the people of God," he said very loudly. "They will give me their own strength and fortitude." There were nine or ten gathered to meet him, and they came out with "Praise be!" and "The Lord be thanked" as piously as if they were in St. Paul's. There was then a little bit of coughing, and a little rustling of clothes, while they waited for him to ladle out some more blessed words. "You poor scattered stones," he said, "raked from the destruction of Christ's field. You wandering sheep compassed around with dangers. On what evil days have you fallen!" This set one old dame crying, and I could see Mr. Milton's nostrils quivering as he scented her tears.

Imitate his voice again, Goose. It is like having him in the room.

"I know full well that we will soon be hunted, as David was by Saul and his acursed courtiers. I know that we will be barbarously oppressed and scurrilously derided. But we cannot make our obeisance to any earthly king or live within the kingdom of Antichrist. We serve only the King of Kings, who does not sit in Whitehall or in Richmond but in the Temple of Heaven!" They all started murmuring then. I thought they were moaning, but they were praying. "Your voices to me are like the sound of the sea. And it brings to my mind that some of you will be my companions on that voyage to the new land. We set forth upon an ocean whose waters will wash away a thousand tears. The iron yoke of conformity will leave no slavish print upon our necks. No, indeed. We will be shipped in Christ's service to the western world. Oh, what an illustrious passage it is!" I thought it was a very illustrious passage indeed. Never had I heard so many words running upon one another. "Long is the way, and hard, but I am reminded of that man who forsook all the greatness of Egypt and chose a troublesome journey through the wilderness, for his faithful eyes were fixed upon an incorruptible reward. And our work, brethren, is also wilderness work. Oh, let us plough and hoe!" I began to marvel at him then. He could put on a better act than any street acrobat or ballad singer I had ever seen. It was a thing of beauty, Kate. It was delicious.

The next morning he arose as fresh and as quick as a stripling. "We must look to our provisions," he said, after he had finished praying by the window of the almshouse where we lodged. It looked out upon a neat little dairy, with its own cow.

I know that dairy. The cow is called Jane.

You must tell Mr. Milton the news. "We cannot cross nine hundred leagues of ocean with a bare cupboard," he said to me.

"That is true, sir. It is not a ditch to leap over with a staff."

"You cannot leap, Goosequill, but you can write. You can look before you leap but I cannot look before I write. That is why you must use my pen and not your feet." He was in so sprightly a mood that he could have gabbled forever in this vein, so I coughed politely. "What is it now?"

"Are you expressing the wish that I should make up a list?"

"Wish. List. Yes. Beef. Write down beef. Bread and peas. Did the brethren recommend oatmeal?"

"They did, sir. I also recommended beer."

"A small casket, no more." I shook my head, but said nothing. "Mustard and vinegar for our meat. Legs of mutton. They are to be stewed and packed up with butter in earthen pots."

"We have no pots."

"The Lord will provide."

"In Barnstaple?"

"It is a godly town. But, if you must, take some coins to the pannier market. We will also need cheese, honey and biscuit."

"May I mention burnt wine? It is a comfortable thing for our stomachs."

"But not for our heads and tongues, Goosequill. You are too forward. You distract me." I could see that his eyes were moving rapidly within their sockets. Like this.

Oh, Goose, you must not. It is horrid.

"We must carry in our private case," he said to me, "some green ginger and conserve of roses. We need prunes and wormwood. Nutmeg and cinnamon, and the juice of lemons."

"And the juice of some good English spirits, sir?"

"We have those already."

"I was thinking of something a little stronger."

"Goosequill. Come here." I put down my pen and, since I already knew something of his wayward humor, I approached him cautiously. He rose from his chair and, with a perfect aim, slapped me lightly on the right cheek. "Now write down water-gruel and fine flour."

Then came the day of general embarkation. We could hear the sheep and cattle being led to the holds, but our master remained in his little chamber. He was crouched in his chair, sighing. "It is almost noon," I said to him as gently as I could. The groaning and lamenting of the animals had become very loud. "Our fellow voyagers are congregating by the harbor." Still he did not move. "Mr. Milton, it is time."

I touched his shoulder, and he rose as suddenly as if he had been summoned. "A hard time. To be parted from my own dear country and to pitch tent in the wilderness—" He was about to say something else, but he checked himself. "Well. No more. Let us go forward together."

We walked to the quayside by a back lane which led from the almshouses to the harbor. "Watch your footing," I said. "Devon mud ahead!" Excuse me, Kate, but you do have mud in Devon.

"I wish to be guided, Goosequill, not deafened."

"Very good, sir. Cobbles by you," I whispered as we turned the corner. "If I may be allowed to mention them. Oh, there she is. The *Gabriel*." And there was the sea, Kate, which I had not known before. How wide and deep it was I could not tell, but I had heard that giants and dragons and devils all lurked somewhere within it. So it was not a very pleasant sight. Kate?

I was thinking of the day we took to our ship. It was a few

months before you, Goose, in the autumn. My dear old father was weeping so hard that I could not look upon him, so I went below the deck and hugged little Jane so tightly that she started crying. It was a whole world of tears. Well. Go on, Goose. Tell me what happened next. Cheer me.

There was not much cheer at this time, Kate. "She is a vessel of huge bulk," Mr. Milton said when we came up to the ship. "I can hear her all around me."

"Large enough, sir. Not of our London standard, of course, but she is very broad."

"Three hundred tons." Someone had started talking to us without so much as an introduction. "Forty mariners. Twenty pieces of ordnance."

"And who may you be?" Mr. Milton said in his fine way.

"Daniel Farrel, sir. Captain of the *Gabriel.*" Farrel by name, I thought, and barrel by nature. He was all toughened and weathered, and I suspected that there was a great deal of ale within him somewhere.

"How many travel with us, good Captain?"

"One hundred and twenty souls, Mr. Milton. We call them planters on the manifest, in case we are stopped in these waters, but they are all brethren."

They were going aboard as we spoke, with as much noise and chaos and crying as you remember. Their bellows, cartwheels, barrows, ladders, pitchforks, axletrees, locks, lanterns, were all being stored away beneath the decks. One old bird of Barnstaple was crowing to her neighbor, "A fine country, that has no locks or ladders in it!" Mr. Milton turned his head towards her and, oh, she did quail. There is nothing like the stare of a blind man to bring you to your senses. The blessed brethren were all still walking onto the *Gabriel* with their knives and iron pans, their rugs and blankets, their sacks of corn and bundles of salt. But it was not Noah's Ark, Kate, not with some of them in tears and others looking as forlorn as the dogs tossed at Shrovetide. They wore those coats of canvas to protect themselves against the tar, and so they looked even more doleful. There was a leather dresser, met by us in the almshouse, who marched up the plank singing ''Jesus My King''; but he stopped soon enough when his voice was drowned out by the groans of the cattle below. One young hopeful was pushing his lame wife ahead of him in a little wheeled cart, while a fellow who looked like a carpenter was trying to hush his child. It was all very lamentable, Kate, and I could see no joy in it at all. I wish you had been with me on that voyage. Then we could all have been more cheerful.

Captain Farrel returned to us, and urged us to go aboard. ''Make everything comfortable about you, Mr. Milton.'' He had drunk some more ale, and was splitting ever so slightly at the seams. ''There is nothing to fear.''

''I know it, good Captain. The hand of God cradles us. He will be with us day and night.''

He was not with us on that particular night, unfortunately. We set sail at the third watch, with a fine wind taking us out to sea, when a sudden gale turned upon us from the south. So we were forced to make for shelter at Milford Haven, which is, my dear wife, in the country of Wales. When I told Mr. Milton, he started to stroke his hands across the little wooden table in our quarters. ''We have come into Pembrokeshire, then. Fourteen leagues distance.''

''Truly?''

"Do I ever lie?" He reached out and caught hold of me. *"Quaestio haec nascitur unde tibi?"*

What was that, Goose?

It was Latin.

What did it mean?

It meant, "Whatever are you thinking of?"

"I am thinking," I replied, "of some little entertainment to pass away the time."

"Ah," he said. "I almost forgot to tell you." He went over to his private chest and, feeling delicately in his usual way, brought out a little book bound in white calves' leather. I knew the skin from Smithfield. "This," he said, "will be our maritime chronicle."

"Sir?"

"Our journal of the sea. We will voyage across an ocean, Goosequill. But we will also traverse the minds of men—" There was a sudden movement of the ship, and he raised his head into the air. "A strong wind takes us. Do you hear it? It is the breath of God testing whether our ballast is just and our cables strong."

"But listen, sir. Something else. The mariners are calling the anchors home. We must be sailing again."

"Again upon the ocean. Forlorn and wild. It makes the heart beat faster."

"Yes, sir. But is it excitement or is it fear?"

FOUR

April 2, 1660. A troublesome sea, with a multitude of persons heaving up their guts. "We must expect," said my reverend master, "a perpetual disturbance on this our dark voyage. Pass me that green ginger." He chewed a bit of it, and spat it from his mouth into his hand. Then he put the pieces in the pocket of his kersey coat. "Recall to your mind that we are crossing fathomless and unquiet deeps." The ship was in such a roll that we were being tossed all around our quarters, and he clung to me to save himself from sprawling upon his arse. "But then we must concede, Goosequill, that in this fallen world all mixed and elemental things must struggle in contraries." At that he retched, and I quickly brought a pot for him to vomit up his bowels.

April 5, 1660. The daughter of one John Rose, a hosier, has grown sick with many blue spots upon her breast. They are like the tokens of the London plague which took off half Smithfield no more than a year ago. "I wish," he said, "that we had an apothecary's shop within the ship's bounds."

"I wish," I said, "that we had an inn to drown our fears in."

"In which to drown our fears. But then we have the discordance of *inn* with *in*."

"Sir?"

"Calm yourself with some wormwood. The Lord loves a peaceful heart."

The sea was as quiet as glass; indeed we had been becalmed since seven of the clock in the morning until noon. So I led him out upon the deck and, as soon as we entered the light, his eyes flickered in their sockets. I took him to the rail, and he leaned out over the water. "I wish," he said, "that I could see the bottom of this monstrous world."

"To view the sea serpents? Fishy dragons and suchlike?"

"Atlantis might lie beneath us, with all its watery domes and towers. That would be a true wonder."

April 7, 1660. The girl had not caught the plague contagion, but the spots were a sign of the smallpox, which has now destroyed her. She was buried in the sea by Captain Farrel and her parents, all of them as solemn as midnight. The sailors tied a great bullet around her neck and another to her legs, and then they turned her out at a porthole while giving fire to their guns. They asked Mr. Milton to make an oration over her body, but he pleaded sickness and fatigue. He remained in our lodgings until she was well sunk beneath the waves.

April 9, 1660. Today he began a letter to one Reginald de la Pole, a clerk of the old abolished Council. "Loving friend," he said, "we heartily salute you. No. First add *Laus Deo* to the top of the page."

"Which is to say?"

"Which is to say, keep silent or be struck down." He lolled in his elbow chair, which the captain had lent to him, smiling to himself while he dictated his epistle (as he called it). Never have I heard so many grave words coming from so cheerful a countenance. "There cannot be a more ill-boding sign to a nation," he said, "than when the inhabitants, to avoid insufferable grievance at home, are enforced by heaps to forsake their native country. Yet we have been compelled to leave our own dear England for the wide ocean and the savage deserts of America—"

"I remembered you to say that it will be very pleasant."

"Do you wish to stand at the helm with a basket of stones around your neck?"

"Very cruel and ingenious, sir."

"—savage deserts of America, where the poor afflicted remnants of our martyred countrymen, our poor expulsed brethren of New England, sit on the seashore, counting the hours till our arrival with their sighs and falling tears."

"Oh Lord." I did not know whether to admire him for his prose, or fear him for his prophecy.

"But we can never and in no wise be persuaded or compelled to return home. With mature wisdom, deliberate virtue and clear affection we intend to restore our lost liberties in the sad wilderness."

"The captain speaks of flourishing towns and villages."

He raised his fist in the air, and shook it fiercely at me, so I said no more. "Change of air changes not our minds. We shall reach our steady hands"—he unfurled his fist then—"as steady as they may be in this misinformed and wearied life of man, to renew our lost heritage, our tenures and our freeholds, our native and domestic charters. Time will run back, and fetch the age of gold. That is enough now, Goosequill. It is a weary business, coining words."

April 12, 1660. There is an organ on board this ship! Captain Farrel told my godly master that it had been taken as cargo on the last journey from Gravesend and, its owner dying of cabin fever before reaching land, it has never yet been played. Mr. Milton could hardly keep his hands from trembling at the news. "My father loved music," he said to the captain, "and likewise he taught me well. We need a sweet air on a journey such as this." So we were led down beneath the hatches into the forward hold, but he stopped before he entered it and asked me to fetch his black gown. "I cannot wear kersey while I play," he said. "It is not fit."

"I'll fit you," I said as I went back through the passages. "I'll fit you tight."

He was waiting impatiently for me, but I made sure to dress him slow and reverential. Then we processed into the hold, and the captain pointed to a piece of cloth in a corner. "There she lies, as quiet as the day we took her on board."

I removed the cloth, which was as dusty as an old virgin. "It is only a small thing," I said. I had expected all the pipes and pedals of St. Paul's.

When he put his fingers on the instrument, he sighed. "It is a portative organ. Is there a chair or stool?" A sea chest was found and, when he sat upon it, he sighed again. "Some of our traveling brethren consider music to be the harmony of fallen angels. But why should the devil have the best tunes? Our good English airs have no taint of the mass about them." He could reach the pedals with his feet and pretty soon he was playing and singing like a ballad seller. It was no devotional air, either, but that piece of sad nonsense, "Go, Crystal Tears," which is always to be heard in Cornhill and suchlike.

April 13, 1660. His voice, like that of some conjuror, has stirred up a storm. At first light I heard the call, "Yonkers, take in the topsail!" and then, a moment later, "Furl the mainsail!" It was so loud that it roused me from the sweetest dream I have ever yet enjoyed. I was flying over the rooftops of London! I thought to wake my master but, on looking into his corner, I saw that he was already at his prayers. So I rose quietly, and crept out upon the deck. And what a prospect it was. The fair sky had vanished, and brought on a scene of cloud as dark as a churchyard wall. There was a strong blast coming from the north, and the sailors were running here and there and everywhere calling to one another to lower this or pull that. I hurried back to our quarters with news of the coming tempest. He was still at his prayers and did not so much as move until he had cried "Amen!" in a loud voice. I supposed that he was about to blast at me for bursting in upon his devotions, but instead he smiled. "You are about to tell me that we have entered obscure and uncouth weather. But I am sure that our captain will not forsake the helm. Lead me to the deck, please, so that the spray can touch my face."

"You will feel more than spray, sir. The billows are lofty and raging."

"Then you must tie me to your body with a piece of strong cord."

"So we sink or swim together?"

"We already live in the vale of death, Goosequill." I guided him into the air and, holding onto his waist tightly with both my arms wrapped around him, I stood firm while he put up his face to the wind and the water. "Wave rolling after wave," he shouted to me through the growing storm. "Their tops must ascend the sky!"

"Near enough," I shouted back. I could see the mariners trying to undergird the ship with cable, to keep her sides together, and Mr. Milton still laughed. He tried to speak to me again but his words were mingled with the shouts of the captain and bos'n as well as the roaring of the waters.

"This eternal tempest, Goosequill, never to be calmed—"

"Bear up the helm! Keep full!"

"Like the wakeful trump of doom—"

"Done. Done."

"Which thunders through the deep!"

"Is all ready again?"

"Yeah. Yeah."

A sudden jolting dashed our bodies so that I could scarcely keep my grip upon him, and a flood of water hurled the unfixed goods across the deck. Oh, how the wind howled! But my master, with the water streaming across his blind eyes, called out, "Bring me ice and snow and hail and stormy gusts!"

"You have enough already! Come away now!" I dragged him with all my strength from the open deck, just as the ship foundered in a wave so great and dark that I thought we might never rise again. I pushed him into the passage where we were tossed and pitched, until we were hurled into our cabin by a sudden sideways moving of the vessel. He collapsed, all in a heap, upon his canvas sheet; he was cold, dead cold, and I saw him bite his arm and hand to bring some warmth of the blood back into them. "It is a great thing," he said, "to hear the voice of God. Do you not think so, Goosequill?" I was still shivering and chattering so that I could scarcely speak. "Did you feel His presence around you?" Then he lay down upon his narrow bed, and slept.

The storm had subsided by noon, and in the sudden quiet I could hear the voice of Captain Farrel in the passageway. "Scrub her," he was saying. "Make clean the whole ship. Surgeon, look to those who have been harmed. Purser, record their names, if you please." He was as calm as if he had never left dry land. He knocked upon our door, and called out. "Mr. Milton, sir, all well. The storm is spent."

My master tried to rise from his bed, but fell back.

April 14, 1660. He has caught an ague, or fever, from sleeping in his soaking clothes. "I am thirsty," he said. "I never was so thirsty after fame, or destitute of—" I put a can of rainwater up to his lips, and he drank it eagerly. "I was destined of a child," he whispered. Then he broke off, and a moment later closed his blind eyes. "Did you know that the candle in Bread Street is never snuffed out until the third hour of the night? I cannot tell you of my wearisome labors and studious workings. Bread Street. Milk Street. Wood Street."

"I know them."

"Are you the constable or the scavenger? The conduit on Cheap is foully blocked."

"Hush, sir."

He shivered in his nakedness, although I had put enough sheets and cloths over him to warm the man on the moon. "This late chill will freeze my early thaw. My love of ease will chill my ardor."

"Sleep. Do sleep."

"I have caught a great fever, Goosequill, have I not? I freeze, but there is a rude lump of heat somewhere within my breast."

"A cold, sir."

"Tom."

"You have caught a cold from the storm and the sea."

He slept fitfully for an hour or more, while I busied myself ordering our cabin after the boisterous winds had turned it about. Then he began to speak again. "They call me Lady, do they?" I put the water to his lips. "Brothelers. Bottle seekers. Some more water, please."

"Can I get you some raisins? Or a little piece of ginger?"

"Go to the market, and buy some beans. Then we can seek the giant." He was smiling up at me. "I tell you this, good boy. I have never left your company without some plain gain of human wisdom." He could hear the brethren on the deck singing "Jesus, Who Reigns." "I am drinking His water now," he said. Then he slept again.

April 15, 1660. The cook told me that all the corn on board has bred worms and now stinks. It would never have happened in Leadenhall. I was walking on the deck, my master safely sleeping after the storm in his head, when there was a great commotion behind me. A stripling was being slung overboard with a rope tied around his arms and waist. "What is this?" I asked the captain's boy, a most slow and shambling creature. "Is he being ducked into the sea?"

"Oh, no, no, no. You saw that yesterday in the storm— well, it was not a storm but truly a tempest." He was always very labored and precise of speech; he had been taken on board,

I gathered from the sailors' rumors, because he was the captain's bastard. "You know that we did thoroughly search the ship for cracks or splits or holes?"

"Yes. I know."

"It was a great search which took six hours. No, seven hours. Seven if you are to count the respite for cheese and ale which, being heavy work, was very welcome to Mr. Rogers and the others."

"Go on, do."

"Did you not hear the cries for pitch and suchlike? Well, in that search some leaks were found and mended."

"And?"

"This is the last. It is not an easy task but it is so necessary that the captain has promised a bottle from his cellar, if it can be truly called a cellar since it is not under the ground. What might you call it, Goosequill? A vat of the sea?"

"So they sling him overboard to prevent a leak?"

There was a general shout when the sailor raised his hand high, and signaled that he had stopped up the hole. "In so many words, yes."

I went down to our quarters where Mr. Milton was sitting upright in his bed. "What was that hubbub?"

"The sailors have cured our last wound, sir."

"And I have also cured mine." He laughed, and I could see that he was now thoroughly mended. "We rise from the waves victorious, just as I emerge from my own bad weather. Pass me that pot. I have not pissed all night."

"Another leak!"

"Turn your back, you infidel." I stood away from him as he passed his water. "It may be that your studies have not inclined you to perform great things, Goosequill, but at least it may be given you to celebrate the works of those that do." He had returned to his old self.

April 20, 1660. Some of our travelers still lie with the small-pox and the calenture—but two deaths only, which, as the captain says, is no great business on a voyage such as this. He told Mr. Milton that those who did not wholly wish to leave England are always the first to sicken. My master shook his head. "Ours is a sad case," he said. "Our true English fortitude has disappeared with our true English liberties. Thank you for that lesson, my dear Captain."

April 24, 1660. A sailor, one Thomas Ficket, has been discovered to have bargained with a child—he sold her a little painted box, worth no more than threepence, in return for three biscuits a day for all the voyage. He has already received about thirty from the squab, and had thereupon sold them to others. This was a greedy guts indeed, and the captain caused to have his hands tied behind his back before he was hauled under the keel. My master, on hearing the news, insisted on attending the ceremony upon the deck. "In Good Mother England there would have been a whipping," he said as he came out into the air. "But this has a more watery justice to it." One of the brethren had heard him recall "Good Mother England" and asked him what he meant by it, now that we were fleeing her. "I said good mother, my friend, not holy mother. Our mother is now down in the mire. Where is that wanton mariner?"

"He is being led out instantly, sir," I said. "He is allowed a prayer."

"I am glad to hear it. Where had I reached?"

"Mother was in the dirt, sir."

"I had often thought that God had England under the special indulgent eye of His providence, and so it seemed in the best and purest times of Edward VI." Three of the brethren, who were now listening to him intently, murmured in agreement. "But then there came Mary's time." There was a groan from them. "That wicked and drunken papist who could not open her mouth without the strong stench of avarice and superstition, that viper of sedition who tried to exercise her raving and bestial tyranny over our nation, so to enfeeble us that we would fall wounded into the dragnet of the Antichrist in Rome. Well, we removed her corruption as we would shake fire from out of our bosoms. Yet a king seeks to effeminate us again. You know how a good mother may take her child and hold it over a pit, so that it may learn to fear? Now we know how to fear." He stopped short and laughed. "What was your question, good sir? I suspect that you would like an answer while the years are still green upon your head? No. Wait a little. The criminal approaches the bar."

The sailor Ficket was marched onto the deck, and tied firmly with a rope. Mr. Milton remained very still as Ficket was tossed over the side and went down, screaming, beneath the keel. He came up again, still screaming, and was hauled upon the deck. I looked into his face, all bruised and bloody, covered in weed and dirt: He was staring straight at my master and, as he was led past us to the hold, he called out, "I am still hissing hot after my fall!"

Mr. Milton took my arm at that moment. "Let us return," he said, "now that the sentence is complete."

"What was Ficket's meaning?"

"Nothing. Wild words." He seemed strangely troubled.

"He is a man in solitude, and thinks to ease himself of his misery." He leaned upon me as heavily as a drunken man against a post, and I steered him carefully down the passage. "You know, Goosequill, loneliness is the first thing that God knew to be not good. You have heard the story?"

"Sir?"

"Of man's first disobedience? One day I will tell it to you."

"Was it in paradise?"

"It was. Our first and final place of rest." He was not yet as old as Paul's steeple, as they say, but he was tired enough. "We cannot endure the estate we are in, however valiant we may appear." I took him into our quarters, where instantly he lay down upon his bed. "They asked me why I deserted England—"

"Not in those words, sir."

"I will tell you why. I gave grave advice uttered with freedom in the public cause. Is that reason enough?"

"More than enough."

His spirits seemed revived, and he roused himself from his bed. "What was I but Cromwell's hand? I was his Latin secretary only, but how many secret writings and deeds might be blamed upon a blind man? Of course I had written several honest tracts and pamphlets for the sake of the good old cause, and rumors had already reached me that my works were to be burned by the common hangman. I had given my severe judgment on the king late beheaded, and I knew well enough that I would be taken as soon as the new vagabond king stepped upon our land. Look on this." He felt within his kersey coat, and from an interior pocket brought out some raw lumps of sugar. I did not know he kept any there and, as sly as any magpie, he must have eaten them only when I left the cabin. "Where is my little table?"

"Here."

He put down three pieces of the sugar in order. "Here is the Court at Whitehall. Here is the Parliament. And here was I in Petty France. What do you say of that?"

"Close."

"Too close. I was compassed around with dangers, and with evil tongues. Universal reproach, Goosequill, is far worse to bear than violence. Mechanics, citizens, apprentices—"

"I was one!"

He put out his hand to stop me. "All will be corrupted by those blaspheming king's men into an inconstant and image-doting rabble. The honest liberty of free speech will become once more as dumb as any beast."

"Beasts are never dumb, sir. They make enough noise in Smithfield to wake your dead grandmother." He reached out to strike me. "I am employing free speech, sir! Remember honest liberty!"

"I shall be the judge of what is to be free." He smiled to himself. "You will not, in your dumb state, recall days just recently passed. Gone was the yoke of patient and manly discipline which the Council had imposed upon our nation, and from the old papal stews there crawled out the spawn of taverns and dicing houses, the ragged infantry of braves and hacksters so void of knowledge, so backward, and so malignant that they had already threatened to strike me in the very street where I lived. I was conveyed a report that my chambers were to be searched, my trunks and studies sealed up. Then I laid my own plans. My wife had died two years before, but I could not take my daughters with me."

"You have daughters?" I was so astonished at this latest piece of news, as well concealed as his lumps of sugar, that I whistled.

"Two of them. They never did wish to accompany me. To be the offspring of a proscribed man is danger enough, but to assist in his escape—well, it would have been worse than folly on their part. With the help of my old clerk, I fled that night." He took up the lumps of sugar and put them back inside his pocket.

April 25, 1660. He complains that he is weary of the ship diet of smoked fish, salted beef, and the like. "Bring me good bacon and buttered peas," he said to me. "Bring me a bag pudding."

"How?"

"Beg or borrow, Goosequill. No. Better yet. . . ." He went over to a trunk, felt its lock, and then opened it with one of the keys which he kept in a bunch around his neck. "I was engaged on some translations of the psalms before I left London. Barter one of them for some currants and some flour. These godly pilgrims will willingly forsake a particle of their hoarded provisions for the benefit of more spiritual fare." I doubted it, but I said nothing. "Search out for me the hundred-and-seventh psalm. It has the line marked in red, 'He causeth them to wander in the wilderness where there is no way.' "

It took me a thousand years to find it, but then I called out, "I have it! It has 'wander' and 'wilderness' with a cross beside them!"

"Take it and wander out of doors. Go."

I brought it to a family of godwits (as the ruder sort of sailors called them), the Bableighs of Ilfracombe: they were on their knees as soon as any gust of wind took the sails, praying and lamenting like Bedlamites, so would prove easy fish to fry. I passed them reciting my master's translated verses in a low voice.

"What is that, good young man?" Mr. Bableigh came up to me at once, ready to bow and scrape at any piece of biblicality.

"Oh, sir. These are Mr. Milton's own words on the wilderness work before us."

"Oh, praise the Lord! Does he instruct us or console us?"

"My master is of a very consoling turn of mind."

"I know it."

"But he offers right pious words of teaching." I put my hand upon his shoulder. "He has singled you out, sir."

"Thanks be to God!"

"He wishes you to be the bearers of this sacred poem in the new world." I presented it to him, and he took it with great reverence. "He wants nothing in return."

"Nothing? Except our prayers, I hope?"

"Indeed so." I weighed his words, and gave them back in equal measure. "Your prayers will be heartening to him. They are very necessary, as he told me before I came to you, and altogether delicious." I paused. "But I fear for him, Mr. Bableigh."

He clutched my arm, and looked so close into my face that his was only an inch away. "Fear? Lord save us, what is it?"

"The ship's diet is very hard upon his tender stomach."

"Truly he has the bowels of St. Paul."

"I say the same to him. St. Paul is always on my lips." I hesitated, but only for a moment. "I wonder if you have a little bit of oatmeal, or pottage, to administer to his tenderness?"

These Puritans were great graspers and little givers, as I had discovered by watching them, but even the godly Bableigh could not wriggle out of my net. "We have but little, Mr. Goosequill."

"We need less than little, Mr. Bableigh."

"Of course, of course. Some pottage, did you say?"

"Some currants and raisins within it?"

A little while after, I carried back a tasty bit of bag pudding to my master.

May 1, 1660. All day in a mist, with nothing around us to be seen. When I told him this, he smiled. "Evil May Day," he said. "It has always been such." Then, without anyone to lead him, he went above. So I followed.

It was hot enough, even in the clouded air. "Like the smoke from some pot in a cookshop," I said. It was so quiet, too, we could have heard a fly cough.

"Do you hear the mainsail whispering, Goose? Every sound has an echo in this stillness."

"It is not natural, sir. It is like some enchantment."

"It has been said that demons, if they wish, cover corporeal things with a fascinating mist of invisibility. But this has always been the wisdom of those who dwell in the night of superstition and old time. If it were really so, then my blindness would have condemned me to a thoroughly damned world. Take heart, Goosequill, we will soon proceed to regions of wide air."

He spoke the truth, and by dawn of the next day all was clear again.

May 3, 1660. I saw last night what before I never had seen. About ten of the clock, two fires settled upon the mainmast. When I first glimpsed them I thought I must have drunk too much of the strong water which I share with the captain's boy, but then another voyager saw them and cried out in alarm. They were like the flames of two great candles; they flickered and flared in the darkness and, all at once, the mariners set up a loud "Halloo!" The captain's boy was watching them beside me, wide-eyed and still very much in drink. "Do you know what they call them, Goose?"

"No." I was still wondering at them as they burned.

"St. Elmo's fire. Can you hear them crackle?" It was like the sound of sausages being turned upon a spit. "Do you wish to know why the sailors are all clapping and rejoicing?" He was as slow as ever, even in drink. "They are rejoicing because these fires always come before a storm."

"Why laugh in the face of a storm?"

"Two fires prophesy safety at sea." He seemed to sink into a trance then, his eyes bursting out of his head. "They are like the two bright eyes of God looking down upon us."

"More like those of a tiger. Or a big wolf." The lights still glistened and glittered, but then they vanished away as quickly as they had come.

I hurried down to our quarters to tell all to Mr. Milton, but he prevented me from speaking with a motion of his hand. "They are also called by the name of Castor and Pollux," he said. "To the Italians they are known as St. Hermes. By the Spaniards they are named Corpos Santos. They mean nothing at all."

May 4, 1660. A fierce storm, but it soon blew over.

May 6, 1660. I saw two mighty whales. One spouted the ocean through some holes in its head. The water ascended into the air a great height, and the beast made such a pother of puffing and blowing that the sea around him boiled terribly. A sailor told me that if a vessel goes too near it is sucked in. My master said that it sounded like the nave of St. Benet's cracking and falling inward. Oh, Lord!

May 8, 1660. Some more fishy sights. I saw a thing which the mariners call a sunfish: it spreads out its fins like beams on every side. I saw some other things slide past in shoals but, what they were, God knows.

May 11, 1660. There were many creatures called porpoises playing in the ocean, which the sailors believe to be a sign of foul weather. One yonker, Matthew Barnes by name, struck at one of them with a harping iron and hoisted it aboard. We cut some of it into pieces and, when fried, the flesh tasted of bacon or hung beef. I gave some to my master, who thereupon spat it out into his hand. "I understand now why it is sometimes called the sea hag," he said. "Or Marsavius. Not to be confused with 'my Savior,' which it is not." Then he questioned me about its size and shape, as if I were the only person in the world who might tell him truly.

"My sister," I told him that evening, as I prepared a dainty dish of fish and bread crust, "believed that if she stroked her eyes she saw something. It was a little smallness of light, she told me, as through a chink in the door."

"I wish it were the same case with me. When I rub them I see only a spotted blackness. It is woven with an ash-color that is being poured continually downward. When my eyes were not yet thoroughly dimmed, I saw colors flashing out with great vehemence.'' Suddenly he turned his head from side to side, very quickly. ''But then they, too, became obscured. Tell me more about this sunfish. How many little fins or beams did it have? Did they seem in the water like the ring of light around a candle? That is how I imagine them.'' He spread out the slender fingers of his hands in imitation.

''That is it, sir. Exactly.''

''My sight is not completely lost, Goosequill. It is drawn within, and I expect that it will always whet rather than dull my mind. My eyes may have deserted me, but my vision remains.''

I was awoken in the middle of the night by the sound of a moaning. It was my good master; he was sitting in his elbow-chair, rocking to and fro with his arms tightly clasped around his belly. At first I could not hear what he murmured, he moaned so low, but then I made out ''O dark dark dark dark'' repeated over and over again. Then I heard him to say very distinctly, ''But whom God hardens, them also He blinds.'' He rose from his chair, and came towards me. I pretended to sleep still and, when he stood above my pallet, I pressed my eyes close shut. ''In most things as a child helpless,'' he whispered. ''So easily condemned and scorned.'' Then he went back to his chair, and resumed his moaning.

May 15, 1660. It is very thick and foggy weather. We are hardly able to make our way, with as much filth and rubbish floating past the ship as if we were sailing down the pestilential Fleet towards the Thames. I could hear cawdimaudies and seagulls which, according to the captain, always frequent the shores of the land. But we could see nothing by reason of the fog. ''There is something here close by,'' Mr. Milton said to me as we patrolled the deck at noon. ''I can feel it by an inner prompting." We walked a little further. "I can smell it now. Somewhere there is an island, salt and cold." Only a few minutes later the unwholesome fogs parted to give us glimpse of some great island: it lay on our starboard side, and seemed to be entirely made of ice and crystal. It was about three leagues in length (so far as I could judge), with bays and cliffs and capes glittering in the light. My master had already turned his face towards it and, when I pictured it to him, he sighed. "Formed from the breath of God. Tell me how the ice congeals above the sea, and in what striations it falls."

"The ice is marked and hollowed like the pillars before St. Andrew in Leadenhall. Is that what you mean?"

He took in a deep breath of the cold. "And you say that it is dispeopled?"

"Altogether bare and frozen. This is a place to die, sir."

"Is it so? Yet it is said that those who die of the cold feel a sultry air around them just before they expire. The ice and winter's drift can also create a paradise."

"Oh, sir, I see something walking on the ice!"

"Where?"

"There!" I pointed, forgetting for the moment that he was wholly blind, but he followed my direction. "It walks towards a cave of ice. It has vanished now. Perhaps it is some wizard or enchanter?"

"What color was it?"

"Tawny, like a bear. But, sir, it held its head upright."

"So you think it to be some sorcerer dwelling in this land of ice?" I was looking too hard to say anything. "Could it be so? The heretics of Danzig believed that we create the things which we most fear, so that they take substantial form before us. They preached that the devil and all his works were a human illusion. Who knows what wonders of this western world will take the shape of our own frenzies?'' Then the fog and mist closed in again.

May 18, 1660. We took soundings at dawn, and measured thirty-five-fathom water. We were close to the banks of New-found-land, and the sailors cast their hooks for cod-fish. I went down to our quarters, to acquaint Mr. Milton with this news of land. He nodded as briefly as the Dutchman on the clock by the Bluecoat School. ''Have you read a work called *Utopia?*'' he asked.

''No, sir. Unless it might have been sold by the dozen on a hanging day.''

''Hardly so. It concerns a new discovered country. Shall I tell you something else?'' He could not help smiling. ''Its author was an idolatrous blasphemer, and was beheaded.'' The closer we come to our destination, the more lost he seems in his own fancies.

May 22, 1660. I saw a great number of sea-bats, as the captain called them. They are also known as flying fish. ''How large?'' Mr. Milton asked me as we stood upon the deck.

''About the size of a whiting. But with four tinsel wings.''

''How like an angel.''

''Where, sir?'' Mr. Bableigh had approached us. ''Where is that godly sign?''

''It was a metaphor, good sir. I see no angels yet.'' Then he whispered to me, ''Take me below.''

May 23, 1660. We are near to Cape Sable, but it cannot be seen in the mist. It is known as the sandy cape. He sits below, brooding, as dry as sand himself. No other news.

May 24, 1660. One of the voyagers has died of a consumption. We passed by the southern part of Newfound-land, and the sailors danced on the deck when we first caught sight of it. We are now more than eight hundred leagues from England.

May 28, 1660. We have come to anchor! We are by Richmond's Island very near the coast of New England. The brethren knelt in prayer, but my master demanded to be led onto land after the sailors. They had already managed to light a great fire with the wood of old barrels, upon which they cooked some Spanish dolphins lately caught by St. George Islands. The fish were beautified with an admirable variety of glittering colors but, as the captain's boy told me, "All that glisters is not gold." The mariners were singing some tavern ditty with as many oaths as a coal heaver by Scotland Yard—I thought Mr. Milton would have bridled at that but, instead, he smiled. "Someone is cooking liver," he said. "I have not known that smell since I left London." It was the liver taken from the porpoises, already boiled and sauced in vinegar; now it was being fried deliciously, and I gave a piece to him. "Very pleasing to the palate," he said. "More, please." Then we sucked some lemons and, secretly, I imbibed some strong water with the captain's boy.

May 29, 1660. My master is in good spirits but not, as he said, "in as strong a spirit as you were." So he had known, or guessed, but kept silent. We were now thirty leagues from the Bay of Massachusetts, whither we are bound, and he had decided to complete his letter to his former clerk, Reginald de la Pole, with all speed. "Bring out the old draft," he said, "and read back to me the end."

"It is to do with Time fetching an age of gold."

"Satis."

"Sir?"

"Take out your pen. These weeks at sea have not improved your wits." He put two fingers up to his forehead, and it reminded me of a divining twig. "Shall we carry over our argument with a question?"

"By all means."

"So write this. How and in what manner. No. Strike out my first two words." I deleted them with a great flourish of ink. "In what manner shall we now dispose and employ that great hoard of knowledge and illumination with which God has sent us to this new world? No. Begin again. Tear up the letter." He was sadly confused in his thoughts, if not his words, which I took to be a sign of sea weariness. "Dear fellow citizen and brother of London, I, John Milton, greet you with news of our most noble cause. It is one also most worthy to be recorded to all future time, so that posterity informed by your hand will know the triumphant beginning of our many wearisome labors. Long has been the way, and hard, towards the happy land of New England, this blissful seat past the unmapped regions and unknown dangers of the deep. Herein our commonwealth will soon spring up as a pattern of sober and well-ordered living, planted by patience and established in justice. So I have come to espy this bright world, whereof in England fame was not silent, here in hope to find better abode. Soon we shall possess a spacious land, good brother, little inferior to our native country. It is the new-created world that has been long foretold, a fabric wonderful—" He broke off with a groan. "The composition becomes too muddy. It has a dying fall, I think. Or was the preparatory matter too rich, too gorgeous?"

"It is all very luscious, sir." He was doleful, so I tried to cheer him. "I wish we had fruit with us of that sweetness."

He smiled, and patted me on the head. "You ought to know, Goosequill, that some fruit is forbidden us. Now go and check our course with the good captain."

May 30, 1660. We have gone along the coast by Cape Porpoise, still within sight of land. We have passed Black Point and Winter Harbor, so Captain Farrel told me, and will soon be bearing east away from the unlucky Isle of Shoals. "Those names," my master said, "belong to some country of allegory. In such a place we will be able to teach other nations how to live."

June 1, 1660. We sound one hundred and twenty fathoms of water. We are seven leagues off Cape Ann.

June 2, 1660. This day proved stormy and, having lost sight of land, fearing the lee shore, we bore out to sea all night.

June 4, 1660. We were riding by Cape Ann, and at first light I tied my good master to the deck so that he might not miss the end of our perilsome venture across the ocean. We saw our wished-for home in the Massachusetts Bay, but a sudden storm drove us from it.

June 5, 1660. God help us, we are adrift among islands. We have passed Block Island, but the captain has good hope for landfall. No more now.

FIVE

That was the funny thing. I had kept this little diary in my pocket. Here. Look. You notice how the seawater has stained its pages? Oh, Kate, it makes me shiver. Feel me shivering, if you please. And it was there, still in my breeches, when we crept up half-dead upon the shore. I was so bruised by the rocks, and so buffeted by the wreckage of the poor old *Gabriel,* and so dazed by the continual roaring of the ocean, that I was sure I had been down to hell and returned again. Truly. Mr. Milton was lying senseless on the strand, and was in danger of being pulled back by the waves, so I dragged and carried and pushed him higher up the sand bank. There was a fallen tree there, and I propped him against it like an old Jack Sweep on May Day. But he did not holler, not this old Jack. He turned up his face and stared at the sky. The rain was running down into his eyes, but he did not blink once. I sat down beside him, and promptly fell asleep. When I say sleep, Kate, it was more like sleeping and waking all at once for as soon as I closed my eyes I believed I was drowning again. So I started up, then closed my eyes, then started up again. "This is not a feather bed, master, is it?" I said after an hour's waking and shaking.

He did not reply, so I looked around at him. He was murmuring, or moaning, and when I put my ear close to his mouth I heard him say, "Christ save us, Christ save us, Christ save us."

"Well," I said out loud, "someone ought to save us." We were quite alone. For the first time I looked about me carefully and oh, Kate, there are times when it is better to be blind. The bodies of some of the travelers had been washed up, all beaten and bloody——

Goose, say no more. You are about to frighten me.

Then hold my hand while I tell you. There were corpses of cattle and sheep floating in the shallow waters, mixed with planks, timbers, barrels and pieces of mast. But do you know what came into my head? That old song, "London Bridge is broken down, broken down, broken down." I thought I saw a foal floating near to the shore, but, when I looked again, I saw that it was the body of the captain's boy. He had drunk his last strong water.

Oh, Goose. How can you be so merry about it? Look, you are smiling again.

I was not merry then, Kate, I can assure you of that. I lay down and wept. I roared. But then I stopped. There was a noise behind me, and I turned quickly. You know, Kate, it was the noise of the earth! There, beyond the sand dunes and the tall grasses, was a bright green wilderness. I had never seen the like before——great bushes and plants and grasses, wonderful big trees with vines and creepers coiling up around them. It would be fair to say that we never glimpse such things on Hounslow Heath. All we have there are ditches. And whores.

Goose!

I never touched them. I have a great respect for my health.

And there was steam everywhere, coming from the trees and bushes, together with a powerful rich scent of life. Of growing things. So here we are, I thought. Life and death come together. And now, Kate, there is a little piece of that life within your belly.

I know it. I cannot feel her yet, but I know that she is there.

Is she to be a female, then?

Oh yes. Stop petting me, Goose, and go on with the story.

So then I walked down to the edge of the water, making sure that I stayed away from the corpses of the brethren. But there was a figure, lying face down among the dunes, which seemed to be moving slightly. So I ran towards it. Yet it was only a hat and a coat, no person within, which had somehow been preserved together by the sea. They were drying nicely in the sun, and I considered whether we might have need of them. I had only my breeches but, when I turned back to look at our good master, I realized that he was wearing nothing at all. The sea had undone him in more than one sense and, if I may be so bold, he was stark naked. Well, as they say at Houndsditch, better a bad bargain than no bargain at all—so I took the clothes and walked back to him. "Come, sir," I said. "Let me cover you."

What is Houndsditch, Goose?

Dogs. Dead dogs. And a stream. Now Mr. Milton had raised his two arms in the air, as if he were about to preach something. But he still kept on saying, "Christ save us, Christ save us, Christ save us."

"I am beginning to think, sir, that we must shift to save ourselves." So I draped him with the coat. Then I put the hat on my own head, to ward off the heat of the sun, and returned to the shoreline to search for food or water or anything. At first I had no luck at all, but I suddenly spotted two cheeses tied together with a full barrel of butter which had been driven upon the shore. One of the brethren was lying, dead, a little way off. He must have been carrying the cheese and butter in his arms as he drowned. He looked like this. Oh, Kate, I'm sorry. I never meant to frighten you. Now that there are two of you, if you understand me. There was this little knapsack tied around the dead man's shoulders, and I was eager to see what it might contain. "Excuse me, sir," I said, "but I doubt that you will need a knapsack in heaven." I untied it from him and, when I opened it out, I found a flint and a knife wrapped in an oiled leather pouch. "No need for a flint or fire where you are going, sir, I hope." It did me good to talk to him that way. I think it made us all feel more comfortable.

I gathered up everything, together with the knapsack, and carried them back to Mr. Milton. I wonder where he *has* gone, Kate. He had stopped his moaning by the time I returned, and now he looked at me as helplessly as our little Jane about to sleep. "There there," I said to him, "all will be well."

I had seen a goat floating in some water close to us, so I went down to the ocean to bring it ashore. It was a nasty business, to reach among the corpses, and I had the strangest feeling that they might take my hands and hold me down beneath the waves. But I got hold of its legs, and pulled the poor creature up to the shore. With my new flint I made a fire among some branches I collected; they were so sodden by the tempest that they smoked and smoldered for a while, but eventually they burst into flame. I put a little piece of goat flesh on my knife, and began to roast it. "Meat, sir?" I asked him.

"Tell me, Goosequill, is ours to be a present or a lingering death?"

"Neither, sir, if you eat this good meat."

"What might it be?"

"Goat. Found by a miracle." He seemed to turn up his nose at that. "Well, if you like, you can live off groundnuts and acorns."

"No. Goat will be sufficient in our present plight. Is it sweet?"

"Gorgeous. Here, taste a little."

He ate some and then looked towards me helplessly again. "Moisture," he said. "I need moisture for my parched gums."

"Give me a moment, sir."

"Only a moment, please. I thirst."

I looked around, as confident as if we were by the pipes in Shoreditch, and then I spied one of the rocks. "Someone is looking after you, Mr. Milton."

"I know it."

"There is still water here which the sun has not dried." I led him towards it, and guided his hand to the pits and hollows where the rainwater had gathered. He bent over and drank. When he had finished he wiped his mouth with his hand.

Oh no, Goose. He is always so neat. So delicate in his manners. His linen is so clean that I scarcely need to wash it. And when he eats, he makes sure to wipe his knife with a cloth at the end of the meal.

Without you to serve him, Kate, he would hardly eat at all.

It is true, Goose, that you need no persuasion. To eat and to drink. I hope, by the way, that is only water in your glass.

May I have the honor of entertaining you with my story for a little longer? So when our dear master had drunk his fill, he seemed to look around. "This place is as silent as midnight," he said. "Are we alone, Goose? Have any survived?"

"I see no one at all, sir. Not in life, that is."

"It must have been one of the hardest and saddest storms known since the days of the apostle Paul."

"Very likely. Do you know what I am thinking?"

"What are you thinking, Goosequill?"

"I am thinking that we should get out of the sun."

"And find some overgrown covert?"

"Exactly so."

"I do feel it upon me now. Is the sun very large here?"

"Enormous. This is a strange place, sir, where sea and wood and sand and grass are all mingled."

"And as sun-blasted as Arabia?"

"Worse, I should think. Yet it is all green enough. I saw some grass yonder, springing up after the storm. It was so long that it must grow up to a man's face. It had a greater stalk and broader blade than any I have known in England."

"What is to be expected? There are no scythes or cows in this uncouth place."

"There are some dead ones now, sir."

"Yes. Tell me about the *Gabriel*."

So we sat down together in the shade of the rock. I drew circles in the sand so that I would not have to look up at the horrible corpses, while I described to him what I had already seen that day. He listened carefully, with his head bowed also. "Enough now," he said, after I had told him about the pilgrim with the knapsack on his back. "This is some world of evil in which God has thought fit to place us. Why otherwise should we have been cast up by a whirlwind, with so many people lost? We have been saved for a purpose, Goosequill. We have been fated to another wandering in a wilderness, on the understanding that this wilderness is an allegory for the whole of fallen nature. Merciful heaven, what noise was that?''

Goose, why are you groaning?

I am imitating the noise that we heard, Kate, something like a sigh and a groan mixed. And, yes, there is more than water in my glass. At this point Mr. Milton grabbed my arm. ''Could it be some robber calling to his fellows?''

''Men would have no reason to travel here, sir.''

''Perhaps not a man. Perhaps a savage.'' We heard the same noise a moment later. ''Keep down your head!'' But I was so curious that I peered over the rock and then, Kate, I gave out a squeak like an old door. No, I shall not imitate it now. ''What is it?'' he whispered fiercely. ''Speak.''

''It is a bear, sir. Bigger than any I ever saw in London. And it is black.''

''Hell's gate has opened. What is it doing?''

''It is feasting on some dead fish cast up by the storm. It is guzzling them peacefully enough. There is probably no danger to be feared from it.'' But even as I watched, it began to straighten up and sniff the air. It was as tall as the puppet in Cloth Fair, truly, and then it started wandering towards us. I knew that it had smelled the remains of the dead goat, so very nimbly I sped towards the cinders of the fire. I took up some skin and charred pieces of flesh, and flung them as far as I could towards the ocean in the hope that the bear might follow.

What is Cloth Fair?

Cloth Fair is a fair where they sell cloth. This bear did not turn. So I picked up the carcass of the goat, and hurled it towards him so that he might stop and eat. Still he ambled our way. Not with any menace, as far as I could tell, but like an old man out for a stroll in the air. But his tread was heavier than that of any old man I had ever met, and Mr. Milton was all quivering at the sound. He grabbed my arm, and pulled me down into the shadow of the rock. "Run now," he whispered.

"Only if you run with me."

"How can a blind man outstrip a bear? Where are your wits? Go."

"No. I stay with you."

But the bear was now almost upon us, and I could smell his breath like stale salt-fish reserved from overnight. Then Mr. Milton rose up from our hiding place, stood erect, and pointed his right arm at the creature. Like this. It would be enough to frighten Gog or Magog, I can tell you, with his blind eyes and his hair all streaming wild. I will not scream, Kate, I promise, but I will raise my voice a little. "Hence, loathed animal," he shouted, "of Cerberus and blackest midnight born! Go! Find some cell where brooding darkness spreads his jealous wings. Go, I say!" The creature just stared at him; then it sucked one of its paws, turned away and began running back to the forests behind us.

I was utterly astonished. "Was that some kind of magic spell?"

"It was." Mr. Milton was breathing heavily.

I know how he excites himself with his speeches, Goose. He is never calm after them. Did he sweat?

He did indeed. But then he wiped his face with the sleeve of the cloak I had salvaged for him. "We are two candles in this wilderness," he said after he had dried himself, "chasing out the darkness. Well, Goosequill, my own words have cheered me. Ask me what we must do next."

"What must we do next, master?"

"We must roam through wood and through waste, over hill and over dale! I will follow your younger feet, since my blindness leaves me lagging after. In other words, dear Goosequill, we will plod on. We will tread these western fields."

I had known him drunk on words before, since he was a great tippler of his own phrases, but I had never known him so exultant. "In which direction shall we travel then, sir?"

"Irregular motions may be necessary on earth sometimes, Goosequill. But we shall not shrink back from our destiny. We shall go on with the strength of divine assistance. We shall find fresh woods and pastures new. Is there more food?" I gathered pieces of the cooked flesh which I had thrown towards that bear, and he ate them eagerly.

That evening we sat beside the fire.

Just as we are doing now, Goose?

It was less snug and cozy, Kate. I had found some wood from the wreck, and I blew upon the timber as it hissed and crackled in the silence. He did not speak, but seemed to look into the heart of the fire. What could he have seen there, but the heat itself?

He saw stories, Goose, as we do. When I sit with him sometimes, he will speak of ancient things. Of old kings, and buried cities, and suchlike. Mr. Milton is fond of his ruins.

He looked like one that night. "It is growing cold," he said at last, wrapping his newfound cloak around him. Then we were quiet again. I started humming some little tune, but he carried on speaking as if there had been no silence at all. "I hope that we have not traveled too close to the frozen zone. That would be unfortunate indeed. Are you benumbed?"

I could not help but laugh. "What was that word?"

"Benumbed. Frozen. Pinched with cold."

"Oh no. It is warm enough for me."

"Then you are not benumbed."

"If you say so."

"I do so say."

We sat quietly again, and he put his head to one side so that he could listen to the flames. I loved to watch him at those times and guess, from the movements and expressions of his face, what he was thinking.

Oh, Goose, I know of that. When his nose twitches, it means that he is about to say something humorous. When there is a little crease upon his forehead, he is thinking of a quotation. When it grows larger, he is about to come out with his own words. Am I right?

Yes, Kate. And on this occasion a very large crease appeared. "Do you believe, Goosequill, that there will be some western millennium?"

"Perhaps there may be some Goosequillennium, sir."

"We have been led into this wilderness by some strong motion. I have not yet fully learned the intent behind it, and perhaps I need not know it. What concerns our knowledge, God reveals." He had scarcely finished when we heard the most terrible sounds from the interior. May I howl for you, Kate? There. That did me good. "What desolate noise was that?" he asked me.

My hair stood up like bristles. "Beasts, sir."

"Ravening creatures of the night?"

"Wolves, I think."

"Quench the flame." He was trembling as greatly as if he had swallowed down quicksilver. "Put out the fire!" So I smothered it with my hat and we both sat quaking in the darkness. "I have heard reports," he whispered, "of their assaults upon travelers in Germany. How much more fierce might they be in this wilderness?"

"What shall we do then, sir?"

"Pray." He began to murmur to himself. "Who brought me hither will bring me hence." He was giving a very good impression of a chandler reciting his accounts. "Teach me to know what I can suffer, and how I must obey. Who best can suffer, best can do."

I crept over to an outcrop of rock, and peered into the night. I could see lanterns being carried here and there among the woods, but of course, Kate, these were the very eyes of the roaming wolves! They set up their howling once again, which was enough to make the whole earth ring like a church bell, but Mr. Milton had somehow composed himself. "They are moving away from us," he told me firmly. "They are traveling inland. God be thanked." You know how he is always right? So I rekindled the fire, and we slept.

The next day we began our journey into the unknown territory. First of all we knelt down and prayed. I could manage only a little bit of devotion but, while he rocked to and fro on his knees, I packed our bread and cheese in the knapsack. Then I took his hand, and led him away from the shore. He stumbled over the shells and small stones, but I kept as solemn as a mule while he made continual yelps. "What flints are these?" he asked me.

"Mere pebbles, sir."

"They feel to me like boulders and cobbles. I shall be cut to death, and my feet will die first." He was getting into an ill temper, and suddenly turned upon me. "Will you stop forever twirling your hair, like some seamstress at her thread! It distracts me." I was still holding his hand, so he must have sensed my movement. "Of course our Lord survived thirty days in the wilderness. I must learn to follow His divine example."

"Better to follow me first, sir. There is a path and even ground ahead of us." It was a dainty piece of cliff, somewhat like our hills in Islington, and I led him upwards.

Not as large as our Devon hills, then? They are beautifully made, Goose. I miss them.

We have only a few hills in London, Kate, but we have Cornhill.

We have moors where the wild beasts roam.

We have Moorfields, where the wild men are imprisoned.

We have the sea.

We have the Marshalsea. Now that we are at evens, may I return? So I lead him up this hill which is smaller than any in Devon. "Ah," he said, "clear air. So pure and so wholesome that we might take our sustenance from it."

"If it is all one to you, I prefer to keep my cheese. Now here is a sight."

We had come out upon a level area at the summit, and I could see ahead of me valleys and hills, woods and lakes, and white mountains in the far distance. When I pictured them to him, he clapped his hands. "We have come out of Sodom into the land of Canaan! Nature has poured forth her bounties with——" He put out his arms, like this, and somehow overbalanced himself. That was when he slipped over the edge of the cliff. I screamed, but stopped when I saw that he had slid only three or four feet into the arms of a waiting tree. Somehow he had got entangled in the bushes beneath it and had his arms around its trunk. "What is it, Goosequill?"

"It is a tree, sir."

"I know it is a tree. But what type or kind?" Already he was running his hands along it, and sniffing the bark.

"Might it be an oak?" I helped him to his feet, and dusted off his coat. "Or a pine?"

"You are a true boy of Farringdon ward. You would not know an acorn from a berry."

"But I know my knife." I had taken it from the knapsack, where it had been having a perfectly comfortable journey with the flint, and cut into the wood. "It is red. Like a stave."

"Yes indeed. This is a holy tree, Goosequill." He was embracing it again, but I stood beside him in case he took another fall. "The cedar. It smells as sweet as juniper, does it not? No more than a foot in girth. Tell me how high."

"As high as my old master's house in Leadenhall."

"Which was?"

"Not very high at all."

"Enough. This tree, fool, is such as Solomon used for the building of his temple in Jerusalem. No doubt it is an emblem of the many temples which will one day rise in this land, and yet——" He looked up into its branches. "Not very tall, you say?"

"No, Mr. Milton. Quite short."

"Certainly it seems a little inferior to the cedars of Lebanon, so much commended in the Scriptures. If sacred works are our guide, then nature's work is wanting here."

"I am your guide, sir, at the present time. Would you prefer to continue rolling down the cliff, or to walk with me?"

"A hard choice, Goose. But perhaps I will follow you."

So we walked all that day, but not before slaking our thirst at a little spring which gushed out from some rocks nearby. Now where there is a spring, as you will know from your Devon days, there will eventually be a stream, and where there is a stream, there will soon be a river. That is, as Mr. Milton said, an adamantine law. And, fortunately, a watery law too. So we were much heartened as we continued our journey through the wilderness, and by dusk we came upon a clearing at the edge of a great forest. All the ground was scorched and blackened but, when I pictured this to our dear friend, he sniffed the air. "A bolt of flame," he said. "It has always been believed that those territories smitten by lightning are deemed sacred. This is a holy place." It looked to me as if the area had been burned and wasted by someone, but I kept my peace. You know how quiet and thoughtful I can be?

No, Goose.

Instead I collected some wood and, having made a fire, we sat and munched upon our cheese. We might have been at Greenwich, Kate, after the fair. Please not to ask me anything about Greenwich. Except that there were these rowdy crickets singing all around us. I am accustomed to them now, but at that time they sounded very sharp. I was about to object but Mr. Milton was nodding his head to their chirrups, just as if he had been listening to some nimble trickster on a clavichord. Then the lights came. They were hovering in the air a few yards distant, and I suddenly thought that there were wolves approaching. So I leapt up, spilling all my cheese onto the ground, and screamed. He sprang up, too, and screamed with me. Of course I realized then that these lights were too small to be the eyes of any creature, and there were so many that the air itself seemed to be on fire.

"I am sorry to have disturbed you," I said, "but there are very many sparkles flying up to the sky."

"You have ruined my supper for the sake of glowworms. Have you never seen them before? They litter the fields of Lambeth."

"But there are so many here. Thousands upon thousands."

"This land, then, has its own light." He had calmed down a little. "In the voices of the crickets, it also has its music."

I picked up the remains of the cheese, and handed them to my master. "If it had its own towns and cities and harbors, too, then we would be merry enough. I grant you that." That was the end of our second day in the wilderness, Kate. Kate, may I have a kiss now? Are you growing sleepy, Kate? Put your head upon my shoulder. There. Do you remember how you used to rest upon me when we sat together? What was that book we once read? *A Letter of Advice Concerning Marriage.*

You never took any advice, Goose.

But I was your guide, was I not? And, if I could lead Mr. Milton through the forests, I might be able to lead you to bed now. Oh, Kate.

.   .   .

Shall I continue now, after our delicious supper? Is Jane yet asleep? No strong water tonight, Kate, I promise. I will be the very pattern of a storyteller. I will not digress, as Mr. Milton might say. I will not embroider. We were woken before dawn by the stinging of the flies. Worse than their bites was my thirst, though, and just before the sun rose I took Mr. Milton to some bushes and grasses on the edge of the clearing. Together we licked the dew from their leaves and then he knelt down to pray, with me saying "Amen!" in all the wrong places.

"Have you noticed something?" he asked me afterwards.

"I have not."

"There are no larks. At least I have heard none."

"Oh, but there are birds enough. I have seen flights of them in the distance, looking like our pigeons."

"It was a pigeon which came upon the deck of the *Gabriel*. Do you recall? We will in future know them as birds of false promise."

We were eating butter out of the pots, licking our fingers like schoolboys. "I had a dream last night, Goosequill, which may presage much. I dreamed that we were in a great forest, and that many turtledoves sat upon green boughs. They watched over us, and their cooing resembled the sound of a calm sea which environed us. But then the flies woke me."

"Oh Lord, sir. There is never a dream so grand that the world will not defeat it."

"Yes. The heat and the dust break through." He wiped his fingers on his cloak. "Which reminds me that I must wash. I am in decay, Goose. I am living as some anchorite in my own filth."

"That is very shocking, sir. But we have hopes for a river, do we not? Or a running stream?" I looked around earnestly, as if I had not already looked a hundred times before. "We have the forest here, through which we could cut a narrow track. Away from it is a land of tall grasses which looks firm enough, but it may hide a salt marsh or a swamp. I cannot choose."

"Choice is but reason. When God made Adam, He gave him freedom to choose. Which way is it to be?"

"Could it be your decision, sir? I am not so resolved in my mind as you."

"So you seek the help of a blind man, do you?" He was pleased with his own wit. "Well, I am content to be our guide." He stood up and seemed to scent the air; his nostrils flared, but he lifted up his head only to sneeze.

"God's blessing, sir."

"Thank you, Goosequill. We go this way." He started striding towards the forest, but then stopped at the very border of the trees. It was all thickly overgrown, and he brushed something from his hair. "May I borrow your hat, please? I have a horror of crawling things."

"Snakes?"

"Serpents." He had such an expression upon his face, Kate, that he might have just seen one. "And what else are we likely to find as we wander? No doubt natives. Indians. Savages. Pagans. All around us."

"No, sir. You are not in London now." What is the matter, Kate?

There are no savages in London, are there? Or pagans?

Plenty of them. Except that they wear cloaks and hats like the rest of us. Mr. Milton sighed at my mention of London. "I wish to God that I was returned there," he said. "I thought we might have raised Eden in this wilderness, but now—"

"Back to the houses and the sewers?"

"Oh yes."

"The jail and the executioner?"

"What have we here but a divine punishment, more serious by far?"

"If I find a shoe, sir, I will take out the thread."

"Why so?"

"So that you might hang yourself with it."

"No, Goosequill, for then I am afraid that you would be compelled to a solitary life. Lead on."

We entered the forest, and I took care to mark each tree with my knife as we made our slow way among dense boughs, underbrush and fallen trees. After a few minutes he sniffed the air. "There is a scent of water somewhere," he said. "To our left hand."

At that moment I saw a rough path or track ahead of us, and I ran towards it with a loud "Halloo!"

I know that "Halloo," Goose. You are always making it when you run or leap or dance.

Or when I catch sight of you, at first light. "It looks as if some little horses have galloped here," I told him. "I see the marks of tiny hoofs!"

"Deer. What else is there?"

Just then some rabbits scattered among the bushes. But our voices had alarmed more than those timid things, and two creatures glided from one tree to another. They resembled squirrels, but I had never yet seen squirrels with wings. "Bats, sir."

"Bats at day? I hardly think so."

"But there is a track, sir, as plain as my hat. Your hat."

"Go forward, then. It may lead us, like the deer, to water."

So we made our way along this little track, which began to slope downwards so sharply that I held on tight to my master for fear of his slipping: he was always good at rolling down hills. He had no more breath than a turkey at Christmas and when we paused for the nourishment of the air, as he put it, we heard the sound of water. With one accord we slipped and crawled down the rest of the path, which must have been the side of some valley into which we had strayed, until I could see a stream glittering among the bushes. But it was no stream at all, Kate, it was a river. "As wide as the Thames!" I shouted, and all at once I jumped in it. "There will be fish! Fish and water and more besides!"

Our master stood uncertainly by the bank, and put his hand over the surface of the river as if he could sense how deep it was. Then he knelt down and touched it while I heard him murmuring, "I pray that this may be a true balm and cordial." He cupped his hands and drank the water, before bathing his neck and face. I was splashing around like a dog in a pond, and some of the water hit him. "Mind my hat! Goosequill, I love your frolicsome revels—"

"You can call me Duck, sir, not Goose!"

"—but already my coat is damp and heavy enough for two men."

"Remove it, then. This is not Lambeth Marsh. Here we are free!"

"I know it. Loosen my clothes, then, if you please." I ceased my tumbling, and came to heel. "Good. Now, Goosequill, will you leave me to my libations?"

"Libations?"

"I am not of an effeminate mind—"

"Oh no, sir."

"But I would like to cleanse myself in peaceful solitude."

"In a word, go?"

"Precisely so."

I started walking backwards along the bank, still facing him. "I am going. I am going. I am going." I stumbled upon some root, and fell among tall grasses. "I am gone, sir. Quite gone." I looked at him for a moment more, and wondered at his body so white and pure that it showed no signs of aging.

Is it so, Goose?

Like the body of a girl. But not so soft and pleasant to touch as yours, Kate.

Do stop stroking me. And pass me that thread, if you please. I must occupy myself while you talk.

I know how I could occupy you, Kate.

Goose! Stop it.

So I decided to explore further. Not you, Kate. The forest. I had a mind to wander, now that I was refreshed, so I scrambled up another part of the bank, where I came upon a space of ground. It was all overgrown with bushes, and from some of them hung a dark berry in many luscious clusters. As luscious as your mouth. I tasted one, and it was sweet. As sweet as your lips. "Since we are all destitute of plants and victuals," I said to myself, in Mr. Milton's voice, "you may pluck this purple food and even chew its pulp." I ate another. "What ambrosial fruitage."

That is very like him, Goose. He is always so eloquent.

There was a tree on the edge of this bushy plot, and I caught sight of some golden fruit suspended from one of its branches; it was like some bright apple bathed in light, Kate, and was as large as the crown of a woman's hat. I could not resist touching it but, when I put out my hand, it dissolved all at once into a cloud of wasps. Not so much a cloud as a storm, though, and I was stung upon my neck and hands. Here, here and here. Why are you laughing? I roared like the bear who had almost stumbled upon us, and rushed down to the river, where my master was still cleaning himself in the water. "What infernal noise is this, Goosequill?"

"I have been stung! All over!"

"In ancient times, bees were supposed to guard places of oracle and divination." I noticed, even through my pain, that his hands were covering his private parts. "Have you become a seer?"

"I see nothing, sir."

"Then we are alike." He turned his back to me as modestly as a maiden. "Yet even if we cannot see, we can think. Is that not right?"

I was very sore, and not prepared for his philosophy at that particular moment. "I suppose that is so."

"Tell me what you think, then, of this river."

"It is very beautiful."

"I can only dream of beauty. Think again."

"It will provide food and drink for us."

"Good. Now tell me where it will lead."

"Inland, sir."

"You have it. It will lead us, in time, to a mill or house or village. All the chronicles of ancient Britain tell us that rivers are the natural place of settlement. You will remember, of course, that a second Troy rose beside the Thames."

"I do not recall it precisely, sir. But I was young then."

"And a fool still. Come. Turn your back upon me as I leave the water. We will march forward presently." I helped to dress him, and then brought some of the sweet berries I had found. "I can hear," he said, "the murmuring of flies and the splash of the fish as they leap from the water." He finished his fruit, and wiped the juice from his chin with the sleeve of his cloak. "But do you know what I see?"

"What do you see?"

"I see lines of words murmuring and calling to one another."

I did not understand him then and I do not understand him now, but I was diverted. "Oh Lord, sir! Here is something you have not heard as yet," I said. "Swans have just turned the bend in the river. They come towards us."

"Is it so?"

"Just like our swans in England. We used to stone them by the old London Bridge." He frowned at that. "But we never caught any of them."

"You are as bad as the swan-eating and canary-sucking prelates who rule us now."

"I used to see them eating by the Fleet ditch. I wondered how so fair a bird could touch anything so foul."

"It is the nature of a beast. Do they drift?"

"They drift."

"And they do not fear us. *Ambulate.*"

"Sir?"

"You have gawped enough. Lead me on to further wonders."

So we started our journey inland, by way of the riverbank itself, which curled and twisted among the rocks and grasses. It was exceedingly warm, but we walked beneath the shade of many trees that grew there. We had traveled for a mile or so when I came to a sudden halt. "Hush, sir. There is something monstrous in the water near us."

He clutched my shoulder and whispered, "What finny beast is it?"

"He is like some dog or cat in the water. He paddles. Oh no. He comes ashore." My master held on to me more tightly. "He is like a mole before, and like a goose behind. Oh Lord, sir, he has a tail like the sole of a shoe. What is he?"

"Ah, now I know." He took his hand from me. "No need to fear. I have read of it."

"I wish that were a comfort. You have read of many things."

"It is something like an otter mixed with a rabbit. I have read that it builds houses with the boughs of trees. Somewhat like our English emmets. It will not harm us."

It was then I noticed, as we turned another bend in the river, that some logs were laid across the water. This was no animal's home, Kate. It was a bridge. And what did I see now but a man, in shirt and breeches, walking across it with a pole in his hand!

Will you cut this thread for me, Goose? I am listening.

"Huzzah!" I screamed. "Hoorah! Here!"

I am still listening, but you are hurting my ears.

"What is it now?" Mr. Milton asked me with a trembling in his voice.

"A man, sir! A living Englishman! Huzzah!" I stood on tiptoe, and took my master's hat from his head, and waved it in the air. The gentleman on the bridge waved back, in as familiar a manner as if we were just passing down Old Jewry.

What is Old Jewry, Goose?

The Hebrews used to live there once, but now it is all merchants and tailors. May I be permitted to reach the end of this history? "We are from London!" I called out. "We have come from London!"

We hastened up to him, my hand upon my master's arm, and the stranger still did not seem at all surprised. "You have come a long way, then," he said.

"Yes indeed." It seemed that Mr. Milton now wished to speak for us. "I thought we had trespassed beyond the bounds of our pilgrim people. But from your voice, sir, I know your origin. God be praised!"

"Who are you?"

He drew himself up, and put his hand upon my shoulder in a highly dignified manner. "I am John Milton. I am the good old cause."

SIX

Dearly beloved brother in Christ, Reginald Pole, I, John Milton, greet you in the name of the good old cause. In your last letter, full of civility, good will, and singular affection for us and our new Republic, you requested another profitable and fruitful chapter from our own divinely inspired history. How could I refuse so heartfelt and devoted a plea? In my last epistle I informed you of my desperate journey after the shipwreck, both of goods and hopes; wherein I was accompanied by a poor and credulous boy, with whom it was God's will I should be further burdened. Nevertheless I was led by my inner sight to an Englishman dwelling in the wilderness, and it was he who, like the disciple of Edom, first brought news of my arrival to the godly people of the region. They were waiting patiently for me when I came, with sure and steady pace, into their settlement. The name of John Milton was not unknown to them, and indeed some of my tracts against the episcopacy had been urgently distributed among the towns of New England many months before. The news of my sudden but not unpropitious arrival was soon widely known, and it became the common report that I had fled the wrath of an unjust and impious king. I had left

Egypt in order to find another Israel, and the grave brethren of New Tiverton were gathered in readiness to greet me. They had assembled in their small wooden meetinghouse, a humble dwelling humbly consecrated to God, and from far off I heard them chanting hymns. But, first, may I go back a little? You have also asked me for homilies and fables from Christ's new land. I have so much to impart to you, good fellow laborer in the vineyard, that I am not undisposed to mix the poetry of history with its plain prose. I have never condemned the employment of mild and agreeable matter, as long as it be not wanton, among high and tragic stuff; there is no harm to be taken from jocose interludes within our epic theme, so long as they are not inclined to gratify a corrupt and idle taste. Such is not your case, dear Pole, and so most willingly do I grant your request.

It was the man named Eleazer Lusher who carried the news of our strange coming. He had discovered my poor companion and myself beside a river, and had at once taken us to his cabin at the further end of that valley through which we had wandered with many sighs and tears. I soon knew it to be a roughly built wooden cottage plastered with clay, though, to the credulous and ignorant child who accompanied me, it was "as grand as Whitehall Palace" after our long journey. Mr. Lusher lived in solitude, and obtained milk and cheese and other such items by bartering the skins of beavers which he hunted. Yet he seemed content with his seclusion and, as I narrated the events of our storm and shipwreck (with many asides from the boy), he listened quietly and solemnly. No doubt he once suffered from some impediment of the tongue, because he replied with great hesitation and deliberation; I knew from his voice that he was looking down at the ground as he spoke to me. "That is why I found you by the

Sakonnet," he said after I had completed the account of my inland journey. "You were shipwrecked on the rocks past Sakonnet Point. It is a hard coast for those unaccustomed to it."

He fed us with baked fish and corn meal, in the manner of the earliest Christians, and pressed us to imbibe copious quantities of milk which were not unwelcome. The distracting child with me, known as Goosequill, guzzled it mightily and I was moved to rebuke him. I wished to learn more of this region to which we had come. "Can you tell me, Mr. Lusher, about the principalities and powers of this place?"

"You mean?"

"Who rules?"

So then, with many difficulties and silences as he strove to compose his halting speech, he informed me of the nature and extent of the territories to which I had come. We were in the land of the Wampanoags (in this barbarous and heathen world, Mr. Pole, the very words themselves seem to be demons), whose sachem or chief, Wamsutta, had been most unaptly re-named "Alexander" by the English; he now resided in Wachuset, which had been more piously called "Mount Hope" by our settlers. This land was in turn surrounded by other tribes of unholy name. The Pokanokets to the southeast, with the Nausets beyond them; to our west were the Narragansetts, and beyond them the savage Pequots who, by God's loving grace, had been all but extirpated by the brethren ten years ago. Our whole land was now known as New Plymouth, named after that wonder-working settlement which had been established by the admirable providence of Christ on a site known to the Indians as Pocasset or Patuxet.

I begged him for fewer heathen and savage names. Aggawam, Nanepashemet, Chobocco, Naumkeag—these were more strange to me, I said, than Gehenna, Vallombrosa, Tophet or Goshen where the devils of scripture had once made their home. The wayward and superstitious Goosequill was elated, however, and clapped with delight when he learned that the recently named Thames, to the west, had once been known as Pequot. When Mr. Lusher earnestly informed us that Englishmen were known as *Wanux,* the boy began excitedly walking around the cabin and chanting "I am Wanux!"

"You must forgive him, Mr. Lusher," I said. "I fear that our sufferings have severely tried his wits."

"Oh no, sir. He may refresh our own. We can be a sad sort here."

So spoke the lonely hunter, withdrawn by choice from the company of the elect. But there was no sadness when I was led towards their meetinghouse, two days later, nothing but a general murmuring of "Praise be!" and "Praise the Lord!" from the assembled brethren. Of course I no longer wore the verminous garments foolishly given to me by the boy, but was instead dressed in a plain russet cloak with a white band around my neck. It was decent, and fitting, without being penitential. I had also acquired a wooden staff for this solemn occasion, and proceeded slowly along the central aisle with my hand upon Goosequill's shoulder. I had hoped to do without his aid, sluggard as he was, but I could not be sure of my footing on these hastily constructed boards.

"This is he," one of the elect whispered. "He enters like a prophet."

I had intended no such resemblance, and bowed my head in humility before I turned to them. "Your presence, friends, revives me. You see me in pain and long-endured suffering, but tax not divine disposal. I thought myself changed, almost fallen, when I found myself cast upon a land so unlike the place from which I had come. But all was not lost. To be weak, good people, is to be miserable. My indomitable will maintained me. Yet you know that it was not my strength. No. It was not."

I heard them echo my words satisfactorily with "Not at all!" and "No indeed!"

"Trusting in God who called me to this land, leaving friends and native soil far behind, I wandered willingly through boggy fens and swamps, through desert and morass—" I paused, and the silence reassured me that they were listening intently. "So with lonely steps I have made my way towards this place foretold, across the oceanic void immense. And now I see a goodly prospect. I see fortunate fields, and groves, and flowery vales."

The boy had informed me, before my arrival, that the brethren were "sickly pale" and, if I recall his vulgar phrase, "looking as tired as a bottle-head on Sunday morning." *Horribile dictu!* Yet oh, Mr. Pole, how revived they seemed as they called out "Hallelujah!" and "Praise be!" after my oration.

One of their number came forward. (I trust that you will be interested in the plain words of the brethren, simple fragments of a history that will inspire those left in my dear old forsaken country. Scatter this history, Reginald, over the land of England. Disseminate it without delay.) "Seaborn Jervis," the pious man informed me.

"I beg your pardon?"

"Seaborn, sir. I was reborn on our crossing of the ocean. I issued through the navel of Christ."

"It was excellently done."

"And now by general consent I have been enrolled to plead with you."

"Do not talk of pleading, Mr. Seaborn, when I come here as a poor errant soul myself."

"Jervis, sir. Mr. Jervis. May I speak something of immediate and present concern to us all?"

"Indeed you may."

"I have been entrusted with the news that this is no place for settlement."

"Truly there is no abiding city upon this earth."

"No, sir. I mean that we have always intended to build our godly town elsewhere. The air here is too rank with many vapors."

"Is it pestilential?"

"I thought it smelled like Tothill Fields," the boy by my side said.

I took the opportunity of squeezing his shoulder until he groaned. "Forgive my servant. He is prone to worldly allusions."

"It is very swampy air here, sir," continued Mr. Jervis with as pious an air as before. "At first we thought to establish ourselves by a spacious lake, which was reputed by our previous brethren to be clearer than the holy lake of Genezereth in Palestine."

"Which was so clear it seemed another sky!"

"But then we learned that it was three hundred miles distant."

"That would be a pilgrimage indeed."

"But now we have found a fertile place near this river, which we hope to subdue to our will."

"Is it a *vacuum domicilium*?"

"Sir?"

"Is it empty of people? Are there no claims upon it?"

I sensed that the congregation had been listening carefully to this exchange, and a woman at the back called out, "Only the barbarians! Only the pagan savages!"

"That is Humility Tilly, sir," Mr. Jervis advised me in a low tone. "She is brimful of piety."

"Who are these pagans of which she is so eloquent?"

"The heathen natives. They called the land Machapquake." He hesitated, and I knew at once that he was to speak of purchase. "But they were easily parted from it."

The interruption from Humility Tilly moved some of the congregation to intervene in the same pious spirit. I heard one of them cry, "Seven miles square got for seven coats!"

Seaborn Jervis was still very restrained in my presence, and I admired him for it. "Forgive their enthusiasm, sir."

"Enthusiasm is a godly gift."

"We obtained the land for seven coats, as they say, together with a few simple tools of our own making. The savages also wished for ten and a half yards of cotton cloth, which after deliberation we granted them. It was a fair bargain, and now the land is within our patent."

"A good price indeed. Repeat to me its name, if you please?"

"Machapquake in the savage tongue. But—" The good Jervis hesitated once more. "But we would wish to call it New Milton."

"Is it really so?" I stared ahead, and waited for him to speak again.

"We have agreed among us, sir, knowing full well of your godly work in our dear mother country, and being acquainted with your right noble mind in pursuit of the general good— well, sir, may we ask you to frame for us a little commonwealth and polity? Will you be our author and prime architect?"

I heard the mad boy by my side whisper "Oh Lord," yet I chose not to admonish him in this bright hour of my life. "Yes," I said. "I will."

At once there was a general chorus of "God be praised!" and "God is present here," which pleased me. I heard the good Jervis turn upon his heels and announce to his brethren that "Our yoke is lifted!"

There was a rustling among them, and from the air and movement I sensed that one had left his seat and was now approaching me. "Much has been done, good sir, to ease your task. We have conferred together and granted twenty acres of land to each of our families."

"Who speaks to me now?"

"Preserved Cotton, sir."

"A holy name, no doubt."

"So our acreage is divided nicely. And, if I may use these names in this godly assembly, we have granted one cow and two goats to each family. As for the planting of corn—"

I took my arm from Goosequill's shoulder, and raised it in the air. "Good Master Preserved Cotton, God will grant increase and prosperity to his own people. Have no doubt of that. Shall we advance into the healthful air?" I have always been of a reserved and fastidious temper, Mr. Pole, believing that cleanliness brings us closer to the pure spirit of God. In this assembly house it had already become uncomfortably warm and close, and I told the boy to lead me through the congregation, in slow and reverent steps, towards the open door. I heard the brethren sighing as I passed them, and then they followed me into the white light of New England.

While they gathered about me, I turned my face towards the sun. To my left hand I could smell all the odors from the lush vegetation of the forest: this godly settlement was by a wilderness indeed. But I took heart, and struck the earth three times with my staff. "This is no Sabbath assembly," I told them. "I shall not make a lecture. You shall not need an hourglass, good people, to measure my exhortations. I say only this. The beginning of nations, those excepted of whom the sacred books have spoken, is to this day unknown or else obscured and blemished by fables. But we will need to spin no stories here. You poor wandering people, so beloved of God, have come into this vast recess only because you prefer hard liberty before the easy yoke of servile pomp. Though I see you not, I hear your grave and solemn words. I know you to be no less noble and well fitted to the liberty of a commonwealth than were the ancient Greeks and Romans." An infant cried and, as it was soothed, I remained quiet and took the opportunity of composing my last words. "I share with you hopes of a glorious rising commonwealth. I see the prospect of another world, the happy seat of some new race, a bright isle and clime where one day, by policy and long process of time, will rise a mighty empire. Long has been the way, and hard, that from the hell of impiety and sacrilege has led you towards this dawn. But now let there be light indeed!"

SEVEN

Do you remember, Kate, how it was that we first met?

I never said a word to you, Goose.

Oh, yes, you did. You were a chatterbox.

I was not.

Yes, you were. But you were not alone. Our good master was spinning out enough words for the brethren to make his tongue ache. Yet who could ask him to be dumb as well as blind? Do you recall that barn they called a meetinghouse? I led him outside, and he made a great display of words.

Among those wooden huts we had, Goose. And those tents of cloth.

You looked as if you were wearing tents as well. Everything was patched and mended, so that you might have been sprung from the sturdy beggars of Shadwell. Except that none of you were sturdy at all. If you forgive me for saying it, Kate, you all looked as if you were wasting away. This is no New Tiverton, I said to myself, this is some New Wen. Then I saw you.

You came over to me when little Jane started crying. Do you remember it, Goose? Do you remember what first you said to me?

I told you what a pretty miss you were.

No, you did not. You gave ever such a funny look at Jane. "Now, that is a child," you said, "and no mistake. My sister was the same exactly. Howled on the hour."

I was pleased to be told that it was not your own. That it was your brother's child. That his wife had perished on the crossing. And all the time I was thinking that you had the prettiest face I had seen since I left England. And then I asked you your name.

"Jervis, sir. Katherine Jervis."

"A fine name. And you can call me Goosequill."

"May I ask you somewhat, Mr. Goosequill?"

"You may."

"How is it that you were chosen to guide Mr. Milton?"

"I entered His Majesty's service by chance."

"His Majesty?"

"That is what I call him, sometimes. He does not care for the title. Or so he pretends." I winked at you, Kate, and you burst out laughing.

I did not. I was cradling the baby at the time.

Oh, yes, you did. "I thought you would have as long a face as the others, miss, but I was mistaken."

"There cannot be much laughter in a place such as this, Mr. Goosequill."

"Goosequill. Plain Goosequill."

"We have very little reason to be merry."

"Oh, you can laugh in a wilderness with no trouble at all. As my master would say, it just takes a fluctuation of the mouth."

You laughed again, and it was as pleasant a surprise as a strawberry in winter. "Is it so easy, then?"

"As easy as a London jury. But tell me, Katherine, why did you come here?"

"I promised to keep company with my brother's wife. Then, as I told you, she died upon the ocean. So now I raise her child. It is God's will."

"Who told you that?"

"My brother, Seaborn Jervis. After her death upon the voyage, he became very devout."

"That is often the case, unfortunately. So he built this church here, did he?"

"Oh no, Mr. Goosequill. That was Indian. When we found the barn, abandoned, we encamped around it."

"So my master spoke in a savage church? He will be highly gratified by that."

Goose, you never said anything of this. You are inventing it. We never spoke so. You asked my name, and then you just stood there whistling and shuffling your feet. Do you remember that patchwork colored coat you wore then? You had pinned a flower to it, and you kept your hat pushed back upon your head.

That was so I might twirl my hair. It was ever so flourishing in those days.

Do you mind that I cut it and make it neat?

No. Not at all. Especially when I can lay my head upon your lap, just so, and you can stroke it for me. Do you remember when, on the very next day, the horrible Culpepper came from New Plymouth with his Indian boy?

No. You never told me. You were shy with me then.

"Mr. Culpepper has long been a student of my pamphlets," my master said to me, when we were given news of his arrival. "I am informed that he particularly admired *The Reason of Church Government Urg'd Against Prelaty* and *Considerations Touching the Likeliest Means to Remove Hirelings Out of the Church*. No doubt he longs to greet me."

I did not long to greet him, after your dear and holy brother Seaborn told me all about his ministry. Is that the word for it? His name was Nathaniel Culpepper, known as "Wonder Working" Culpepper because of his work among the "Praying Indians," who were the poor souls converted to Christianity under his instruction. Seaborn said that the savages had once heard the voice of their god in the thunder, but now they heard it through "Wonder Working" Culpepper. He was certainly loud enough, and when he greeted us with a bellowing "Rejoice! Rejoice!" I noticed our master to flinch and step back. He had a large, red, fleshy face which reminded me of the butchers in the Smithfield shambles, and he pricked his horse as fiercely as a thief in the night. You must have seen him, Kate.

I have some memory of him, Goose, but everything was so new and strange that I scarcely—

It was strange to me, too, because then I saw riding behind him a young Indian native. He was the first I ever had glimpsed.

Were you frightened, Goose? I know that I was, when I first saw them.

No. I was extremely interested. In fact I was staring so hard at him that he turned his face away politely. And do you know what he was wearing?

Those mantles of feathers?

He was dressed in English clothes with a holland shirt, white neck-cloth and very neat stockings. I described him quietly to Mr. Milton as he approached, and our master murmured "Indeed, indeed" in his usual way. Then the boy was introduced to us by the loud Reverend Culpepper as "a godly person from without" who had been given the name Joseph. I could only wonder if he wore these same clothes in the forest, and I knew that my master also wished to learn more when he asked Culpepper about his "little heathen flock."

"It pleased God," the "wonder worker" replied, "to visit the tribes with an infectious murrain. Ten years ago He had permitted Satan to stir up the Indians against diverse Englishmen, but the plague then hit them with such a mortal stroke that they died in heaps as they lay in their wigwams. They expired like rotten sheep. It was all God's work."

Mr. Milton held on tightly to my shoulder. "How so? It seems to me like some newfound Golgotha."

"Oh no, sir. No, indeed. There you show the prejudices of our old country, if I may say so. Those who survived crawled up on all fours to our town for a little water and victuals. They were ready then for salvation and, when I told them that God had given Englishmen power to keep the plague buried in the ground, they called out for divine mercy and assistance. It was all very uplifting."

"Indeed."

"They are like children, good sir, who need force to tame and quiet them." I kept on glancing at the Indian boy, since I was not sure whether he understood the harsh words of this "wonder worker"; but he stood patiently behind his master, with his arms folded and his eyes fixed straight ahead. "The way of the wicked is darkness, Mr. Milton—"

"I know it."

"—and this race of foolish heathen was wont to stumble at they knew not what. Now they kiss and embrace the Bible like any godly Englishman. My boy here, Joseph, is perfectly subject to me. *Cowautam?*"

You spoke that well, Goose.

You always tell me I am a heathen, so I learn the heathen language. But none of us knew it then, and Mr. Milton inclined his head to one side as if to hear it better. "What was that?"

"I asked Joseph if he understood me."

The boy now looked directly at the holy Culpepper. *"Kuk-kakittow,"* he replied.

"As much to say, Mr. Milton, that he hears me." Our master repeated the strange word softly to himself. "I shall ask him to speak English to you, sir, if you wish. Joseph, *awanagusantowosh.*"

"Two sleeps we walk. One sleep we come here."

"Askuttaaquompsin, Joseph. English it for them."

"What cheer, friends, what cheer?"

He had pronounced the words just like a Londoner, and I could not help but whistle. Mr. Milton took a deep breath, and still held on to my shoulder. "What may this mean, Mr. Culpepper? The language of Englishmen pronounced by the tongue of a brute, and human sense expressed! Of what complexion is he?"

"They are said to be born white, sir, but their mothers make a bath of walnut leaves so that they can be washed with a tawny color."

"Is it so?"

"Well." He had the most ill-tempered laugh I ever heard.

"I do have reason to doubt these reports. May I quote from the prophet Jeremiah?"

"You may indeed."

" 'Can the Ethiopian change his skin, or the leopard his spots? Then may ye also do good that are accustomed to do evil.' Chapter thirteen, I believe, verse twenty-three."

"But, white or tawny, what is their origin? Did they receive some crawling life from the sun and mud?"

"Some say that these pagans come from the Tartars or the Scythians. Others say they are the offspring of the dispersed Jews."

Our master called for two chairs, and settled down very comfortably. You know how he loves his discussions and his disquisitions. "Surely you do not mean the ten tribes that Salmanasar carried captive out of their own country?"

"The same. We read it in the second book of Kings, sir."

"Chapter seventeen? That is an extraordinary thing, if it be true. Yet, I grant you, it is said that they followed heathen ways—"

"More extraordinary still, Mr. Milton, is the belief that the savages of this country originally come of the scattered Trojans. Brutus is said to have led them out of Latium."

"But these people can have no literature from that age of the world."

"Canceled, sir. Worn out of use. Now mere wild words." The wonder worker cleared his throat. "Wild men, too. And licentious."

My master leaned forward, as thirsty as a flea upon a bullock. "You must explain yourself, Mr. Culpepper."

"They commit much filthiness among themselves. There is

lust and lechery in their native places. Gaming. Harlotting. They have no foresight, sir. They are addicted to idleness and lying."

"Yet no doubt it fits their shadowy apprehensions. If they are the vagabond sweepings of a former race, we must expect a broken and disjointed people. Truly I pity their sad and doleful plight."

"I am soaked in pity too, sir, but you must never forget that they are also savages and therefore vain and crafty."

"Perhaps their blood has dried up with overmuch sun and fire?"

"It is possible." The good reverend moved his chair closer. "And what is more, their government is generally monarchical."

Our master drew in his breath. "I might have known it." Then he waved in the general direction of the woods and forests beyond us. "I see now that we are indeed on the edge of the wilderness, on the very brim of a noted corruption."

"Oh verily."

"I tremble to think of the sordid sperm engendered by their lustiness. How do you keep them in good order?"

"Oh, sir, it is best to encourage them with some small gift such as an apple or a biscuit. Of course they know nothing of money. God caused them to give us fish at a very cheap rate last winter."

I was tired of the wonder worker's canting and, since they were entertaining each other like Cheapside gossips, I decided to start a conversation with the Indian boy. "Goosequill," I said, striking my chest. Then I pointed to him, and raised my hands in the air as if I were a living question mark.

"*Mummeecheess,*" he said.

"Not Joseph at all?" He shook his head. "So what's this blessed old godly fool talking about?"

He saw me look at "Wonder Working" Culpepper with as much friendliness as a hanging man looks at the rope, and seemed to guess something of my meaning. Then he murmured "*Manowessas,*" and looked ferocious.

"Well, my boy, that sounds very interesting. Why don't we take a walk and discuss it? Would you care to share a cup of something?" I put both hands up to my mouth, as if I were drinking from a goblet, and he smiled. "We are going to study the Scriptures," I called out to Mr. Milton. "Do we have your permission?"

He waved me away without so much as a nod in my direction, so Joseph—or I beg his pardon, Mummeecheess—ambled off with me towards the forest. It came to pass that I happily found a flask of strong water somewhere about my person.

I can believe that, Goose.

Thank you for your confidence in me, Kate. May I drink to your health later? So within a short time the boy and I were very companionable. "Tree," I said, pointing to the trunk against which we were leaning.

"*Mihtuk.*"

"Wind." I waved my hands towards the branches swaying in the breeze, and blew the air out through my cheeks.

"*Waupi.*"

"Earth." I pointed to the forest floor.

"*Auke.*"

"You are a good fellow."

Joseph put his hand upon my chest. *"Wautaconauog.* Coat man. English man."

"I do wear a coat, yes. Useful in a London winter."

"Chauquaqock. Knife men. English men." He was pointing towards the settlement of the brethren. "Hearts of stone."

"I know it. These pious folk are not so sweet-tempered as they might be."

"They come from under the world to take our world."

"It looks very much like it, doesn't it? So why don't we have another drink to their ruin?"

We soon finished the last of the strong water, and started running through the forest with a few "Huzzahs!" and "Halloos!" which I taught him. He was swift while I was happy and you know, Kate, in that wild place I felt free. Do you remember Eleazer Lusher? He was the first Englishman Mr. Milton and I had met in our wanderings. I envied him then. I envied his liberty.

You have asked me about him before, Goose. He was the one who wore the skin of a bear like an Indian. I used to see him every Monday morning, when he came to barter with us. He brought with him furs and meats, while we gave him milk and cheese and suchlike. He was a quiet man. He lived alone, I think.

You are right as always, Kate. He lived within the forest. Well, I suggested to Mr. Milton that he was the man to tell us more about these Indians. Our master was now very interested, after his enlightening conversation with the Reverend Culpepper, and so I approached Eleazer in the market.

Monday morning?

As you say. He agreed to converse with us and, as Mr. Milton put it, instruct us in their heathen devices. So on the following morning he took us back to his wooden cabin by the river. Of course we had to enter the forest, and Mr. Milton gripped my hand when he felt the darkness closing about him. "Are there snakes hereabouts?" he asked.

"Oh yes." Do you recall that Eleazer had a slow and halting voice? I think it had something to do with his beard.

He never really spoke to me, Goose. He was a shy man.

He was not so shy in the forest. "The natives find snakes excellent for agues and pains, Mr. Milton. So they eat them alive."

Our master held even more tightly to my hand. "These serpents love the dark and tangled forest," he whispered. "They love foul weeds and muddy waters."

"*Askook,*" Eleazer said suddenly, startling us both. "That is what they call them."

"All this should be uprooted and burned." Mr. Milton was still whispering. "He should learn to prune."

Within an hour we had reached the cabin and Eleazer led us inside. Although it was hot enough to roast chestnuts in the palm of my hand, he lit a fire just beyond the threshold; the smoke from it, as he said, would ward off the great green flies and the gurnippers.

So then we sat down upon two wooden benches, and our master began. "We are children of London, Mr. Lusher, and know little of savage customs." I could have laughed at that, but I decided to act polite and cough instead. "Teach us, if you please, the native ways."

Mr. Lusher stared down at his shoes, as if they might be persuaded to do the talking for him. "It is hard to know how to begin—"

"I am told that they are no better than wild beasts. I am told that they delight in massacre."

"Oh no. Not at all. They can be vain and haughty, but they are not truly savage. They love society, even the wildest of them. They dote upon their children, too, spoiling them in everything."

"Indeed."

"They are as upright as many Englishmen. They call themselves *Ninnuock,* which signifies mankind." He was silent for a minute. "May I relate a history to you? It is the tale of an Englishman who lived among the Indians."

Oh, Goose, can this be true?

Exactly what Mr. Milton asked him. "Can it possibly be true?"

"It is, sir, in every particular."

"Monstrous. Horrible. Go on."

"There was once an Englishman who betook himself to the woods, and there lived by hunting which was his only sustainment. He had trained a young wolf as his dog, just as the Indians do: it was brought up tame, but maintained a ravening nature against all sorts of creatures. Of course this Englishman was always in his worst clothes, without a band and with a foul linen cap pulled close to his eyes. He was, you might say, neither Englishman nor native."

"Absolutely fearful!"

"Then at the beginning of the summer, when the Indians

removed from the thick woods to the open fields, this Englishman's wolf was gone very suddenly. It had followed the other
wolves, you see, which had accompanied the natives to their
new home. But he had loved that animal, his only companion in
the wilderness, and determined to take it back by any means
within his power. He found the trail left by the Indians, and
discovered that they were encamped a mile eastwards on plain
ground near to the shore. But of course they had seen him long
before he came upon them, and all at once he found himself
surrounded by their warriors brandishing bows and long staves.
He called out to them in his own language "Peace! Peace!" and
then he tried to convey to them that his wolf had gone. *"Anum!"*
he said, which was their term for dog. *"Anum!"* And then he
added, *"Nnishishem"* which means "I am alone." At this their
whole manner changed, since there is no race more hospitable
to strangers who do not prove themselves to be enemies. That is
why they are known to entertain the English in their houses,
providing the best victuals they can."

"I can believe that," I said. "They are good fellows." Mr.
Milton silenced me with a gesture.

"So very merrily, and with great good will, they took the
Englishman back to their wigwams, where indeed he was joy-
fully reunited with his wolf. The natives may make grave utter-
ances, sir—" he looked up from his shoes, and gazed at our
master. "But they are by nature a cheerful people. And so it fell
out that this Englishman, without company for so long, determined to live among them and free himself from the havoc of
enemies or wild beasts. He went near naked amongst them and
used their manners until, in time, he became a proper savage."

"This is terrible beyond words." Mr. Milton shifted uncomfortably on the wooden bench. "Did he commit uncleanness with any young Indian women?"

"Oh no. Not that. Yet he fished with them, and ate with them, and slept with them. He sailed with them in their canoes."

"I have heard of those," I said. "They are somewhat like our fishing boats, are they?"

"They make them out of birch rinds sewn together with the roots of white cedar trees—"

Of course our master was not interested in any such matter. "You seem to have great knowledge of these savage things, Mr. Lusher."

"Yes indeed. I was the one who lived among the Indians."

Our master rose from his seat at once and motioned me to be gone. "A narrative of great interest, sir. But we must bid farewell to you now."

Eleazer must have been surprised, because he stared at me for a moment without saying anything. I just rolled my eyes. Stop, Goose. You look like a corn dolly.

So then Eleazer asked us if he could guide us homeward. "No, sir. We know our path. Come, boy." Mr. Milton took my arm, and we marched out of the wooden cabin onto the forest path. Eleazer hovered by the door, I waved, and then he went back in again. As soon as we entered the forest, we were grazed on by flies. "This wilderness is a foul contagion," he said, "when it breed monsters such as these."

"What monsters, sir?"

"You know well enough." We walked on in silence for a while, while I made sure that we followed the right path.

"Virgil informs us that a race of men came from the trunks of trees, Goosequill. Unspeakable changes. Noah's descendants lived in forests after the Flood." I led him firmly forward but, still, he loved to wander in his words. "Who lingered in woods but lepers and vagabonds and hermits? Then Dionysus took the frenzied citizens of Thebes into a forest, did he not? *Velut silvis, ubi passim palantis error*— oh!" He had slipped upon a fallen branch, and toppled into swampy ground. He was soon sunk to his ankles in the mud but, as nimble as a link-boy with his light, I stepped upon two stones and pulled him free. He was now in a thoroughly bad humor. "I hate a plashy fen!" he muttered as I hauled him onto dry ground. "We must purge ourselves of these sloughs and quagmires." Then he added, after we had found the right path, "I must explain to our brethren the necessity of discipline and good order. We cannot allow our-selves to be entangled in rank weeds or environed with pestilent vapors."

"So what do you propose, sir?"

"We must remedy the soil. We must build bridges. We must create roads across these rotten bogs. We must recover this terrible wasteland. We must make maps!"

I led him by the hand, until I could see clear sky above us. "Mr. Lusher told us a strange story indeed."

"Vile. Loathsome beyond all measure. I cannot dwell on it." At that moment he was stung upon the hand by a large fly, and he yelled out in pain. "When we come to divide the territory of New Milton," he continued, after sucking his palm, "we must build stone walls and mighty trenches to protect ourselves against the inroads of the pagan enemy." I did not know what particular enemy he meant, Kate, but I knew better than to question him about it. They say that a burned child dreads the fire. "We must be fenced about and armed!"

By the time we arrived back at the settlement, he was already planning and calculating. We were lodged in that tent made of canvas cloth. Do you remember it?

Oh yes, Goose, it was a scandal. You had draped it with the prettiest and brightest flowers, without ever Mr. Milton knowing of it.

Oh, he knew. Alice Seacoal told him.

She is an old gossip, I grant you.

An old shrew. An old— So, Kate, we returned to our tent, and I made him stand outside as I brushed the leaves, dried mud and forest mess from his clothes. "To govern well," he said, as I began to unlace his boots, "is to train up a nation in wisdom and virtue. That is the true nourishment of a land, Goosequill. Godliness."

"Yes, sir. Will you please to lift up your leg a little?"

"I see a mighty and puissant nation arising here. I am no prophet. That would be too high a title for me to claim."

"A little higher still. I cannot remove your boot."

"In this land there are no false charters and tenures, no ancient and unrepealable statutes. We have no lordships or privy counsels clothed in the exterior luster of pomp and glory. All is to be made new. All is to be invented."

"I wish I could invent a boot that came off without labor. There we go. Now the other leg."

"I shall sow the seeds of virtue and public civility amongst this scattered flock, and they shall be ruled by that piety and justice which are the true causes of political happiness. In our fallen state—'' I tugged upon his boot too earnestly, and he reached for the canvas to steady himself. "In our fallen state all human society must proceed from the mind." Once he sets sail upon his words, as you know, he can never be persuaded to change his course.

I have heard him talk in chapters, Goose. In whole books. He is a library all to himself.

You might as well try and stop the wind. "We will create a society sufficient of itself," he said, "in all things conducible to well-being and commodious life. Ours will be the household and city of God."

"But what of the Indians, sir?"

"What of them?"

"What do you propose for them?"

"Oh, that heathen rabble can be dispersed in time. Think nothing of it."

"Are we to benefit them with our learning?" I was smiling, as I borrowed his words, but I kept up a grave voice.

"We cannot slacken the reins at the beginning of our race. The law is our touchstone of sin and conscience, Goosequill, and it cannot be tainted by corrupt indulgence. Lead me within. I must prepare my thoughts."

I stayed outside, and was just starting to clean his boots with some bindweed, when, Kate, I saw you again. You were holding Jane in your arms and singing to her softly under the shade of a tall tree.

It was a sycamore. It was a temperate day, and I was happy.

I came up to you, do you remember? "That's a very shrewd child, to get itself in that position."

"Mr. Goosequill. You scared me."

"I believe that this little thing will turn into a real New Englander." I started playing with Jane's fingers, then, so that I would not have to look at you directly. "Do you think you might be having any yourself?

"Mr. Goosequill!"

"Well, my master says that the brethren will have to people the wilderness."

"I don't think you are one of the brethren at all. I have never seen you at your prayers."

"Oh yes. They pray for a spreading vine, and I pray for a vineyard. And I pray for something else, Katherine Jervis. May I tell you what it is?" You said nothing.

I was too surprised by your rudeness, Goose. I was struck dumb.

So I ventured a little more. "I pray to God that my spiritual ardors will be scattered in one particular direction."

"Go to, Mr. Goosequill, you are a wicked blasphemer."

But you were smiling at me, Kate, so I knew that you were not terribly offended.

I was not smiling. The sun was in my eyes.

I was in your eyes, I think. Then you started whispering nonsense words to Jane. Dada. Lala. Tala. And suchlike. It reminded me of the words Mummeecheess had taught me.

They were good Devonian words. Hert. Zlape. Gurden. Luve.

I know it now, Kate. I know that your heart slept in the garden of love. But I did not know it then. And what was that ditty you were singing to the babe? I can hear it in my head, but I cannot recall the words exactly.

About the maypole, Goose, we dance all around,
And with garlands of pinks or of roses crowned,
While to each pretty lass we give a green gown——

That was the point you had reached when Mr. Milton called for me from the tent. I took my chance then, and gave you a little kiss upon the cheek.

I don't remember anything of the kind, Goose. I am sure I would have blushed. I might even have slapped you.

You did blush, and I kissed you again. Then I hurried back to our master. He wanted to compose some mighty speech before we all made our journey to the site of New Milton, so I took up my charcoal pencil and my scrap of paper. We rehearsed it while he strode up and down. "Do you think, Goose, that I should bring in the moral fable of Hercules?"

"The strong man?"

"Undoubtedly. Have you not heard of his labors?"

"I had a friend in the Hercules Tavern who said he was worked very hard."

"None of your absurdities. Yet you remind me that it will seem to these good people a pagan analogy. I must find a more pious example."

It was the day before our journey and so his words, Kate, were fresh from the oven. Everyone had to be gathered together in a circle, before he would begin. "It is not known what wise and eloquent man first persuaded his race into civil society, but my own task is little different. Mine is a high enterprise, and a hard, which I can perform only with temperance and incessant prayer, with continual watchings and labors in your cause. But I am content.'' He made one of his dramatic pauses. ''I am content to be your judge, your magistrate and your shepherd.''

''God be praised!'' Do you remember how Humility Tilly was always breaking out into praises and rejoicings?

Sometimes I wish she would break out in plague-spots. Is it uncharitable to hate someone, Goose?

Highly. I don't believe our master was overjoyed by her either, but he never showed it. ''I know your voice, dear Humility,'' he said, ''and I thank you. I shall guide my inward sight towards the good of family, church and commonwealth. No man shall be more patient in hearing causes, more inquisitive in examining, more exact in doing justice. But I am only an instrument—''

''No! No!'' Humility was doing it again.

''—under some power and counsel higher and better than can be human, working to a general good in this fallen world.''

''A sanctified vehicle is being poured upon our heads!''

That sounds like one of Alice Seacoal's sayings.

It was. ''There may be some,'' he went on, ''who incline to think that I undertake a task too great or difficult for my years and lowly state.''

''Woe to them all!'' Humility was never to be outdone by Dame Alice. Oh no.

''These are not inconsequent opinions. The Grecians and the Romans, the Italians and the Carthaginians, impious though they were, did of their own accord reject a sovereign sway. That is why I utterly abhor any arbitrary rule or government. You have not traveled so far to have another king set up before you. So, after we have journeyed in faith to New Milton, we shall establish a free and general assembly. If it is pleasing to you all.''

"It is, good sir!"

"Who speaks?"

"Phineas Sanctified Coffin, sir."

"Sanctified, God bless you."

That evening he called your brother to sit with him.

Seaborn loves to talk.

But not as much as Mr. Milton. "Take notes," he said to me. "Item. We must have an ingenious carpenter."

"We have, sir," your brother said. "Master Hubbard has already turned a beech into three godly chairs for my own family."

"Good. We also require someone that is skilled in the trade of fishing. And a fowler. We must have meat. Rich meat." There was a rustling in the trees behind us, and our blind friend turned around quickly.

"Only a wild cat, sir," I whispered. "Looking for food."

"Please be so good to remember, too, that we must have a brickmaker and a tiler to improve our dwellings." He turned around again, and listened for a moment. "We will need a cunning joiner. And a cooper."

"The Lord Jesus has provided us with men and tools, sir. We have come armed for our wilderness work."

"The only true tools, Mr. Jervis, are discipline and orderly proceeding. We must be as eager to discipline ourselves as some are to tutor their horses or their hawks." The smell of the forest was so rank in the evening, Kate, that I almost fainted away.

Poor Goosey.

And then I heard some strange creature calling from the forest. I believe they call it a loon. It sounds like this.

Goose, that is the barking of a dog.

If it was a dog, it had been crossed with a seagull. But Mr. Milton just went on talking. "Nothing in this world is more urgent and important for the life of man than rigor and control. Have you and your brethren considered my proposal for a general assembly?"

"We have, sir, and we find no fault with it."

"Then we must settle matters of wages and of hire, of revenue and taxes." He turned around for a third time, although the cat was long gone. "A little English ordering, and we will tame all the wild things."

EIGHT

My brother in Christ, Reginald, dear friend and confederate in the Lord, what else may I tell you of our pilgrimage? We began our journey on the morning after I had exhorted the brethren to train themselves in the discipline of good government. The site of New Milton was only five miles from our settlement of New Tiverton, but we were compelled to make our way through horrid woods and swamps; it was of course intended that I should lead the procession of our two hundred souls but, being blind by the will of God, I deemed it more fit to follow at a slower pace. Several times was I hindered by thickets, and by fallen or broken trees, so that, like Remaliah, King of Israel, I grew weary of the way. Then we came out upon a plain of scrubgrass, which seemed all the drier and hotter after the dankness of the woods. "It is not as plain a plain as the brethren would like," the boy Goosequill told me. "Some of them have been very much cut and scratched by the bushes. Those without buskins are as bloody as a pig after Lent." Yet it was not exhaustion alone that impeded our march. The sun's heat beat down upon the sweet fern, the scent of it so strong upon the plain that, as I was informed later, many of the brethren were close to fainting away.

I was powerfully affected by the cloying odor, I admit it, yet it brought to my mind an analogy. "Nineveh," I said to my foolish boy. "This is the very air of Nineveh." For a moment I dwelled among the prophets of old, until his whistling brought me back to our present plight. "You know, Goosequill, I cannot be a king. Mine must be a temporary and elective sway."

"I do know it. You have told them so."

"I shall not like Brutus be forced to reign. Otherwise I shall be no better than the pharaoh who now sits upon London." I leaned upon my boy's shoulder, overcome for a moment by the warmth and dirt of the world. "No man should take up that scepter which many have found so hot. It is so hot."

"We will be there shortly, sir. Mr. Jervis says that it is very close."

"Hercules was not begot in one night or by a casual heat. Do you think I babble like a wanton? No indeed. I must shine openly under a clear sky. My own actions must be held up as a mirror before my face."

"No need for a mirror now, sir. You will see your reflection in that river yonder, just behind the trees." We had, praise God, come to the end of our journey.

At dawn on the next day the dear brethren began their labors. The weaker vessels among them pleaded weariness, but I informed them that they were engaged in sanctified work and that the fields now called them to toil—when a people slacken, I said, they might as well lay down their necks before some wily tyrant. Indeed, dear Reginald, I had started to devise schemes for building and farming. The site of our new town was upon meadowland, well watered by springs, and I soon marked it out for pasture and for orchards; the plain itself, over which we had traveled, was then partitioned as a plot where streets and buildings might presently arise. The younger men had already been instructed (in our sadly betrayed mother country where, as I know with much sorrow, you still reside among sighs and tears) how to lay down the stone for streets, how to dig ditches, how to hew and hack the wood for their houses; others were now at my request divided into small bands in order to fell trees or to plough the necessary planting ground. I exhorted the women to perform such tasks as burning brushwood, gathering up stones for the streets, and picking bog iron from the surrounding ponds. The brethren also began to erect fences and stake out boundaries; there were to be meadows for their cattle and gardens for their fruit, but I had reminded them of the urgent necessity of a prison to contain the evil seed and of a meetinghouse to protect the good. "What a Christian republic will be raised here," I told Humility Tilly, a widowed woman of great piety and patience. "What a new tabernacle of saving grace!"

You will be pleased to hear that our church was completed some six weeks later. The first assembly of the settlers was called to celebrate this blessed instauration with a ceremony of prayer and godly hymns, but I had decided that the solemn occasion should also be used to ratify my position as chief magistrate and shepherd of the flock. "Merit without free choice is not sufficient," I told them as they gathered upon the plain. "There must be clear suffrage, vote and election!"

The clown by my side shouted out "Hurrah!," but I could not bring myself to chastise him for his godly enthusiasm.

"And who will be the taskmaster of these elective ceremonies? May I call upon Seaborn Jervis?" All of the brethren, men and women alike, were then given a scrap of paper; those who wished to vote for me were to make some kind of mark, while those opposed to my agency were expected to leave their papers blank. Mr. Jervis instructed them to line up in a single file, with their papers folded in half. "Your hat," I whispered to Goosequill. "Put out your hat as a vessel for their tokens!" He whistled under his breath as they proceeded past and dropped their papers within. "It is a good and prudent work to be able to guide one family," I told one of the flock, a slaughterer and butcher who had become known to me as Job "Defiant in the Lord," "but to govern a nation piously and justly is a task of the greatest size."

"If there is to be a nation which governs like this," Goosequill muttered, "then we will need plenty of hats."

"You show us a divine example," Job replied, "in allowing us to cast our votes."

"No, no, it is not so. Where men are equal they ought to have an equal interest in government. We are entirely free by nature. Goosequill, your whistling pierces my ears. Will you now count the slips without more noise?"

The boy murmured something about being "free" himself, but I struck him with my staff in a gently chiding manner. He must have piled the tokens high upon the table before us, and announced my election in dumb show, since I was all at once overwhelmed by the salutes of the brethren. "The first act of our assembly has been fulfilled," I told them. "You remind me of the apostles of the church who made open proclamations in such a forum. But may I ask you this? May I advise you to adopt the civil government which Jethro proposed to Moses? Are we not also Israelites in the wilderness?'' There was a moment's silence, since the good people had in their enthusiasm momentarily forgotten the passage from Exodus to which I referred. ''It is otiose, of course, to recall to your minds what is already imprinted on your hearts. I mean, as you know, that laws and rights must be established. Freemen will choose the other magistrates, who with me will sit in supreme council. And so from works of law we will aspire to works of faith.''

I led them in solemn procession towards the meetinghouse where, after many devout prayers, our business was begun. Two necessary acts were passed by acclamation. One prohibited the ploughing with horses by the tail, and the other most severely forbade the burning of oats in the straw. I then recalled to their minds the importance of frugal economy, and recommended to them that the price of staple commodities should be fixed. Forgive me, dear elect brother, for these worldly allusions. Yet it is right and proper that you should learn every jot and tittle of our wilderness work. Who knows when it may fall upon you, and our scattered brethren in England, to commence it? A penny was deemed to buy four eggs or a quart of milk, while butter and cheese were to be sold at sixpence a pound. The like controls were voted upon wheat, oats, peas, barley, beef and pork. I informed the brethren that fish had already been found so plentiful that no fixed price was necessary, but cows were so much prized that their price should be raised to twelve pounds sterling. There was no further discussion.

In truth I was content to move from earthly considerations to that saving medicine inherited from God, the necessity of just punishment. Job ''Defiant in the Lord,'' whose grave voice was now known to me, proposed that those found drunk should be whipped. There were loud cries of support, of course, but I bid them to be silent. "You who are so minded," I told them, "hold up your hands." Goosequill whispered the result to me. "You that are otherwise minded, hold up yours."

"Only me," the foolish child murmured in my ear.

In the same fashion other holy laws were passed without dissent. Anyone seen to be kissing a woman in the street was to be whipped, scolding wives were to be gagged and set at a corner for six hours, and those heard swearing or cursing were to be burned through the tongue with a hot iron. Witches and adulterers were to be put to death in the sight of the whole community. I sensed night approaching as we debated the burning of the witches and, although I was naturally reluctant to prevent their godly deliberations, I thought it best to close our assembly with words in praise of our sweetest and mildest manner of paternal discipline.

My guide and fool led me back to my newly built dwelling. "I suppose," he said, "that you could burn them for being drunk. Or hang them for swearing. That would be very holy."

"Punishment, Goose, is sometimes necessary to tame and quiet."

"If you say so."

"I do say so." The boy remained silent for once. "We cannot have uncleanness or enmity or contentions."

"But we can have burnings, can we?"

"Have you not heard that judgment comes in flames?"

"I have also heard that it is easy to start a fire, but very troublesome to put one out."

I felt a just anger coming upon me then, so I took him by

the shoulders and thrust him out of doors. "But it is no trouble to put you out. Go. Leave me."

I sat quietly for a few minutes, contemplating all the events of a day so remarkable in our history, when I decided that I should walk out into the air to calm myself. I made my way alone, of course, but God guided me to that spot where the four streets of our town had been marked to come together. There in the dark, dear brother in the Lord, I gazed westward towards the unknown territories.

NINE

Poor Mr. Milton. I miss him, Goose. Was he always the same?

Very similar, Kate. Wherever he is, I am sure that he follows the old road. Awake at four, when the birds have hardly stirred. Then he was accustomed to wash his hands in the water that I left in a bowl beside his bed. I will not mention the fact that he relieved himself in an earth-closet just by the garden. Then he returned to his room, which I have not mentioned that he left, and knelt down upon the wooden floor. It was as hard as a Flemish sausage, but he always remained at his devotions until the clock struck five. At that precise moment he exclaimed "Amen!" and called out for "Nourishment!" I would be waiting outside his chamber with a pewter dish containing no more than bread soaked in milk, but I carried it with enough solemnity to grace a funeral service.

He always eats slowly, Goose.

And he carefully wiped his mouth after every bite with a linen cloth. Then he rinsed his hands before settling down in that plain wooden chair. Do you know the one, which creaks in winter? Well, here, for the next hour, he would listen to me reading from his blessed Old Testament. He had tried teaching me a bit of Greek, but I could never get my tongue around the syllables: when I attempted the sounds, he put his hands up to his ears and moaned. It was the end of that venture and, ever afterwards, I recited plain English. He heard you, Kate, on the day we reached the end of Eccles cakes. Excuse me. Ecclesiastes. Do you remember how glad I was?

I always thought that you devised some plan with him.

A plan? Oh no, Kate. I had no part in it. I was thoroughly surprised.

Did he wish us to be together?

I hardly think so. I truly believe it to have been chance. "Who is that singing?" he asked me after the reading was over. You were playing with Jane a short distance from the house at the time.

"Excuse her, sir." I was all ready to go outside, and hush you. Would you have forgiven me?

Indeed I would. I was so respectful of him that I would have hushed myself. I was a little respectful of you, Goose, if you must know. To have so fine and grand a master.

As grand as a sultan, isn't he? "She cannot help but sing in the mornings," I said to him. "I will tell her to be quiet."

"No. No need. Her voice is a little like the sound of the forest birds, do you think?"

"Oh yes, sir."

"And she is called?"

"Katherine Jervis."

"You know her well?"

"I have heard her before."

"I swear, with a voice such as that, she must be handsome. Is she so?"

I had never known him ask such a question before and, I admit it, I blushed the same color as a flower seller's cap. "I suppose she might be. She is a young woman."

"Call her into the garden, so that I may talk to her through the casement."

Do you remember me running outside, and whispering to you? "Katherine, Katherine. Mr. Milton wishes to talk to you."

"What have I done?"

"You have done nothing at all. He wishes to hear you."

"Me?"

"He wishes to hear your voice."

I watched you walk into the garden, with Jane in your arms. Then you stood on the path, and looked at me nervously when Mr. Milton spoke. "Sing me that air again." I knew that he was sitting by the window, just out of sight. "If you will." Then you sang that old Devon song. What is it called? "The Sparrow and the Thrush."

I was very bashful, Goose. I believe there was a trembling in my voice.

Mr. Milton was silent for a moment or so after you had finished, and you soothed the baby. "You are called Katherine, are you not? The sister of Seaborn Jervis?"

"Yes, sir."

"A saintly family, I am sure. Can you read, Katherine?"

"Oh yes. I read the holy book to my father at home. We were all taught to understand God's word."

"Come within. Goosequill will lead you."

I had some notion of his plan for you then, and I could not help smiling when I took your hand.

I was so surprised when I came into the house, Goose. It was so plain. Neat and plain. I had expected more furnishings, and quilted stuff, but there were just those old chairs, a table and a bed.

Not forgetting the iron spit for his meat, and the copper kettle on its chain.

And there are the stools, of course. As well as the shelf of books. And you were always there, too, Goose.

You know that Phineas Coffin offered to build him a larger house? He had declined it. "I am merely shepherd of the flock," he said. "I require a simple plainness. Nothing grand or spacious, if you please. I do not gape after possessions except those that be homespun." I did suggest that he might enjoy some proper bedding, but he put his hand on my shoulder while he spoke to Phineas and the others over my head. "I fear, good people, that this silly boy speaks out of the heat of youth. You know the voice of the sluggard? Make us easy, make us rich, make us lofty."

I was used to his tricks by now, and paid no heed. "Not even a simple pillow?"

"And then all comes to this. Make us lawless."

"Only a few feathers?"

"No rich furniture—"

"Goose feathers, perhaps?"

"And no delicious fare."

That was why he was sitting on a plain oak chair when you came into the room. He had his Bible open before him and he had taken care to have his forefinger resting on the page. "Might you read this passage to me, Katherine Jervis?" You looked at it for only a moment.

"May I read it as I am accustomed, sir? In my Devon speech? My dear father loved this part."

Well, I was astonished, Kate, when you spouted forth. Spout it again for me, will you?

Tha zong uv zongs, wich es Zolamin's. Let'n kiss my way tha kisses nv'es mowth: vur thy luv es better thin wine. Becuz uv tha saver uv thy gude hointmints thy neame es as hointmint powerd vorth, thervaur da tha vargins luv tha. Dra ma, we wull ruun arter tha: tha king ith brort ma inta es chimbers: we wull be glad an rayjoice in tha, we wull raymimber thy luv moar thin wine: tha uprite luv tha. I am black, bit comly, aw ye daters uv Jurewslim—

That was where our master stopped you, but I believe that he was smiling. "Do you also recite it in plain English?"

"Oh yes, sir. I was taught it by a dame in Barnstaple."

"I sense you to be courteous and modest. Is she neat in her dress, Goosequill?"

"As neat as a cloth maker's stall, sir."

"Well, Katherine Jervis, I am sure you will copy our mother Eve before she conversed with the serpent. Do you cook?"

"Almond custard, sir. Artichoke pie. Damson marmalade."

He smiled again and that, Kate, is how you came into our service. It was not all lavender, though, was it? We soon had you cleaning, and washing our clothes, while I watched over little Jane. But, as I warned you at the time, the biggest baby of all was Mr. Milton. Everything had to be as ordered and as regular as the bells of St. Magnus, with those four tapers on the mantel to measure out his time.

I grew tired of lighting them, Goose. Time for his eating, time for his studying, time for his shepherding the flock, time for his recreation.

After he had eaten his morning broth, he always listened to your sweet voice reading from the Scriptures. He knew that I listened, too, but he used to call out to me as if I were in another room. "Take up your packsaddle, Goose, your day's work is now begun!"

You always had the quill behind your ear. It made me laugh.

I had those quills from a vulture, since Eleazer Lusher told me that they made the best text-pens. When I explained this to Mr. Milton, he scowled at me. "How can I take flight," he said, "on the wings of so malign a creature?"

"They make a strong hand, sir."

"Well, it is true that I need a good hand to milk me. Proceed, proceed." So every morning, at nine o'clock, after you had gone, he would lie down upon his bed and dictate to me. We continued with his blessed translation of the psalms, although I swear that he prepared them in his sleep: they came out so precise, and so musical, that he might have been reading them from a book. There were days when he was so filled with words that he called me to his side in the evening. "I have my vespers," he said, "as well as my matins." If he had worked me harder, there could have been a burial service. We translated one hundred and fifty of them, Kate, and when we came to the end I gave my own rendition of "Praise Ye the Lord." I cheered, and waved the quill in circles around my head. He was pleased, too, but he did not care to show it. "Do you think," he said, "that we should now move from the Old Testament to the New?"

"Oh yes, sir. At once. My pen is not yet dry, and we could use the rest of the ink."

"Perhaps a series of epistles to the elders of our scattered communities? I might exhort them somewhat."

"Exhaust them," I whispered under my breath.

"I once wrote in a similar spirit to the Swiss cantons, although it is true that their ministers were of a far more scholarly disposition. No. It would be wasted on the pilgrims here. They are godly, but they are rough."

Of course it was not all prayer and labor, Goose. Do you remember the day when my brother told him that a pair of virginals had been brought by those weavers from Dorset just arrived? He told Seaborn to take it from them at once.

Oh yes. I recall it. "It is not right, good Mr. Jervis, that profane hands should force rude notes into the air." So it was carried into his own house. He was sitting in a corner at the time, with his head bowed as if he were deep in thought, but I could see his ears twitching when two of the holy brethren brought it within. Have you ever seen ears twitch, Kate? Watch. As soon as they were gone, he leapt up. "This will be the womb," he said, "of sweet airs and melodies. I always tell you that we must force ourselves to slacken the cords of intense thought and labor."

"I don't know about cords, but these strings are very dusty."

He ignored me, as was his way, and ran his hands across the keys. "You know that my father was greatly addicted to music. I used to sing to him often. Monteverdi. Henry Lawes. Even the papist Dowland.''

"Do you recall the organ upon the *Gabriel,* sir?''

He shook his head. ''That is not a thought I wish to revolve in my breast, Goose. Not now.'' Then he sat down to play, and began to sing in his sweet sad voice which was like the sound of the wind in the walls of old ruinous St. Michael's:

> *"O Lord thou knowest what things be past*
> *And thus the things that be*
> *Thou knowest also what is to come*
> *Nothing is hid from Thee."*

You were in the garden at the time, Kate. You were kneeling before your bed of sweet herbs, and I watched you through the window. You stood up when he began to sing, and you remained very still.

> *"Thou seest my sorrows what they are*
> *My grief is known to Thee*
> *And there is none that can remove*
> *Or take the same from me."*

I love his voice, Goose. Somehow it seems to fit with all the sounds of the wilderness. Do you understand me?

I understand you very well. I even told him so. ''That song is sad enough, Mr. Milton.''

''This is a sad time.''

''Yes indeed. And a sad place, too.''

133

"Of course." But then, for no reason in the world, we both burst out into laughter. "Go into the garden," he said to me. "Compose yourself among the marjoram and sorrel."

He orders that garden as if it were the courtyard of Bedlam, Kate. And before you ask me, Bedlam is a pleasant spot in the middle of fields. A great many people visit it for their recreation. There was a time to husband the fruit, a time to prune the trees, a time to cut the hedges, a time to pluck up the weeds among the plants.

A time to walk at twilight, Goose, with you holding his right arm and me taking the other.

Do you remember that evening we saw the monster? "It is a pleasant and shady spot now, Katherine," he said. "It fits my calm solitariness."

"Thank you, sir. Goosequill tended the branches. They are too high for me."

"And how spring our tended plants? How blows the citron grove?"

"Oh, sir, they are pretty."

"Their scent is my delight. I seem to be wandering through flowing odors of myrrh and balm." He stopped suddenly upon the path, and I almost tripped over him. "Can I smell hellebore?"

"You can, sir. It makes a good potion for sleeping."

"Root it out, Katherine. At once. Its name is tainted because it is the devil's herb. It leaves people slugging in bed while others are at work. Help her, Goosequill." So we fell upon our knees but then, as we dug into the earth to root out the most offending plant, our fingers touched. Oh Kate.

Goose. Stop it.

He was wandering up and down the narrow path, in an ill humor. "You asked me yesterday, Katherine, if we should plant apple trees in the garden. I grant it a pleasing fruit, but I am told that in this wilderness it may have dangerous and suspicious properties. So beware the apple." Our fingers were still touching, and we were smiling at one another.

We all began to stroll companionably, after the plant had been uprooted, and then once again he stopped as suddenly as a chair-man in a gale. "What is that sound of humming, Goose?"

"A bee?"

"It is not a bee. It is somewhat louder."

"Could it be what they call here a hornet?" I was peering nervously among the flowers, because there are creatures in this new land which disagree with my refined tastes.

"No. It has a different note."

Then I saw it.

It was the prettiest little thing, Goose.

"Oh Lord, sir," I said, "it is a bird. A tiny bird, sir. No bigger than a hornet."

"How can that be? Look again."

"It *is* a bird. It has little silken feathers and feet as tiny as those of a spider. It is all alive with color and motion, Mr. Milton, it moves so quickly! It is like a little burst of glittering light."

He stepped backwards, with something like a frown upon his face. "What kind of feathered creature may it be, then?"

"Oh look. It puts its beak into the flower and hovers there."

"It must be some deformed work of nature, some freakish progeny of flies and crows."

"No, not that. It is far too beautiful."

"Come away, Goosequill. There are nameless things in this wilderness world with which it may be folly to deal. I feel sure that this creature is the fruit of some monstrous coupling. Come away." So he led us both from the garden.

But I turned back to watch the little bird. It was so delightful, Goose, going on its sweet journey from blossom to blossom.

That was not the only monster in the garden. Oh no. Do you recall I had left him one afternoon, sprawled in that old hammock which I have set up for him between two cedars? It was hot enough for the devil, even in that early spring, and Mr. Milton was wearing only a linen shirt with his breeches—with his white russet hat upon his head, he looked like, excuse me, Kate, a Devonian gardener. I had already walked onto the main street—on my way to you, of course—when I suddenly heard the most vociferous scream. I ran back as fast as ever I could, calling out, "What is it? What is it?" I could see Mr. Milton with his knees drawn up in the hammock.

"Oh, Goosequill, it was a rattle."

"What?"

"Is it on the ground beneath me? Is it rearing up its head? Is it swaying towards me?"

I rushed into the house, and then entered the garden through the back door. All was quiet, for a moment, but then I also heard this rattle. Mr. Milton screamed again, but then he shouted out, "You serpent! Subtlest beast of all the field!" There was silence, and I do believe the snake had heard him. "You labyrinth of many rounds self-rolled! You creature slyly stored with poison!"

At this moment Preserved Cotton ran towards the garden hedge. "What is the matter, Mr. Milton?"

"Oh dear brother. There is a serpent here. It surrounds me with its coils, I think."

"Wait, sir. Do nothing at all. I will fetch my son."

"Will that be Zephaniah Cotton?"

"It will."

"Thank God for this deliverance!"

You know Zephaniah as well as I, Kate, and you know what a terrible pleasure he takes in the trapping and killing of snakes; I have seen him catch the creatures by their tails and whirl them around his head with as much enjoyment as a conjuror at Greenwich Fair.

I never did like him, Goose. Sometimes he looks at me with the strangest expression upon his face. As if he would like to trap and catch me.

I have already spoken to him, and he will not so much as blink in your direction again. So he came into the garden at once, all smiles, with a long pole and a piece of sharpened stone. "Oh, Mr. Milton," he said. "This is a big one."

"Where is it, good Zephaniah?"

"A little way off from you. No need for alarm, sir. This devil will never reach you." I saw our master wipe his forehead with his palm. "It is longer than a yard, sir. It has a little neck, but I have known them to swallow a live chicken as big as one we would give threepence for in England." The idiot was talking loudly as he approached the snake which now I saw for the first time, curled upon the ground. "He need not have killed you in any event, sir. If you are bitten, you need only take a saucer of salad oil and chew on some snake-weed." I looked hard, and could make out its yellow belly with all black and green markings upon its back. "The savages call him *askook!*" Zephaniah shouted out the word as he rushed upon the beast, struck off its head with the sharpened stone and then beat it with the pole. "It is dead, Mr. Milton. It is all gashed and mangled."

"I thank you, Zephaniah. It is well done." Then he turned his face in my direction. "Where are you, Goosequill? Help me from this hammock, if you please. My limbs grow stiff."

"I am with you now, sir."

"I was near to death. I might have been savaged by the fangs of the serpent."

Zephaniah liked to see me knocked in a corner, as it were, since I knew even then that he had conceived a great fancy for you. "Poison as black as ink, Mr. Milton," he whispered. "Fangs like diamond points."

"Precisely so. Has it been removed from my garden?" Zephaniah draped it upon his pole, and threw it across the hedge onto the path beyond. Mr. Milton heard the thud of the carcass, and smiled broadly. "Today we have been saved from great danger. Without any help from my servant whose attentions, I understand, were desired elsewhere." The snake killer sniggered, and pointed at me. I said nothing, but helped Mr. Milton from the hammock. He was now in a good humor, after being released from his panic fear. "It is still a delicious grove," he said to no one in particular. "It is still a garden planted with the trees of God. No serpent can destroy this!"

TEN

So, dear brother Reginald, I was delivered from the fangs of the serpent by miracle. And how I praised the Lord, when I understood how He had preserved me for my work in the wilderness! It was by divine dispensation, I have no doubt, that these first months passed quietly and orderly under my jurisdiction. But we were not without many laborious sighs: the brethren were compelled to plant in untilled earth, like the servants of Jehu, tearing up the bushy land with their hoes and sometimes with their godly hands. Yet even in the work of nature providence was our guide. Grains of rye had been brought from England but, once we had enclosed fields for corn, it was made known to me that local grain purchased from our neighbors was far more fruitful and could even furnish two harvests. There had been rain and thunder at the beginning of our first year, bringing mosquitoes and other great insects in large numbers, but then the weather had changed. So in our own gardens we began to sow pumpkins, wild onions and other vegetable fruits. "Let no man," I said to them, "make a jest of pumpkins. With these the Lord has been pleased to feed his people." Our little town then also began to grow. By the early months of 1661, we rejoiced in four complete streets meeting on the plain.

I described it to Nathaniel "Wonder Working" Culpepper, a very profitable and spiritual minister from New Plymouth, who had decided once again to visit me for pious converse. "Our little town," I told him, as we walked in my garden, "is in form like that of a fleur-de-lys, do you not think?"

"Sir?"

"A flower de luce." I used the London pronunciation to suit his rougher ear.

"I have no time for flowers, Mr. Milton. I am planting true vines."

I chided him gently. "But think of Solomon's song, when in allegory Christ awakes the Church. Are there not plentiful gardens and flowers to be found there?" The good shepherd seemed not to recall the passage, but without any word of reproof I changed our theme. "Where is that Indian boy who traveled with you last year? Was his name Mummee, or some such?"

"He is gone."

"Gone?"

"Dead. He was caught in the act of stealing a horse. So he was hanged, as the law requires. It was no loss, since he had turned disobedient and sullenly inclined."

"I am sad to hear of it."

"Death is a necessary discipline, Mr. Milton, in a place such as this."

All at once, as he uttered "death" in my ear, there was a great noise rushing above me through the sky. "Do you hear it,

Mr. Culpepper? Do you hear that sound coming from the south? Can it be guns and cannon?"

"Not guns, sir." I heard him smile—is that possible, Reginald Pole, to hear a smile? "The pigeons have returned."

"What birds make such a thunder?"

"They are like our dove-house pigeons." He has a precise and literal manner, which is sometimes restful. "Only they have long tails like magpies. They always come here in the spring."

The noise grew louder still, and the flocks of birds became so thickly strewn across the sky that I felt them blot out the sun. "The winged air is dark with plumes," I said. "There is something monstrous in their flight."

"Generally it continues four or five hours. We have tried to drive them from their track, with the peltings of small shot. But nothing alters their course."

"Millions upon millions with the same anticipation of their end."

"They will build among the pine trees to the northeast of us. The sun never sees the ground because of the obstruction of their nests."

"This is a fearful thing, do you not think, this living shadow at noonday?" He made no answer, and spoke upon the price of beans.

On the following morning I construed an allegory for this great migration, pronouncing my words carefully to the foolish boy who insists upon staying by my side. "Their steady and purposeful flight," I said, "puts me in remembrance of those laws of human society maintained by the will of God, continued in outward peace and welfare within a great commonwealth."

I was about to continue with certain allusions upon the theme of brotherhood, when he stopped me in my own flight. "The boys and girls are already gathered in the schoolroom, sir. Do I hear them at their prayers?"

"Would you know a prayer if you heard one, you savage? Bring me my gown."

They were indeed at their devotions when I hastened into the little school that I have caused to be erected. We had no stones but those which were striped or spotted, and no benches but those which were roughly hewn out of beech wood, but in the sight of God there can be no stain or mark in the shrine of learning. So it was that I heard the pious voice of a child as I entered the room.

"Our lord and master, sweetest Jesus, who, while yet a boy of twelve years disputed in such manner among those doctors of the Temple at Jerusalem that all were amazed at Thy most excellent wisdom, we ask Thee that in this school of which Thou art head and patron we may walk in the path of Thy learning."

"Very well said, good William Cogeshall. And how may we follow that divine path, Jonah?"

I knew this Jonah to be a slow and stubborn boy, with no more sense than an ant. No doubt he had been watching one crawl upon the ground, even as I spoke to him, and he merely blurted out, "Good master, the Indians make them in the forest."

I knew where he was seated and, stepping over to him, I took his left ear. "We must be just," I said, twisting it in my hand. "Watchful." Another twist. "And accurate." The silly boy gave a mild cry, and I relented. "Jonah Saybrook, I condemn you to hard labor in the deep mines of knowledge. One psalm to be learned by rote each day. Now, Martha, will you take up the lesson of the moral law?"

"That which is grounded on the principles of nature and right reason is commonly called the moral law."

"You speak very methodically and profitably. Go on." As Martha Rainwell, the daughter of a pious carpenter, recited the moral sentences from Drake's *Simple Rules and Examples for a Christian Child,* I considered once more the lessons which I might draw from the great flight of the birds. She had reached the divine homily on repentance, when I stopped her. "If all of you keep to these precepts, and instruct those who come after you, then our little colony will spread knowledge and religion through all parts of this new land. Our natural heat will revive those who still lie numb and neglected." I heard a shout somewhere within the settlement, but I paused only for a moment. "What nation will be more industrious at home, more potent and honorable abroad? Our commonwealth may then indeed attain the general power and union of a whole republic, something quite new upon the earth—" Suddenly I heard calls of "Peace peace," followed by "Good morrow, good morrow, good morrow." A party of native Indians, dear brother Reginald, had come into New Milton!

Jonah Saybrook cried out that we were to be cooked and eaten, but I ordered him to be silent. "They may be heathen, but they are not savage. All of you remain quiet and attentive to your studies. I shall be gone from you a little while." I left the schoolroom with grave step and, calling for Goosequill, walked onto the dry earth road near the Indians themselves. I stood in front of the school, and I said nothing. I remained still, but then

I put my arms out towards them. They had seen me at once, of
course, in the black gown and white band which it is my obliga-
tion to wear among the brethren. I heard one of their little
group step forward, stop, and then step forward again. Then he
repeated, in a low tone, "Good morrow, good morrow."

"Good morrow to you, sir." I put my fingers to my eyes.
"I cannot see you, but I hear reverence and authority in your
voice. You are welcome here." Then I recalled a word taught to
me by the man Lusher. *"Npockunnum."* Which is to say, I am
blind.

The native came closer to me, and I could scent the animal
grease smeared upon his skin. He leaned forward and placed a
cord or rope over my head: I touched it, and knew it to be a
necklace of fish shells. I bowed, quite aware that some prize or
honor had been granted to me. Then he spoke to me in his own
language. *"Wunnetunta,"* he said. *"Kekuttokaunta."*

Goosequill was beside me, and translated the heathen
words. "My heart is true. Let us parley."

I asked the boy later how he had understood their language.
"Oh," he said, "I watched the old file's gestures. He put a
hand on his breast, and then on his tongue."

"Very well observed. Tell me, Goose, of their dress. Do
they wear loose garments like the natives of Scotland?"

"Not so primitive as that, sir. The older of them wore the
skins of animals, but they were also draped with mantles made
from the feathers of birds."

"Extraordinary, if they were plucked from the pigeons I
heard in the sky above me."

"The younger men had mantles of red and blue cloth, tied

under their chins like the old wives who sell the chairs in Leadenhall. But I tell you this, sir. I have never seen those wives with vermilion stripes upon their faces, or with the emblems of fish tattooed on their foreheads, or with ear-rings in the shape of birds, or with bracelets of whelk shells.''

"No, it is not the fashion of Leadenhall. You have seen enough to write a volume. But we cannot rely on sight, Goose-quill, when we may also have speech. We must call upon Mr. Lusher to assist us in these delicate parleys.

So it was, dear Reginald, that Eleazer Lusher arrived in New Milton on certain appointed days to act as translator in my discourse with the Indians. It was clear at once that they wished to barter with us, and on their first visit, they had brought with them the skins of beavers and black foxes, horse teeth, seal oil and cakes of maize known to them as *nokake*. In return the good brethren gave them brass kettles and copper pots. At a later date they presented us with shoes tied with deer-gut, and the charita-ble English provided them with dishes and spoons; the Indians furnished us with quantities of maple syrup, too, and in recom-pense we built them wooden doors in place of their old hanging mats. Goosequill informed me that the natives distributed all these goods and materials equally among themselves, and so I made an allusion to Plato's commonwealth. "I don't know any-thing about that, sir," he replied, "but sometimes these savages seem more just than the Englishmen." I made no answer to him, having more burdensome matters to consider.

Their leader, or *sachem,* was known as Cutshausha; but I soon awarded him with the name of Adam Newcome in honor of his first arrival at the settlement. In fact it became evident, through Mr. Lusher's report, that Cutshausha had approached New Milton some months before—and that the first English voice he had heard was my own. I had been talking in the garden, and he had concealed himself behind my hedge; it was not out of fear, he insisted, but curiosity. He had not been naked, he added, but had been wearing a little apron of leather to cover his secret parts. "So your name is well granted, Adam," I replied through the agency of Mr. Lusher. "You dress like our first parents. God has covered you with the skins of beasts to hide our common filthiness."

"Oh sir," Lusher told me, "they live in happiness."

"We are all expelled from paradise, Mr. Lusher."

At this moment Adam Newcome decided to recite an English sentence that, as I discovered later, he had carefully put to memory. "You my friend, John Milton, I desire your worship and your power because I hope you can do great matters this one. We are poor."

"What does he wish for, Mr. Lusher?"

"He wishes his people to work."

Of course I had considered the very same possibility ever since the arrival of the heathen amongst us. The all-wise economy of our pious settlement lacked only a proper stock of laborers, and within a very few days I had agreed with Adam Newcome that his people should work with the settlers in hoeing, in the cutting of wood, and in the building of stone fences or houses. Each of these activities was to be superintended by one of the savage chief's three sons, renamed by me as John Firstfoot, Newcroft Matuxes and Last-born Nanaro. The work began in full earnest soon after. The Indians distributed their food of oysters, bear, dried lobster and moose tongues in exchange for English provision of cheese, butter and eggs. I am sad to relate, dear Reginald Pole, that some of our brethren offered them beer, no doubt honorably and generously; but they were not accustomed to its strength, and I was forced to limit their supplies.

Yet, even despite these just edicts, there were still certain natives who did not feel inclined to labor for us. They began to dice with painted plum stones, when they ought to have been working in the fields, and played a game like cards with stiff rushes. At night many of them sang and danced around their fires just beyond our settlement. I could even hear their chanting from my own chamber. "I thought them to be very like the ancient Britons," I said to my boy one evening, as he served my meal of capon and white broth, "but it seems to me now that they are closer to the wild Irish. Certainly they are very moody and hot-brained, and their mantles of deerskin are not so different in fashion from Irish mantles. They howl like the murderous Irish, too. Do you hear them?"

"They are only singing."

"Barbarous yellings, like the sounds of hell itself."

"It was Increase Dobbs who first gave them the beer, sir. He made a fine profit upon it."

He was always too forward, but I chose to ignore him. "And I have heard news of cannibal tribes not so far distant from us. Did you never read of those heathen Irish who used to feed upon the buttocks of boys and the paps of women? Hollis describes them very well in his *Memorials*." I could not help but sigh, and then sipped from my customary glass of plain water.

"It is the same savagery in all the races and realms of the world. Wherever we go upon this earth, Goosequill, we know nothing but hideous howlings and horrid cries."

"I am sorry to hear of it."

"Yet however ungoverned and wild a race superstition has run, it can yet be overturned by right reason and godly persuasion. It is time, Goose, to uproot this goblin world and its affrightments."

"Sir?"

"It is time to teach our Indians how to pray."

On the following morning I called John Firstfoot, the sachem's oldest son, to my dwelling. I knew that the Indian youth and Goosequill had over the last weeks been teaching each other the rudiments of their languages, and so I asked them to sit together before me. "Tell me about God, dear Firstfoot."

"Mannitt."

"I believe that is your word for the deity." I was affable, yet I was determined.

"Ketan. Wetuomanit. Keesuckquand."

"He is explaining to you, sir, that his people have many gods."

"I am quite aware of that, Goosequill. They are struck with superstition. They might as well worship the moon like the elephants. They might as well be monks. Good dear John Firstfoot, how do you worship your god?" I put out my hands as if in prayer. "Worship?"

Goosequill spoke to the Indian for a few moments, and then replied on his behalf. "They do not worship their god because they say that, being god, he will do them no harm."

"How very extraordinary. Blind heathenism."

I had spoken too sharply, perhaps, since now Firstfoot whispered something to my boy. "He says, sir, not to be angry. He says that they do fear the Englishman's god, because he has subdued them."

"I am glad to hear of it. It is suggestive of proper reverence. Ask him about the devil."

"Oh, they have already told me about that fine gentleman. Do you wish to hear of him?"

"Of course."

"They say that he sometimes comes in the shape of a white boy."

"Another absurdity. White has forever been the shade of purity and virtue. Would they have blackamoors for their angels?"

"But if you recall, sir, they do sometimes call us devils."

I rose from my chair, and went over to my shelves. "They are as ignorant as gypsies. Deluded by their wizards—"

"*Powwows,* sir."

"Forgive me, Goosequill, but I cannot screw my English mouth to these outlandish names." I put out my hand and touched my books. "Wizards only. Peeping and muttering. I am reminded of those papists in their antic copes parading upon the stage of their high altar." I came back to my chair. "Spreading mists of incense and the clamor of cheap bells. Tell me, Firstfoot, have you always believed your wizards?"

Goosequill translated the question, and again replied for him. "He says, sir, that they know no time when they were not as they are now."

"I see. The same old circulating dance, with its false and dazzling fires on which men stumble and are burned. Do you know my meaning, Goose?"

"If it was that dance I witnessed—"

"Tradition, you fool. It will be a perpetual cankerworm until the world's end. Yet we must bestir ourselves and tread it under. John Firstfoot, I must speak to all your people."

"*Cowautam?*" The boy asked the Indian and he signaled that he did, indeed, understand my words.

"I will excite their minds with the desire to know."

So it was that, two weeks after this conversation, I met the elders of the tribe in solemn convocation in order to discuss matters of faith. Eleazer Lusher had once more agreed to act as an interpreter, since I could not trust my boy to be a diligent translator, and I began with an oration to satisfy the savage heart. "I dreamed I was here," I said, "and I saw a church rising out of the ground."

I heard one of their number call out *"Mamaskishaui!"* but Mr. Lusher did not translate it.

I knew where the native stood and, turning my face towards him, courteously requested him to describe the nature of his deities. He seemed reluctant to discuss any such matter, but he was persuaded by Eleazer Lusher who replied on his behalf. "He is telling you that their great god, *Cawtantowwit,* has his cave in the southwest from where the warm winds come."

"I see."

"But they also have many strange relations of one Wetucks, a man that wrought great miracles among them and prophesied truly."

"No doubt some devil's pastime."

"He walked upon the waters. He was said to have descended from heaven."

"Another gaudy superstition. What is this heaven of theirs?"

Eleazer once more questioned the Indian, whom I suspected now to be himself attached to wizardry and magic. "It is a place of very fair soil, Mr. Milton. They want neither for meats or for clothes. It is but wishing and they have them."

"We may as well be entranced by the pomp and gay show of the papists. Please to go on."

"The people in heaven do nothing. The fields yield corn, beans and pumpkins without any tillage."

"Truly? No doubt there are apple trees and suchlike."

Eleazer consulted the presumed wizard. "Always green, and always flourishing."

I could not help but laugh. "No serpents, I hope."

The savage could have understood nothing of this, but I heard him walk up to me and stand before my chair. "The Englishman's god is all one fly," he whispered, "and the Englishman is all one squaw." Then he spat upon my face. There was immediate consternation among the Indians, who had never witnessed any of their number strike or insult an Englishman in this way. I did not move. I sat there until the tumult had subsided. "This day," I said quietly, "I make a solemn covenant with God to root out heathen superstition. I will not allow idols or ceremonies or candles at noonday or any such pettifoggery. Enough."

Two days later the brethren of New Milton, in their own assembly, published a warrant ordering the constable to suppress powwowing and heathen idolatry anywhere within the patent of the settlement; I then suggested that an edict also be issued to extirpate any such practices, if discovered, among the Indian tribes who bartered with us. I was urged to be patient, however, since it would prove dangerous to move against all of the Indians. So I decreed instead that our redeemed people could employ, or trade with, only those praying Indians who embraced the truth revealed in the Old and New Testaments. At the same time, dear Reginald, I instituted praying schools, and on the first Sunday of the month following twenty native men and women intoned the Lord's Prayer. I had taken great pains to learn the words in their own language, so that I might lead them in the recital. *"Nooshun kesukqut, quttianatamunch koowesuonk."* In these weekly classes I also began to preach to them in the order of doctrine, question, answer, reason and use. *"Kukketas-sootamoonk peyaimoutch."* It occurred to me that I should display to them clocks and mechanical instruments designed by Englishmen for the greater glory of God, and afterwards the natives lined up to kiss the Holy Bible which I held in my hands. On that occasion, also, with the help of Eleazer Lusher, I had announced *"Pausuck naunt manit."* There is only one god. Of course I could never become accustomed to the smell of bears' grease upon their skins, and I insisted that all praying Indians should wear English clothes. I explained their old condition in one word—*Cowauwaunemun,* they were out of the right path—but I had good reason to hope that the allusion would please them with its reference to their own old tracks within the forest. They told me that their god had created man and woman out of a tree which had become, as it were, the root of mankind. At that I had grown more concerned. "No. No. What is the word, Eleazer, for hearken to me?"

"Netopkihkta."

"Please to translate what else I tell them. God took a rib from Adam and out of that rib He made one woman." I had deliberately chosen the simplest words. "When Adam saw the woman, he said 'This is my bone.' You must forget your old superstitious stories." I left them then, and returned to my meditations.

ELEVEN

And that was the day we became betrothed. When I got down upon my knee and gave the ring to you, Kate.

Oh yes. You told me that it had been bequeathed to you. Your grandmother had died of a fit at Sadlers Wells, you said, and left it to you. As soon as I saw it, I knew it was Indian.

I admitted to it, Kate. After several minutes, I know, but I went down on my knees again and heartily begged forgiveness. Look how sweet it sits upon your finger. When Newcroft Matuxes sold it to me, he said that it was a token of happiness.

You told me that it was a sign of many children to come!

Same thing, Kate. Or so they say. Do you still have that book I presented to you? What was it called? It had the strangest title.

A Discourse of Women Shewing Their Imperfections Alphabetically. I was highly offended.

It was a lark, Kate. I never wanted to hurt your feelings.

I blamed it upon Mr. Milton, of course.

You had noticed that his temper was not improving, I remember. "He has become very difficult," you were saying as we strolled through the forest that day. "More masterful."

"More narrow, you mean. He has grown worse than the others."

"Not as bad as some of them, Goose. He sings still. And I heard him whispering to a dove pigeon the other morning."

"I agree that he can be merry, Kate. But he can also be harsh. I think he feels his loneliness here."

"But there are so many of us now."

"No. There is no one who is his equal. He told me once that he contemplated some great work. But then, he said, who will read it here, Goose? The trees and stones?"

"I thought he cherished the brethren?"

"A good Christian, I am sure, every inch of him."

"But he thinks that we are God's people."

"So he declares at his precious assemblies. But he is not as fond of them as he appears to be. He likes to govern them, certainly. But I have heard him sigh and yawn after they have left him."

"Is it so, Goose?"

"Yes. It is so. He loves the mastery, and the ordering, but sometimes I think he is truly lost in this place."

"I suppose that, after London, it must seem a wilderness to him?"

"Oh, the world is his wilderness. He is a very disappointed man."

"He is a blind man. Isn't that misery enough?"

"He suffers something more. Much more." We were hand in hand at the time. You were wearing that lovely little bonnet which Sarah Venn had made. "You know, Kate, there are times when I find him by the window, looking towards the sky. I could swear then that he sees something."

"He is probably listening to the birds."

"No. He gazes upwards. And sometimes he makes a motion with his hand, as if he were writing something down. I know he tried once, because he spilled the ink. 'I could not wait for you,' he said to me. 'Look at your hands,' I told him. 'They're black.' 'Like a savage,' he replied. And then he laughed."

We were in our favorite part, where the trees and bushes make that clearing. What do you call it? Our own wooden O. And then we settled down very comfortably upon the grass. "Can you do me the pleasure of singing a little, Kate?"

"What shall it be, Goose?"

"What about that old favorite, 'Comfort Me with Apples'?"

So you warbled, while I closed my eyes and lay back upon the ground. I had never heard a lovelier song in all my life. You know what happened next?

Goose. Say nothing more.

Why put your fingers up to your ears? It was all perfectly natural. I took you by the waist, and lowered you very gently.

Goose. I am blushing.

I was very gentle, wasn't I?

Goose.

Oh Kate.

I returned to Mr. Milton's house a few hours later, whistling very loudly to signal my arrival. I found him in the garden, lying in the famous hammock. "Ah, Goosequill. You find me at a propitious hour."

"Yes, sir. I feel propitious."

"I am raising the savages to a knowledge of their Savior."

I did not know if he meant himself or someone else. "I am glad to hear it."

"Thank you. It would be a mighty thing to establish a nation of God in this western world." He rolled out of his hammock, and took my arm. "What a majestic chronicle might be unrolled to future ages! Think of Diodorus among the Greeks, and Livy among the Latins."

"I am trying, sir."

"I shall be Milton among the Americans! And you shall write it down."

"To your dictate, I hope?"

"Of course. The events of our history will be recorded as a monument to further ages. You shall have a pen of iron, like Job, for iron deeds! You may begin now."

TWELVE

August 25, 1661. The colony has this last week been much troubled by a plague of caterpillars; where they have come upon trees they have left them bare and wasted, and where they have fallen upon the harvest they have brought it back down to meadowland. I am told that the cartwheels, in their passage, were painted green with the running over great swarms of them. I refrained from mentioning biblical parallels to the good people here, since I do not believe that we are being punished for any impious or wicked thing. Have I not embarked upon the holy work of training the savages in God's word? No, the caterpillars are merely nature.

August 29, 1661. A fellow newly arrived from Lyme, one Daniel Pegginton, came running up to the watch yesterday evening in a state of curious excitement. In heated words he related the appearance of a triton or merman which he saw laying hands upon the side of his little boat. He chopped off one of its hands with his hatchet, he said, and it was in all respects like the hand of a man. Then, taking fright, he threw it back into the water, where the merman itself presently sank, dying the water with its purple blood, and was no more seen. The climate of this land must work strangely upon the minds of men. It may be that the impure traditions and ceremonies of the savages, ripened by the sun, can turn the wits of our settlers. I must hasten on with my holy work, before we are all infected.

September 1, 1661. I taught the Indians that the proper name of the brethren is Particular-Separatist Elect; but they mangled the words so foully in their mouths that I begged them to be silent. How, in future years, will I be able to instruct them in Latin and in Hebrew?

September 7, 1661. The northwest wind has come again and has struck many, English and savage alike, with that sad disease known as the plague of the back. It is an American sickness, since I have never known the like in London, and I have decided to number it among the other killing agues of this region—viz. the black pox, the spotted fever, the griping of the guts, dropsy and sciatica. Yet some of our English diseases are wonderfully absent from the wilderness, among them measels, green sickness, headaches, stones and consumptions. I myself am free always of affliction. I have a healthy *constitution* which, I hope, may be impressed upon our growing new colony of Christian souls.

September 11, 1661. We have been tested. A woman of great shame came to us, after trying herself among the various towns and villages of the brethren hereabouts. She called herself ''Faithful'' Joanna Fortescue and tried to pass herself off as a pious member of our reformed church, but her reputation as a strumpet soon reached us. I had her taken and flogged at the whipping post before sending her back, like her goddess Venus, to the sea. Such harlotting and uncleanness are not to be tolerated in a new world such as ours. How then could our light shine like a beacon to the savage wilderness?

October 5, 1661. An earthquake disordered us yesterday. Between three and four of the afternoon, in clear calm weather, it came with a noise like that of continual thunder or the rattling of coaches in London. It sprang from the western interior, and shook the earth with such violence that the platters and dishes fell from my shelves. Those in the street could not stand without catching hold of the posts, while those in the fields cast down their working tools and fled they knew not whither. The noise and the shaking continued for three minutes, but was presently gone; after another half an hour, there came a second tumult but one that was neither so loud nor so strong as the former. I informed my Indians that we had experienced the wrath of God. Where there is glory, there must also be terror; where there is reverence, there must be fear.

October 7, 1661. We have returned to due order and custom. I have called for a general assembly to consider the apportionment of land to new comers: let it be just and godly, I said, but let it also be methodically strict. This morning some gunpowder exploded, and destroyed Isaiah Fairehead's barn.

October 9, 1661. God seldom sends us rain, but when it arrives from His hand, it is very violent.

October 11, 1661. Adam Newcome, chief of the savages within my patent, led his sons to my door this morning and demanded to address me. I gave him leave, very courteously, and he told me (through the words of one son) that some of the elect had despoiled an Indian grave. His speech to me was in this manner, which I reproduce for the sake of those curious to know the primitive tongue: "When last the glorious light of all the sky was underneath this earth, and birds grew silent, I began to settle and to take repose. Before my eyes were fast closed I saw a vision, at which I was much troubled and trembling, a spirit cried behold who are these wild people who have broken my bones. I implore your aid against the thieves who have come to our land. If this be suffered, I shall not rest within my everlasting habitation." I was affronted by this heathen oration, but I kept my temper and conveyed to Adam Newcome my oath that the despoilation of the grave would be thoroughly examined. But my amanuensis, Goosequill, already knew the facts of this matter. Two of the younger brethren, newly arrived, had been seeking for Indian corn, which, they had been told, was often buried beneath the ground. In burrowing under some deserted barns, two miles from New Milton, they came across some old forsaken bones covered with a cloth made out of two bear skins sown together at full length. Thereupon they had left the bones, and carried the skins back to our godly town. It was a wanton act and, although I have not a groatsworth of reverence for any pagan ceremony, I saw the folly of their theft. It was very ill done. I called for the young men to be apprehended and immediately brought to me. They were soon found, and I ordered them to go down upon their knees to beg pardon of the sachem. They complied, most unwillingly, and then on my peremptory instruction returned to him the bear skins. I gave Adam Newcome a watch as a token of my own compassionate succor. I have no need for it, and I trust that its mechanism will quiet his ancestral spirits. Yet I went to bed uneasy.

October 15, 1661. There came a strange spectacle at dusk yesterday. Three wolves pursued a deer down the main thoroughfare of our blessed town, and it fled towards the river with the ravening beasts following. It was a lesson that there is a wilderness within every zone and under every clime.

October 20, 1661. Increase Dobbs is shut up in some hectic fever, and has grown frenetic. He had come to Humility Tilly, wailing and roaring, saying that he had seen the apparition of a black person in a blue cap running at him with a spindle. Then he fell upon the ground, and complained bitterly of having burning rags thrust into his mouth and nose. Mistress Tilly fainted away, and was revived by Alice Seacoal with some preservative of camphor. Increase Dobbs has proved a more difficult case. We have an apothecary, but one in his dotage who has no right drug to purge him. The stricken Dobbs lives a little away from our town, and no doubt solitude has caused a general discomfort and dejection of mind. I had touched his face once, when he came to me for instruction in the letters of St. Paul on church discipline, and I knew then that he possessed a complexion which would induce him to melancholy. He was taken with a vomiting after his fit, which is a token of some sanative or balsamic ferment within him. I told our not so skillful apothecary to give him chemical sulphur, yet it had no effect: marks appeared upon his skin, as if of branding irons or of bites, and he vomited forth more matter.

October 24, 1661. What is this pestilential murrein running among the people? Mistress Sprat, a godly widow out of Barnstaple, came to me this morning with some rambling narration that she had seen in the river, yesterday at noon, a thing with the head of a man and the tail of a cat with nothing else between. "Go to," I said. "You dream, woman."

"Mr. Milton, it is not a fancy. I cannot gainsay you, and the

Lord knows that we all reverence you, but this was no dream on my poor part. Others beside myself have observed things in that forest which no Englishman or Englishwoman can abide or have seen heretofore.'' She was always of florid style. ''We have seen men in blue shirts continually appearing and disappearing among the trees. We have heard voices.''

''And how is it that no one has informed me of these frenzies?''

''We believe them to be the work of the devil testing us, sir, and did not wish to add to the heaviness of your burdens here. We did not wish to disturb the calm and orderliness of your candid mind.''

I dismissed her. There is a breeding corruption which can lie hid under the show of a full and healthy constitution before breaking out in disease; it seems that, as yet, our laws and ordinances have not been sufficient to curb the demoniac frenzy and moping melancholy which seems to spring up in this wilderness. Yet moonstruck maladies can be cured by the bright sun, and the only sure physic for these disorders is to be gained from the light of discipline and penance. I have ordered a week of fasting and humiliation. Increase Dobbs has died, still raving.

October 27, 1661. It has been decided by the assembly, under the impress of my authority, that Mistress Sprat should be examined for witchcraft. I questioned her carefully in solemn convocation—yet she were but a weak witch, if she were any at all. She had engaged in no dealings with any of our children, as is their general course, but she steadfastly maintained that she had seen these phantasms or apparitions. She further confessed that she had seen objects such as spades and hoes flying about the fields. In a dream, she said, she had seen great towers of light rising out of the ground which we now inhabit; these great piles, she continued, filled the spirits with terror and affrightment. She saw winged chariots and huge roads, at which point her voices cried out, "We knock no more! We knock no more!"

All this idle fancy displeased me, and so I asked her, "Do you, by your own confession, admit that you have had much converse with the devil?"

"Oh no, sir. I am one of the Lord's people. And I will say this. It has been told us that the devil led the savages into this land. Could it be that he reigns still amongst them, and hopes to make us his subjects?"

I ordered her to be silent, and issued a sentence that she be tied to the whipping post for three hours with a gridiron upon her head to make further mock of her.

November 24, 1661. A barbarous murder has been committed. One Noah Winthrop, a chair maker, was found stuffed through the ice in a pond outside the town. His hat and gun lay upon the ice, so that others might suppose he had drowned himself. But it was found that his neck had broken strangely, and at once a jury was empaneled. At first the suspicion fell upon the Indians, since the neck is the savage means of murdering, yet two godly brethren testified that they had seen this Winthrop in furious quarrel with a leather cutter by name Simon Gadbury. Winthrop had been observed to fall upon him, catching at his hair, and more violence was prevented only when a neighbor ran between them. The cause of this quarrel was not yet known, although high words had been spoken. Gadbury was questioned, and at first denied his guilt—yet I could sense from his manner of speaking that he lied and, as chairman of the jury, I called for the neighbor to be questioned once more. He was a tremulous weak-spirited creature, this Samuel Hardinge, a bee-keeper, and could hardly speak out when I called him forth. He held something still within his breast, I knew, so I grew peremptory with him. "They were," he said, "as man and wife."

A terrible groan rose from the jury, but I silenced them with my hand. "Pray go further, Mr. Hardinge."

"I believe them to be—to have been—sodomites." I understood at once why the Lord had been visiting us with apparitions, but I waited for him to continue with his tale. "I believe that they were quarreling over an Indian boy." I put my hands over my ears in horror, yet I could still hear the loud moaning from the assembled brethren.

"This is a burning matter," I said. "Why was it not put before us?"

"I had—I have no proof. I am newly come to your colony, sir—"

"Newly come and newly gone. For your grievous and deceitful silence, Mr. Hardinge, you go by foot away. You are banished forthwith." I could hear the wretched fool sobbing as he was led out of the meetinghouse, but now in fierce joy I called for Simon Gadbury. He had been locked away, and knew nothing of our proceedings. "You stand accused, Mr. Gadbury, of a very grave evil. Do you suspect what it might be?"

"No, Mr. Milton."

"Oh, Mr. Gadbury, do not meddle with me. Do not meddle with fire. You were an acquaintance of the dead man, were you not?"

"I was indeed."

"Oh yes indeed. Are you a pretty little fellow, then?"

"Sir?"

"Do you play the maid?" I pursed my lips, and tossed my head from side to side. "Are you wanton?"

"Truly, Mr. Milton, I am at a stand—"

"You stand. No doubt you squat. You bend. You wriggle. You lie." I clapped my hands for silence once more, as the brethren lamented. "Was there shit-begotten lechery between you and the dead man?"

"Mr. Milton, I—"

"You are accused of sodomitical uncleanness. Do you deny it?"

He could not withstand the force of my godly inspired will and, having confessed to that beastliness, he willingly avowed that he was the murderer—that he had broken the man's neck and stuffed him beneath the ice in Indian fashion. Two days later he was taken from his dungeon, and was burned to death. I decreed that the bones and ashes be thrown into the common cesspool. No more is to be written, or said, of this matter.

December 3, 1661. I always considered this to be a healthful air, so clear and dry that it cooled the crude humors of the body, but now I find it to be of no such healing nature. A savage was raving in the street at dusk yesterday, and I heard loud shouts coming from some of the brethren. I hastened out of doors, and could hear the native crying out *"Mamaskishaui, mamaskishaui!"* I consulted Goosequill, who informed me that the heathen had declared he had the smallpox. I recalled then that Eleazer Lusher had once informed me that the natives can be mightily smitten with our English diseases, having no previous acquaintance with them. The savage fled into the forest in order to die alone, which suggests to me that these people have some form of conscience within their breasts.

December 15, 1661. The infection has spread among the savages, and they have fallen into a lamentable condition. When they lie upon their hard mats the pox breaks, and their skins cleave to the mats themselves. I ordered bedding and linen to be brought to them, but they refused it. So they groan in a gore of blood. The good people here fetch them wood and water; they make fires for them, and bury them when they die. Not one of the elect has grown sick or has been in the least measure tainted by the disease, which leads me to hope that the distemper did not arrive with us into this new world. My prayerful Indians, themselves touched by the contagion, have asked me why they are being punished by the Englishman's god. I assured them that He is also their god, and paraphrased from the first chapter of Isaiah on the just punishment of idolatry and evil. May God clear their minds of all perplexity concerning His will.

December 20, 1661. A story reaches me, fitter for a legend than a history. Preserved Cotton came into my house this morning, to tell me that he and his companions had seen unearthly lights close by them. I caught the substance of it in the haste of his tumbled words, but gave it very little credence: on the previous night, he had observed a great light by the river. Then it ran off, as he put it, and was contracted into the figure of a swine; but after a moment it stood still, flared up and was about three yards square. It was seen so by Mr. Cotton and some other brethren for the space of three or four minutes, when it was joined by another light. They closed in one, and then parted, and closed and parted diverse times until they vanished with dim flashings.

"Will-o'-the-wisps," I said.

"No, Mr. Milton. They were great lights."

"Indian torches?"

"No, sir. They were marvelously quick, coming together and dividing in the twinkling of an eye."

"Have you been feeding on evil meats, Mr. Cotton, which have spread an ill humor?"

"It is always the plainest fare for us, as you know. These lights were not our fantasies."

"If they are not of this earth, Preserved Cotton, then they are the devil's work. God would not choose to reveal Himself in woods and wilderness. You and your fellows go back to your houses and pray that they come not again. Go. Take your leave now, before you also take leave of your senses."

I had no more ready answer than that and, after he had left me, I walked in the garden to clear my thoughts. What if this new land were indeed full of lights and apparitions, as have been reported to me? We knew it to be a wilderness, but what if it were a wild land in more than one sense? Could it truly be the devil's own country?

THIRTEEN

That was how he left the diary, Kate. Do you see here, where I have marked the next day? Nothing. Nothing at all written beneath it. I went to his chamber that following morning, at the accustomed time, but he was nowhere to be seen. He was gone. Clean gone.

I know it, Goose. We have talked it over and over.

There had been no violence or ambush, since nothing had been touched. His bowl of water stood by the bedside with a little film of dust upon its surface. I fear that he has wandered deep into the wilderness, trusting to his inner sight, and lost his way. Oh, Kate, where has he gone?

PART TWO

Fall

ONE

How is it that I have fallen? How can it be permitted to end like this? How can it be permitted to begin like this? I had left the settlement. I was called to the forest. I entered the darkness. I went down into the wood, to see whether the vine flourished and the pomegranates budded. I was wandering among the pillars of trees, I was touching wreathed incense of wood and earth as the wind of green life lifted up my cloak. Such a soft and yielding darkness I had not known since I dreamed of raven down and sable clouds. I heard the names of cedar and of pine, of fir and branching palm. I touched the sacred poetry of trees.

He found a beaten track as wide as an English lane. Oh, briars and brambles, exposed and tangled roots, do not impede me. My eyes are as the eyes of a dove, washed with milk. Infinite milkiness of space. But the blind man stumbles, because he has walked among rocks. He has become lost. There is no echo around him, and he fears the presence of a marsh or swampy ground. Why have I strayed, seeking and finding nothing? This is the wilderness. In the dream of man, this is the place of fear. Druid fear. The evil things that walk by night. Oh, defilement.

Blind mouths. He turns and turns about as the night comes down upon him. I said, I will go up to the palm tree. I will take hold of the boughs thereof. I must rest in the pensive secrecy of some woody cell. I must find a harbor. But where can he find rest, except at the base of some great tree, where he sits and wraps his cloak around himself? Without the company of kind or kin, he blows upon his hands to savor his own warmth. It rains, and I hear the comfort of the showers upon the outer leaves. He sleeps, and he wanders again.

Dawn. Is it dawn? My head is filled with dew, and my locks with the drops of the night. I have put off my cloak, how shall I put it on? Tell me, what is the destination of a blind man in a wood? Is it towards myself? I took off a piece of bark, and I ate it. I licked the moisture from the leaves, and I drank it. I will arise and go. He treads upon living things, not without fear. The world is still a wilderness of words and sighs, like the sighing of the trees. Such heat. Such cries. Here is copulation. Here is the whispering darkness. The vines are tangled in his hair, and the rank odor of weeds surrounds me. Lechery. If I fall, I will be comforted by the slug and the spider. A whiplash of sound comes from the trees, and he bows his head in shame. He smells the earth, as ripe as a charnel house. Something is growing around me.

But now the breeze brings the perfume of fruit. All my hunger and thirst quicken at the sweet scent of that alluring fruit, and I reach out my hand to touch it. To revolve ambrosia in my palm. Delicious. No. Oh no. The blind man, he or I, is taken by the leg and hurled upwards into the air. He is snared, and hanging from a pole. Everything waits expectantly as he sways from the rope, set in an Indian trap. His dark world has been turned upside down. I am like Mahomet's tomb, he shouts aloud, suspended between earth and heaven!

Let there be light. And there was light. The word was light. The world was light. Something is happening. My head has been broken, and is now streaming with light. Light is entering my veins and moving upwards. Downwards. And now the trees are walking towards me. First seen. Creation trees. Green leaves. Emerald sky. These colours are the arms waiting to greet me. The rush of blood, my red sea, has parted the closed lids of my eyes. The blind man, swinging from the rope meant for the deer, can see. From morn to noon he hung, from noon to dewy eve, watching the colors deepen as the day advanced. I can see.

TWO

And so, dear brother in Christ, dear Reginald, I was returned. The blind man, like he who came weeping from Hebron, was given back to his own people. I had been missed for
six weeks and almost despaired of, so great is their love for me,
when I was found, my staff in my hand, walking in the meadows
outside our pious settlement. As I trod upon those blessed
fields, I was glimpsed by two of our laborers. "God be praised,
sir. You have returned to us like Joseph. Well and whole."

"Who is this?"

"Accepted Lister, sir. You once heard me preach upon Ish-
mael."

"It was a good preaching. I remember particularly your
remarks upon the hair of the outcast." I believe that I sighed, so
great had been my struggle in the weeks before. "Will you
now, please, take me to my dwelling? I am tired after my journey."

"At once, sir. My heart leaps up at your deliverance! This
way."

I was led towards my house, and the foolish boy who ministers to me came out laughing and crying all at once. "You're home," he shouted. "You are returned!"

He embraced me, but I remained still. "Oh, Goosequill."

"Yes, Mr. Milton?"

"Take me into the house. The haven." The young woman was waiting there, and greeted me happily. "I am gratified to hear you, Kate. I am content to return under this lowly roof. I have seen enough. I have seen one world begin and end."

"Sir? What is it?"

"No matter, Goose. I have endured much. All is God's will."

"I suppose so, Mr. Milton. But you look half dead from traveling, if I may say so."

"I am half dead."

I am sometimes of a sad imbibing humor, and had no wish to express my suffering. Like Job, I am content to sorrow. So the clown rambled on. "We have cleaned everything very nicely, sir. Even your old pair of compasses shines like a star now. And all your books are dusted down. I took a cloth to them every day."

"I am glad to hear it. Did you remember the pedometer?"

"Polished."

"Good. I must resume my measured walking."

"Kate has performed wonders with the garden, too."

"Oh, Katherine, there is something else. It would please me if you could plant the herbs alphabetically." She was silent. "You understand me, I trust?"

"If you wish it, sir. I know the names well enough——"

"Excellent. Is there fresh spring water in my closet?"

"I changed it every morning, sir." I sensed that he had some secret to impart, and so I remained quiet. "And you will be pleased to hear that Katherine is with child."

"And what other news is there?" I walked over to the open door which led into my garden, but found no savor in the scents of the flowers. It was very warm, yet for some reason I trembled on the threshold.

"What is the matter, sir?"

"Nothing at all, Kate. Whatever could be the matter?" I stared, dear Reginald, into my familiar darkness. "Yet the sun is too strong for me. Take me within. Some tepid water mixed with the camomile herb, please."

A solemn council was called the next morning, formally to welcome my return to the elect; Seaborn Jervis, Job "Defiant in the Lord" and Phineas Sanctified Coffin led the others in prayer as I reverently entered the assembly house. "I have been restored," I told them once their prayers had ended and they had settled down on their wooden benches. "I have been called back from the land of abomination and desolation."

"Thanks be to God."

"You may ask where I have dwelled these past weeks. Well, I will tell you this. Good brothers and sisters, the Lord Christ deemed it expedient that I should dwell among carnal men and wanton people." Of course there was great consternation, with much gnashing of teeth, but I put up my hand to silence them. "Yes, I was compelled to live with the savages." So great a moaning had not been heard since the destruction of Tyre. "But God was pleased to give me a patient and pitiful spirit, even while I lodged with them in their filthy holes."

"His ways are mysterious and mighty!" Good Dame Seacoal was excited to pious speech.

"They luxuriate in sloth. They are filled with insatiate desire."

"It cannot be!"

"There were noisome stenches."

"Oh!"

"The natives pursued such filthy ways that I rejoiced in my blindness. I gave thanks that the Lord saw fit to keep me from the sight of their horrid blasphemies."

"Praise be!"

"And now I am come back to you." No more was said that day, and, dear brother, nothing more was ever said.

Yet the Lord is ever watchful, ever reining in the harness, ever pricking with the goad, and I was not left to wallow in peace. On a Sunday morning in April, two months after my homecoming, the brethren had gathered for our Sabbath assembly. The beating of a drum announces our service, since no bells have yet been cast in this wilderness, and at the appointed time I was led to my place by the boy Goosequill; the elect followed me, according to custom, and sat gravely upon their benches. At their back I had placed an elderly dame with a birch rod to overawe the children—there is no whispering and laughter in paradise, as I had told her, so wherefore should we suffer them here? There were extemporaneous prayers, issuing from the godly mouths of those who felt moved to speak. On this morning Daniel Pegginton murmured a prayer for the eventual redemption of "all those who are without"—by which we mean, dear Reginald, those who are neither precise nor separate. Each

line of the Sixty-first Psalm was then read by the deacon, Seaborn Jervis, before being sung by the congregation; we have no
brass cymbals or trumpets, no instruments of Belial or of Mammon, but I was pleased to think that those sacred words "From
the ends of the earth will I cry unto Thee" were ringing out
over the woods and swamps of this desolation. Our lecturer that
day was William Deakin. He is the butcher of our little colony,
and is known by all to be truly inspired; he is given to sudden
fits of godly utterance, accompanied by bursts of "Hallelujah!
Hallelujah!" with which he is accustomed to finish his sentences. So he has become known as Hallelujah Deakin, and is
often to be heard singing psalms in his little shop. I stop there
myself, before purchasing my meat, and refresh myself with his
ululations. He advanced now to the front of the congregation,
and began to speak. "Our evangelic faith may be told in two
words, my dearest limbs of God. What are they?"

"Faith!" intoned good Humility Tilly.

"Charity!" followed Alice Seacoal.

"Yes, indeed. Faith and charity, which may also be construed as belief and practice. Hallelujah! Listen to those two
words. Grind them within the edifices of your ears. Faith. Charity. We have no need of books which smell of the perfume of
Rome, no need of prayers which stink of candle oil. All with us
is spirit and revelation. What shall I cry?"

"Hallelujah!"

"The Book of Common Prayer is an idol, and its readers are
idolators."

"Hallelujah!"

"It is rotten stuff, abstracted out of the pope's old mass
book, an abominable and loathsome sacrifice in the sight of

God." He paused. "Even as a dead dog!" I was so moved by his discourse that I felt obliged to wipe my forehead with a linen cloth. "I tell you this, dear anointed of the Lord. I tell you of my father in the old country. He had many books in his chamber where there was also corn stored, and he had among these books the Greek testament, the psalms and the Book of Common Prayer all bound together as one volume. He came into that chamber and what, dear flies in God's ointment, what did he find?"

"What was it?" Dame Seacoal was wrought to a pitch of intensity, in which I felt inclined to join her. "Tell us!"

"He found the Common Prayer eaten by mice, every leaf of it, but not any of the other two touched, nor any of his other books harmed. Do you see how the Lord works with us? How He winds us about His sacred finger?"

At that moment I heard sounds of calling and general commotion outside the meeting. "Goosequill," I whispered. "What's this?"

"Some of our Indians, sir, are jumping up and down like—"

"None of your profane similes in this place."

"They say that a party of Englishmen are riding this way. Englishmen and Indian warriors."

"Is it so?" I feared some riotous enemy, but I judged it neither wise nor proper to display my fears to those assembled. Hallelujah Deakin was speaking more loudly, in order to rival the confused noises without, but even he was forced to break off when the sound of many horses' hoofs could plainly be heard. The brethren were now distracted and, sensing the ferment all around me, I rose from my bench and ordered them to be still. I motioned the boy ahead of me and, placing my hand on his right shoulder, proceeded into the open air. The congregation followed me, despite my stern injunction, and raised their voices in astonishment when they came out upon the thoroughfare. "What now?" I muttered to Goosequill.

"Horse-drawn carts, Mr. Milton. Somewhat like those in our London streets."

"What else?"

"Men on horses. Some with flagons in their hands. Some of them singing."

"I hear their lewd voices well enough. Picture them to me before they descend upon us."

"They are wearing clothes, sir, as brightly colored as the drapers' livery. But it is not exactly London dress. Nor is it exactly Indian. It is somewhere betwixt the two. And their hair, sir, is as long as a maiden's." Of course I had feared that these were soldiers come from England to arrest me. But their singing and laughing assured me that they were a ragged regiment, if they were a regiment at all. And yet, who were they? "Oh, their leader, sir, is a man of quaint habit. May I?"

"Yes. But be quick. I can already smell their drunken breath."

"Fellow of sanguine humor. Face very large and ruddy like a bowl of cherries. Beard as red as the tail of a fox. Shall I go on?" I nodded, with as much patience as I could command. "Frock coat of blue, with a green band around his waist. And on his head, oh Lord, a hat of white felt with some feathers sticking from it."

"What creature of Bedlam is this?"

"He wears a sword, sir, and is double-pistoled."

"Not of Bedlam, then, but of the Tower."

"Oh no, sir. He wears them as ornaments. They hang so prettily, and he has put flowers around the handle of his sword."

I betrayed no feeling, but drew myself up as I heard this creature of motley call for his crew to halt. He dismounted, and I heard the jingling of his jewels and beads as he approached. "I am honored to greet you, sir," he said to me.

"The honor is mine. May I be so bold as to ask——"

"My name is Ralph Kempis, sir. Traveling from James Town in Virginia to take possession of my new territory." Could it be that this man had been given some patent from the blasphemous king, and was about to take control of this new land? I could not speak. Might he even be some royal commissioner sent to harass and subdue me? "Is this place, sir, known as Machapquake?"

"No. It is known as New Milton."

"Forgive me, sir. I know that we Englishmen now rule, but was it once known to the Indians by that name?"

"I believe so, yes."

"And therefore I am your new neighbor. I have purchased the land on the other side of the river, known as Sepaconett. But its name will also change."

"How shall we know it, Mr. Kempis?"

"It is to be called Mary Mount."

"Mary Mount?"

"In honour of the Blessed Virgin, sir." I took a step backward, and there was a low groan from the brethren around me. Kempis laughed. "Do I perceive that you are of a different faith? Well, it is a vast land. There is room enough for all."

"Excuse me, Mr. Kempis." I remained as calm as Hezekiah

before the heathens. "We must return to our service. We were listening to some excellent words on idolatry."

"An interesting theme. Well, good day to you, Mr.—"

"Milton. John Milton."

"I am much obliged to you, Mr. Milton." I heard him bow to me with a great flourish that set his ornaments jangling again, but Goosequill told me later that he had smiled up into my face. Oh yes, he knew me well enough by name and repute. Then he mounted his horse, and with a loud "Hurrah" set off again at the head of his troop.

My neighbors in Christ remained still as the procession began to move through our town, but there was a sudden disturbed murmur. "What is it that affrights them, Goose?"

"Three wagons, sir. Of Indian women. Do you wish me to go on?"

"I am afraid. Yet continue." There was then a louder groan from my brethren. "What fresh horror is this?"

"Two priests in black gowns."

"Hellish."

"They carry a statue of the Virgin Mary between them."

"Excremental. This is not to be endured."

"They ride merrily enough. Oh dear. One of them gives you a blessing."

I admit, dear Reginald, that I spat upon the ground. That evening I summoned Seaborn Jervis, Hallelujah Deakin and Preserved Cotton to my humble dwelling; they brought with them Innocent Jones, a farm laborer who had traveled in Virginia before making his way to New England. He was supposed to have heard rumors of Ralph Kempis in that territory, and I was eager for any report. "Tell me more," I said, "of this wanton fellow. This most incogitant woodcock."

"Sir?"

"The Roman whoremaster Kempis."

"He is one of many papists in James Town, sir. It is thick with them. The heat there dries up our true English blood, but they flourish upon it."

"That is no marvel. They are not true Englishmen. They are merely painted ones, like the Indians." I found myself to be smiling. *"Purpurea intexti tollunt aulea Britanni."* Deakin managed only the faintest "hallelujah," so large was his sorrow.

"That's just what I say," Preserved Cotton murmured. "All dressed up in purple. Tolling their bells."

"Verily," said Seaborn Jervis, "of a crooked generation."

Yet I was impatient for more news. "Innocent, I thirst."

"A cordial, sir?"

"No no. Give me your report."

"I believe, sir, that Kempis must be one of those who held plantations in Virginia. I saw one wagon laden with tobacco stuff."

"But you have no certain knowledge of him?"

"No, sir. I was only a laboring man, and desperate to be gone from the wild Catholics."

"And now this monster, this seven-headed hydra, lurks among us. Have you made inquiries, Mr. Jervis, about the purchase?"

"I am told that he holds a letter from the King, and the governor was compelled to grant him a patent."

I fetched a sigh, dear Reginald, from deep within me. "So

now we must contend at our very doors with pride, luxury, drunkenness, whoredom and all the other ills attendant upon the Roman superstition. They think no more of the Living God than of a buzzard idol.''

"Did you see the idol they carried with them?" Hallelujah Deakin was righteously indignant. "They carried it between their legs like some painted squaw.''

"Oh yes indeed." I could barely refrain from crying aloud. "No doubt we shall soon have rich copes and gorgeous altar cloths, pictures and images, gay shows and ceremonial shadows, all the old pomp and glory of the flesh!''

"And those priests, sir, riding upon one horse as if they had come from a tavern.''

"Male whores upon their beasts. It is the figure from Revelation. No doubt they are incontinent and daily drunkards, like every other imposter priest. But we must be careful, gentlemen, now that we are in the wilderness. When men turn papist, they soon lean to the black arts—''

I was interrupted by Goosequill, who came in whistling. He placed a paper in my hand. "It is from Mr. Kempis, sir." I dropped it to the floor with a groan but he picked it up, still whistling, and gave it to me again. "It is a letter, sir. Would you care for me to read it?''

"I do not know if I have the strength for any papist incantation.''

"Shall I burn it, then?''

"No, fool. Read." I heard him break the seal. "Aloud, sir, if you please.''

"It is certainly from Mr. Kempis. He has signed it with a very large hand.''

"I wish it were with his own blood."

"He humbly salutes you, and sends you all fraternal civil greeting. Then with due reverence he invites you to be present at the ceremony."

"Ceremony? What ceremony?"

"The instauration—is that the word? Of Mary Mount."

I refused to attend any such carnival, of course, but it was my solemn duty to learn what idolatrous rites were being prepared on our very borders. So I sent the boy in my place. "Do you really wish," I said, "to commit yourself among the thick of them? Do you dare?"

"They seem very merry, sir."

"Merry becomes Mary, and other putrid trash. Theirs is but false glitter. Be sure they do not deceive you, Goosequill, as they would deceive the Indians with beads and glasses. Beware."

T H R E E

Yet Goosequill had admired the retinue who rode, singing and drinking, into the town; there was so little gaiety, and so little color, in New Milton that sometimes it seemed to him to be no more than a patch of shadow upon the flourishing green land. So he chose to sit with the Indians, patiently learning their language and observing their customs, finding out how they had lived before the Englishmen came. They told him the story of the dream warriors who could still be seen, running at night through the dark forests; they lived off bark and rotten wood; they sat all day in the crouching posture of the sick, but when night came, they hunted the shades of animals with the shades of bow and arrow.

Such stories seemed to Goosequill to be more genuine and more interesting than any words preached by Hallelujah Deakin or Preserved Cotton. With their grave air, with their formal manner, with their dark coats and faded neck-bands, the brethren had no real affinity with this place. Goosequill sensed that they would either die here or somehow manage to subdue it to their will. Only his marriage to Katherine Jervis could reconcile him to life in New Milton—they owned a small wooden house close to Milton's dwelling, and now they worked together as servants and companions to the blind man. So when Ralph Kempis and his followers rode into New Milton, Goosequill felt genuinely elated: here at last were Englishmen who seemed to revel in the wilderness, who wore clothes as bright as the Indians, who sang among the streams and trees. "We hardly need to fear them, sir," he had said to Milton, before he left for the inauguration of Mary Mount. "They may make more noise than the brethren, but there is no harm in them."

"No harm? They are serpents armed with a mortal sting, and you say no harm? They commit the abominations of the beastly whore who sits in Rome. No harm? They spread a universal rottenness and gangrene, wherever they wander. And you say there is no harm."

Goosequill was accustomed to his master's violent outbursts, and he looked at him impassively. "I expect, then, sir, that you cheerfully would burn them all. We love our roasted meats here."

Then Milton smiled. "No, Goose, you are too rash. We must not burn them yet. They may be persuaded to renounce their superstition. I shall instruct them."

Goosequill was smiling, too. "How shall you do that, sir?"

"There is a printer newly come from Weymouth with all the implements of his trade. I shall write them a true and useful treatise."

"Well, master, let us hope they are good enough readers to be worthy of you."

"That is a consideration. They are a rabble, I believe, of papists, fugitives and savages. Could I tune my speech to such mixed auditors?"

"You could send Mr. Deakin to preach at them. Such a sober gentleman would surely prove an example. They would repent at once."

"You are very forward this morning." Milton reached out to cuff his ear, but Goosequill dodged the blow. "So go forward. Go to that most horrid and damnable place. Witness all the vomited paganism of their sensual idolatry."

"And bring it back to you?"

"Go. Now. You will see incense in the evening, and candles at noon."

Goosequill seemed delighted at the prospect, but said nothing beyond his farewell. The next morning he set out for Mary Mount; he rode by the side of the river and by midday reached a wooden bridge which must have been hastily erected by the new arrivals themselves; it was no more than some planks laid across the large stones on the riverbed, but there was a path on the other side. He followed it, and within half an hour he had reached the settlement. He had not known what to expect, but certainly he had not expected this: on an area of open ground, a tall pole had been erected. It was richly decorated, festooned with garlands and with ribbons, and draped with small bells which sounded in the breeze. As he rode closer he could see that it had also been painted with various faces and human figures, depicted in red against a deep blue background. A man came over to him, with his arms outstretched in greeting. "Welcome," he said. "Our first visitor. An Englishman, I see."

"London, sir. Tallboy Rents in Smithfield. A sweet part of town."

The man took a step back, put his hands upon his hips, and whistled. "I was born in Duncan Lane!"

"Known as Drunken Lane?"

"The very same."

"Otherwise known as Roll Again Lane?"

"Of course." He laughed, and shook his head. "What a fine thing it is to meet an old neighbor!" He had noticed that Goosequill kept glancing at the pole. "Have you not seen one of these before?"

"Not in London. No." Yet he had the most fugitive and elusive memory of having glimpsed something of the same kind in his earliest childhood; yes, it had been erected in some fields beyond the city walls. "I do know it," he said. "It is called a maypole."

"A rare sight in London."

"Unknown. As rare as a stage play."

"But now all is changed again. I hope, too, that all may change here."

"And make the brethren merry? I doubt it."

"So do I. Give me your hand, please. My name is Percival Alsop. To my friends and neighbors, Percy."

"Goosequill."

"Oh, so you are a scholar?"

"I speak English like a native, and can count on all ten fingers."

"You have too much wit for the wilderness, sir. You should be at home shelling peas and fighting the watch."

"I would give everything I possess, which is nothing, to see the old city again."

"So what brought you so far from Tallboy Rents? The delicious climate?"

"Oh no." He hesitated. "I was taken up."

"Impressed?"

"I traveled of my own will." He hesitated again, unwilling or embarrassed to mention his association with the brethren. "I come from across the river. Over there yonder. New Milton."

"Indeed? You hardly look like one of the elect, if I may say so."

"You may." He was relieved to be able to express his feelings without any concealment. "I am not elected. I am not precise. I am not separate. I am not godly at all."

"Thanks be to God."

"Precisely."

"And so?"

Goosequill understood the question. "I am secretary to Mr. Milton."

"Truly?" Alsop whistled once more. "I believe that he is a very solemn gentleman."

"Very solemn indeed."

They were silent for a moment, then both of them burst out laughing. "I suppose," Alsop said, "that we must continue this conversation on some other occasion. If you have come from the very reverend Mr. Milton, then I must lead you to the very merry Mr. Kempis. Dismount, neighbor, and follow."

He took Goosequill towards one of the canvas tents which had been erected near the maypole; it had been painted with bright blue and yellow stripes, with a large "K" daubed in red across a mat which hung over the entrance. Goose could hear someone speaking and, just as Alsop led him within, there was a sudden loud burst of laughter. "So we shall have jugglers, and mummers, and gymnic artists." It was Ralph Kempis who spoke; he raised a hand to salute Goosequill, and carried on talking. "We shall have antics and mimics and fortune casters and conjurors. No. We already have our conjuror. Is that not so, Maquisa?" He had addressed an Indian, who was sitting on a wooden stool at the other side of the tent. He looked nothing like the natives who worked in New Milton; his head was entirely shaved, except for a narrow crest of hair, and the preserved body of a small bird hung from his left ear. He did not reply to Kempis's question, but he grinned and shook a bag of jewels or powder. Goosequill smelt the strangest scent, like the perfume of a lily flower, which suddenly seemed to pervade the air. Kempis looked over to him, and smiled. "It keeps away the flies, sir. Now sit down and tell us your business."

"I really have no business, Mr. Kempis. I have come from Mr. Milton." He had rehearsed his words on the journey by horseback, but here they seemed improvised and wretched. "He salutes you and sends you greetings, but his leg is highly inflamed and he cannot travel as yet. And so—" He paused for a moment, embarrassed. "Here I am."

"You come as his legate to our little ceremony?"

"I am to be his eyes and ears."

"But not his mouth, I hope. He has said and written much—" Kempis broke off, and stood up to shake the visitor's hand. "Well, you are welcome. But I must say that I had hoped to see Mr. Milton dance around our maypole."

Goosequill smiled at the sudden vision of his master kicking his legs into the air. "I think, sir, that he would rather dance in hell."

"Oh, but this would be hell for him. I have seen some of his tracts and pamphlets on behalf of the Puritans. He can be a very rough and decided man."

"Now there, Mr. Kempis, I fully agree with you. Very decided indeed."

If Milton had attended the next day's ceremonies, he might well have considered himself to be in some infernal region. The baptism of Mary Mount, as Ralph Kempis had described it, was ordained as a day of revel. At first light a pair of antlers were brought forth from the forest with drums, guns and pistols being sounded for their arrival; they were carried in state by Ralph Kempis to the maypole, whereupon a native boy took the horns and climbed with them to the top of the pole. He bound them there with a rope, to the accompaniment of loud shouts from the crowd below, and at once the inhabitants of this new town began to drink each other's health with bottles of wine and flagons of brewed beer. From the band around his waist, Ralph Kempis took a rolled paper. "I have composed a merry song for us," he shouted over the noise of the revelers, "fitting for the present occasion." He unrolled the paper and, in a deep steady voice, he began to sing:

> "Drink and be merry, merry, merry boys
> Let all your delight be in Hymen's joys,
> Joy to Hymen now that the dance is come,
> About the merry maypole take a run.
> Make green garlands, take bottles out,
> And pass sweet nectar freely about.
> Uncover your head, and fear no harm,
> For here's good liquor to keep it warm!"

Goosequill doubted whether Milton would approve of the cadence or the false rhymes of this song; somehow it seemed to lack, for example, the gravity of his master's verse translations of the Psalms. But he was soon distracted. He was given some cordial of wine and honey in a clay pot, and he drank it down eagerly. Then his hand was taken by an Indian woman, and he found himself following the settlers and natives as they formed a large circle around their maypole, skipping and leaping in the spring morning. Then they broke off, and watched as the Indian men began their own separate dances; they danced alone, one beginning after another had ended, and Goosequill was delighted by the gestures they employed during the performance. One kept one arm behind his back, while another whirled on one leg, and a third jumped up and somehow danced in the air. Suddenly there was a strong smell of spice, or incense, which seemed to rouse them to even greater efforts. But then the loud ringing of a bell stopped the entertainment. From a canvas tent, painted light blue, two priests emerged carrying a statue of Mary between them. Everyone, English and Indian alike, knelt before the image. Even Goosequill fell upon his knees. But he watched with interest as the statue, painted in white and pale blue, was carefully placed in front of the maypole. The priests implored its aid in this vale of tears, and the boy heard that it was blessed among women. There was something about fruit, and then the priests carried the Virgin slowly around the pole before returning to their blue tent. The revelry began again and, all that day, there was dancing and drinking and gaming.

At dusk, Ralph Kempis called Goosequill into his tent. "So what do you make of us?" he asked him. "Do we bob and jump as gaily as the banded Puritans?"

"As different as magpie and mutton, sir. I have never

laughed so much since the draymen secretly pissed into the Clerks Well before the French ambassador tasted its waters."

"I wonder that you can endure New Milton, then. I hear that they are not addicted to laughing there."

"You have heard right. The children sometimes laugh, of course. And Mr. Milton."

"John Milton laughs?"

"Oh yes, he has a very nice sense of humor. There are days when he is something of a spark. 'Precise?' he said to me last week about some of the brethren. 'They are as precise as the wooden teeth of an old maid.' "

"Indeed?"

Goosequill stopped, afraid that he had already said too much; he had come, after all, as an observer rather than as an informer. So he quickly changed the subject. "But why travel from Virginia, Mr. Kempis, if you do not care for the brethren here?"

"Necessity. Hard necessity. The climate there is as hot as Persia, and there was a season of drought just passed when the rivers themselves were dry. We dug into the ground, but all we found were oyster shells and fish bones. We would have been reduced to the same condition, except that we agreed among ourselves to move north into more healthful climes and softer air."

"When did you lead them out of the desert?"

"We are Catholics, Goosequill, not Israelites." He pretended to frown, but could not help laughing. "And I am not their leader. I am only their master of ceremonies."

The Indian conjuror, whom Goosequill had seen before,

came into the tent. *"Uppowock?"* Kempis asked him, and passed him a pouch of tobacco.

Goosequill was intrigued. "We have no such word among our Indians. It signifies this stuff?"

"Oh yes. They venerate their tobacco. They worship it. They cast it into the fire and produce a strange incense. They throw it upon troubled seas in order to calm them. They toss it into the air, chanting, when they have escaped from danger. We all used to dance when we brought it from the fields."

"So you danced one with another?"

"We are not separate, Goosequill. We are together. We have suffered so much hardship, English and Indian alike, that we have become one body. Come. I will show you something which will anger Mr. Milton." He led him towards the blue tent at the edge of the encampment, and pushed up the mat hanging over its entry. There, within, Goosequill could see the statue of the Virgin Mary which the priests had carried around the maypole. Two large candles were burning before it. "Our Lady is our guardian here," Kempis whispered. "But now look upon this." He led him over to an adjacent tent, and opened its entrance. Goosequill peered inside and could see a wooden idol, some four feet in height. It was that of a man or god squatting upon the ground; it had a chain of white beads about its neck, and was colored black and white except for its purple-dyed face. "This is Kiwasa," Kempis told him. "It is the keeper of souls, and is much like our Holy Spirit in His efficacious actions."

"So you have two of them?" Goosequill scratched his head and, in his surprise, began twirling his hair around his finger.

"It is like our Gog and Magog in London, although I never heard that those gentlemen did any good."

Kempis did not seem offended by the comparison. "It is not quite a similar case, Goosequill. We never worship Kiwasa for himself, but keep him for the Indians who wish to preserve the old religion without forgoing their new Catholic faith. There is more assurance for them in maintaining both, and, for my part, I see no harm in it." Goosequill said nothing, principally because he could think of nothing to say. "How would your godly master respond?"

The boy shook his head. "He would not be at a loss for words, Mr. Kempis. I can tell you that. I don't suppose that he would stop talking for weeks."

On his arrival in New Milton the following morning, Goosequill did not go at once to his master's house. He returned to his wife and Jane Jervis, the child whom they had unofficially "adopted" from Seaborn. "Well, Kate," he said, after kissing her many times, "there is a new world after all."

"Where is that, Goose?"

"Over the river, and far away. Mary Mount is like a boiling pot. It is like some painted stage all sprinkled and bedecked with jewels. Oh, Kate, it was wondrous!"

A little while later he attended Milton in his chambers. The blind man was standing by the window, facing out towards the garden, but Goosequill knew that his step had been recognized at once. "Well," Milton said, "what will you tell me? How were those pimps of the Roman whore?"

"Very well, sir."

"Have they already tainted the land with their poisoned breath?"

"Not as far as I could see. But Mr. Kempis does send his greetings."

"Oh yes? That unswilled hog's head. That brain worm." He paused. "You have told me nothing as yet. Suspense in news is torture to me. Speak it out."

"If you are asking me of my opinion, then I scarcely know where to begin. In Mary Mount there were so many sights—"

"May I please know without further jangle?"

"Well, sir." He stared hard at Milton and poked out his tongue. "It would be true to say that they worship the image called Holy Mary."

"I knew that already. It is an everlasting scandal to our new land that they should rake over the ignorance of dead ages. Did you see that painted garbage they call the mass?"

"There was some ceremony."

"No doubt with gold and geegaws fetched from Aaron's old wardrobe, all the Jewish beggary of cloaks and false beards and beads."

Goosequill listened to him with some amusement. "There was also a maypole. With colored bands of cloth."

"What?"

"A maypole, sir."

"The Dark Ages are come again." Milton put a hand up to his forehead. "The huge overshadowing train of error has swept away the sun and the stars!"

"It is only for dancing, Mr. Milton."

"This Kempis has gone beyond all shame and impudence. To worship pillars?"

"No, sir. They do not adore it. As I said, they dance around it."

"It is all one. All one. Get me some clear water, or I faint from the news of this impurity." He sat down upon a small stool, and did not speak again until he had drunk from his bowl. "In past ages, Goosequill, this maypole, this spiritual Babel built to the height of abomination, was the subject of gloating adoration. Once, in our own towns and villages of England, it was pageanted about like some dreadful idol. Now it has returned." And then, unexpectedly, he smiled. "I wonder what Preserved Cotton will say of this? Can you ask him to call upon me, at his leisure?"

In fact Preserved Cotton could not wait to hear news of the "painted harlots" of Mary Mount, and agreed to accompany Goosequill at once. Milton was severe when he entered his chamber. "Preserved Cotton, please to be seated." He waited for a moment. "Has God smitten us with some frenzy from above?"

"Oh Lord, sir, what is it?"

"Some misbegotten thing vaunts and glories beside us."

Preserved Cotton wiped his face, and looked slowly around the room. "Where is it, Mr. Milton?"

"They say their masses. They put on their polluted clothing of ceremony. They take flaminical vestures from their piles of ecclesiastical trash. They worship pale images, Preserved. They have, this day in Mary Mount, erected a maypole!"

"Abomination of desolation, Mr. Milton."

"My words exactly. They hallowed it. They fumed it." Goosequill looked at him in surprise, since he had reported nothing of the kind. "They festooned it with verminous and polluted rags which, as we thought, had dropped overworn from the toiling shoulders of Time.''

"Oh the perverseness, sir!''

"Their settlement, good Preserved, is a mere ague cake coagulated from a tertian fever.''

Preserved Cotton looked wildly at Goosequill, who stared back at him calmly. "Let them eat stones and dirt, sir. Let them cut their wanton tresses!''

"You have a godly, loving heart, Mr. Cotton, which warms mine to pious motions.'' He had grown quickly bored, as Goosequill had guessed. "Might you leave me now, while I ponder on their irreligious and execrable courses?''

Preserved Cotton rose, and clasped his hands before him. "You will be like a tree planted before a damp stream or watery river, Mr. Milton. You will bring forth fruit for us to guzzle.''

"Good day to you.''

As soon as Cotton had left, Goosequill sat down on the chair which he had vacated. He looked at Milton, who had his back turned, and shook his head. "I suppose that is called helping a lame dog over a stile.'' Milton said nothing, but he was smiling. "Now the whole town will be afraid to get up in the morning.''

"Their hours of waking will not change.'' He turned to Goosequill, and he was still smiling. "They will be ever wakeful.''

Goosequill travelled to Mary Mount many times over the next few months. Ostensibly he was there as Milton's "eyes,'' reporting what he had observed, but he enjoyed these visits on his own account. He was particularly interested in the fact that the Indians and the English lived with each other on terms of absolute equality. It also became clear to him that some of the

Englishmen had married squaws, with many children issuing from these unions, but he determined never to mention this to his master. It was too sensitive a point to put to him. "What news of the distracted cuckoos?" Milton would ask him. "How is the worm himself?"

Goosequill had decided to allude only to those matters which would divert or amuse Milton, hoping that, over the months or years, he would become reconciled to Mary Mount. "Mr. Kempis," he said, one evening on his return, "is preparing a stage play."

"What a superlative fool. Nothing but dirt and filth ever came from those creaking boards." He was silent for a few moments. "So what are his preposterous whimsies?"

"It will be a comedy, sir."

"I would expect no less from such a mountebank." Again he was silent. "What is it called?"

"Might it be something like *The Magician* or *The London Magician?*"

"Oh yes, I know it well. I have heard of it, rather." He cleared his throat. "It was written by a preposterous ninny known as Tiddy Jacob. He died on a close-stool. No doubt writing." He got up from his chair, and went over to the window. "When do you see it?"

"I had not planned—"

"Oblige me by attending. We must watch the antics of our Jack-pudding. I would wish that blasphemous mouth of his to be stopped up, it is so foul, but, still, we must keep note of all his riddles and fooleries."

As Goosequill had already guessed, Milton was strangely interested in the designs and ambitions of Ralph Kempis. He did not see him as a fit or suitable adversary—there was no one in the country of that stature—but at least he provided the blind man with material for reflection, gossip, and even sometimes amusement. It often occurred to Goosequill that his master would prefer the company of Kempis to that of the precise separatist brethren with whom he was compelled to live.

So, at Milton's instigation, Goosequill traveled across the river for the staging of *The London Magician.* Mary Mount had become a flourishing settlement, with many gaily colored wooden houses on both sides of a central thoroughfare. The maypole had been found a permanent site on an open space at the edge of the settlement, and statues had been placed in various stone or wooden alcoves throughout the town. The male inhabitants, Indian and English alike, were dressed in the strangest mixture of striped breeches, wide shirts and feathered caps; the women of the settlement preserved decorum by putting ribbons and colored bands across their hips and breasts but, otherwise, they dressed in the same fashion.

The play was to be performed that afternoon, on the feast day of the Visitation of the Blessed Virgin, and Goosequill arrived just as mass was being said on the open ground behind the tavern. He was intrigued by the silver and yellow vestments which the priests wore, but looked on in astonishment as the host was raised into the air; then the Indians and English, kneeling on the firm earth, bowed their heads as the bell rang three times and the incense mounted towards the sky. Eventually he left them and walked over to the tavern, with its sign of the seven stars swinging in the breeze. He waited in its cool interior, listening to the responses of the mass, and passing the time of day with a friendly cat. A few minutes after the mass was over, Ralph Kempis entered with his companions. "What cheer, Quill?" They all knew Goosequill well now and, after ordering beer and strong water, Kempis sat down beside him. "What news from the godly men yonder?"

"They are dancing in the street, as usual."

"And Mr. Milton? Does he send me greetings?"

"Oh yes. He greets the slug and brain worm."

"Very good. What else?"

"He says that you flow with insolence and wine."

"A hit. A palpable hit."

"You are like the apple of Asphaltis appearing good to the sudden eye but, to the taste, turning to cinders."

"So I am the apple of his eye? I am much obliged." They had all begun to eat from two large bowls, filled with flesh and boiled fish mixed with chestnuts and artichokes, and for a while they said nothing.

At the end of the meal Goosequill wiped his mouth with a linen cloth, and burped. "You know, Ralph, one day I will persuade Mr. Milton to come here. You and he must agree on some things. We are all so far from home."

"His home is not my home."

"Yes, but surely in this wilderness—"

"*They* call it a wilderness. We do not."

"But here, of all places on the earth, we ought to live in harmony."

"Tell that to your master."

The London Magician was to be performed later that day, after a procession in honor of the Virgin. The two priests, Lambert Bartelson and Henry Staggins, had called Kempis from the tavern before arranging the settlers and Indians in a straggling line which wound through the main street of Mary Mount. Two young Indians held up the statue of the Blessed Virgin, while the priests followed it with incense and thuribles. The procession made its way out of the town, chanting "Beata Maria," until they arrived at a small shrine near the river. The Virginian Indians themselves had chosen the site—they learned from the Pequots, who had sold the land to Ralph Kempis, that here was situated a spring of sacred water which cured agues and fevers. It was known as *Cowweke Tokeke*—Sleep and Awake— and the powwow of the newly arrived Virginian Indians had decided to build his own dwelling close by. It was he who now helped the two priests to place the statue of the Virgin in its niche among the rocks. Then he stepped back, and began chanting his own prayers. The Englishmen kept off their hats throughout this ceremony, and at the end responded "Amen" in unison.

The London Magician was played on a small wooden stage behind the tavern, in the same area where mass had been said that morning. It was a comedy of prose and verse, written at the beginning of the seventeenth century, which concerned the mixed fortunes of a Cheapside conjuror in search of alchemical gold. Goosequill knew nothing of it and, since stage plays had been banned during the sixteen years of Puritan rule, he had little real memory of any theater. So he was intrigued by the play, just as he had been by the rituals of the mass. Two young Englishmen mounted the stage in old-fashioned clothes, and began to speak to each other in a falsetto which greatly amused the audience.

"Can it be true, Josquin, that all our rings are to be turned to gold?"

"Too true, Ferdinand. In a trice. I cannot abide tarnished silver, can you?"

"It is horrible to me. So unnecessary. And vexatious."

"No longer, Ferdinand. Here is our divine alchemist."

The Indians now gave out loud cries when a native, dressed as an Englishman, stepped onto the wooden platform. He was wearing a black silk cap, with a black gown and white ruffs, but Goosequill recognized him as the conjuror whom he had once met in Ralph Kempis's tent. Maquisa had borrowed the gown from one of the Jesuit priests, and had made his own ruffs out of swan feathers; but the black cap could not conceal his crest of dark hair, and the same small bird hung from his left ear. He was carrying a hollow gourd upon a stick as he came onto the stage; it was filled with stones, or kernels, and rattled loudly when he shook it. He embraced the Englishmen, and then spoke in an Indian dialect which Goosequill had not heard before; but certain words seemed close to the Pequot terms for smoke and fire. Then all at once the conjuror raised his left hand, and from it there came a mist or steam of powder which enveloped the two English actors. When the mist had cleared, they had vanished from the stage. This was a London magician indeed who caused men to disappear, and the whole audience looked on in wonder. Goosequill scarcely believed it, and was even more astonished when the Englishmen were to be seen emerging from the tavern as if they had never left it. The play resumed with Maquisa miming his part as the magician. He pored over old books and globes, he polished mirrors, and he filled chalices with powder or cordial; it was clear that his search for alchemical gold was unsuccessful, and towards the close he danced some ancient step of anger and hostility. Then he picked up one of the chalices, took out its powder and threw it around himself in the air; it seemed to glitter in the evening light, falling so slowly that it might have been dust drifting through the lengthening rays of the sun, and it covered him in brightness. He shouted, clapped his hands, and was gone. Goosequill was standing next to Percival Alsop. "Well, Percy," he said, "Now I can believe that the stars are made of curds and whey and that men on the other side of the world walk upside down. Now anything is possible."

He described the events of that day to Milton, on his return, and the blind man seemed strangely troubled by the reports of the Indian conjuror. "It is not meet," he said. "It is not right. It is not wholesome." He felt his leg, and sighed heavily. It was then that Goosequill impulsively told him about the Indian women of Mary Mount—how certain of them had married Englishmen and had borne their children. At that, Milton stood up, his cheeks flaming, and walked into the garden. Goosequill could hear him muttering and groaning, so in his alarm he went over to the window. Milton was kneeling down and breathing in the scent of the flowers, but then, quite suddenly, he began to uproot the sweetest of them and fling them onto the path. These were Katherine's favorite blooms, planted by her gently and neatly—and now they were being torn out and discarded recklesly. He ran out, shouting that these were proper flowers. "No, Goosequill, you are mistaken. Katherine has let the garden riot. All these are weeds." Milton looked exultant as he spoke, and then he added, "I am calling a solemn meeting of the brethren."

Goosequill did not intend to go back to Mary Mount for a few weeks, until Milton's wrath had been appeased, but he was forced to return much sooner than he wished. His adopted child, Jane Jervis, had become ill. She was suffering from colic and, in the heat of the summer, it had grown so severe that Goosequill and Katherine began to fear for her recovery. The resident apothecary in New Milton prescribed hellebore, but its effects lasted only for an hour or two before the pains resumed. Humility Tilly and Alice Seacoal prayed loudly and often by the child's bed but, since they mixed their pleas for divine assistance with many aspersions on the vanity of earthly well-being, Goosequill was not convinced that their devotions were altogether helpful. "Time to go now, ladies," he said, one morning just after sunrise. "The child is trying to sleep."

Humility Tilly remonstrated with him. "It is for the good of her soul."

"At the moment I am more concerned with her body."

Alice Seacoal put her hand up to her mouth. "That was not well said, young man. The body is merely the vesture."

"—or the pit, Alice."

"It can also be smacked, dear ladies, or lifted out of doors. Now please to leave us." He began bustling them towards the street.

"Mr. Milton would not approve of this!"

"Go! Shoo!"

"I really do believe, Kate," he said when he returned, "that this religion kills rather than cures." It was then that he remembered the sacred shrine of Mary Mount where the statue of the Virgin had been placed. He had been told by Kempis of its healing waters and now, without hesitation, he took horse and rode with Katherine and Jane across the river. His wife had never visited the settlement; she had heard it described as the horn of Babylon or the new Sodom, and was nervous of appearing there as a supplicant.

"Seaborn told me," she said as they rode across the scrub, "that their priests are given blood to drink."

"Oh yes, Katherine. And they use the skin of dead men for their vestments." Her eyes widened. "And they eat the buttocks of babies, as Mr. Milton says, like the wild Irish."

Katherine realized that he was fooling her, and pinched the back of his arm. "Is that what he means by an allegorical sense?"

"They are as peaceable and as amicable as any people in the wide world, Kate. I know he taunts them with the name of beasts and slaves—"

"Yesterday he called them tainted scraps."

"—but they are as kind and gentle as anyone could be. I know that the brethren do not care for the Catholic faith—"

"They only believe what they are told."

"—but there is no harm in it. It is all sounds and sights and sweet smells."

The child was woken by a sudden movement of the horse, and began to cry. Katherine tried to soothe her, and placed her hand above Jane's head to protect her from the sun. "If they can cure this pain," she said, "I will worship sticks or stones or anything."

They reached Mary Mount a short while later and Goosequill, seeking out Ralph Kempis, was at once given permission to take the child to the sacred waters. The powwow had been informed of their arrival, and emerged from his dwelling in a long black cloak made from the skin of a bear. The child did not seem alarmed, however, but smiled as the Indian led them over to the shrine itself. "Good cheer?" he said, in English. "Good cheer?"

"Good cheer, sir." Goosequill pointed towards Jane's stomach. "Sick, sir. Sick here."

The powwow took her, and cradled her in his arms. "Good," he whispered. "Well." The spring itself was a few yards from the shrine, and they could see its waters disappearing among some flat white stones. The powwow laid the child upon a bank beside it, filled a shell with the water, and gently offered it to her. She drank it slowly, all the time gazing up at the old man dressed in a bear skin. Then he gathered the water in his cupped hands and, intoning all the while, poured it upon her forehead. She fell asleep soon after, and the powwow carried her back into the shade of the stone shrine. He laid her at the feet of the Virgin, and murmured some more Indian words. Katherine and Goosequill could hear the noises of the forest around them, and the calls of the animals in the country beyond.

"I hope," Goosequill whispered, "that Our Lady can speak their language."

"It is only a piece of plaster."

"So I am told."

An hour later Jane Jervis awoke and smiled. The pain had gone.

FOUR

Such news as that I heard from the boy would have shaken wise Solomon. Yet, dear Reginald, the report of the noisome ways of Mary Mount filled me with what I trust to be a holy and prophetic rage. The brethren were assembled at my summons, and I spoke to them without delay. "The blasphemous heathens are calling down a terrible vengeance upon themselves," I said. "They have a conjuror. They practice the black arts." There were many sighs and groans, delicious to a pious spirit. "They perform deeds more terrible still. I cannot mention their unlawful acts in this holy place. I cannot—"

Yet then I understood that the Lord called me to plan and to calculate more subtly. I must proceed by degrees of stealthiness, dear brother in Christ, if I am to extirpate the enemy with their swollen bladders and swollen bellies. I must suckle my own people tenderly, training them up to be strong in front of that lustful crew. Am I right, dear brother? Oh, I only hope. So then I spoke to them more calmly. "Yet my illuminating spirit, which has always favored me to do no everyday work, has fastened upon one of their manifold vices. That vice, good brothers and sisters, is drunkenness." I had struck against one root of sin, and could not wait to tear it from the soil of New England. "I shudder to say it, but the papists are daily, gluttonous and incontinent drunkards. Yet we ourselves are not free of vices. Oh no. This corruption is not unknown among us. I myself have smelled strong liquor in these blessed streets. I have heard wanton and untimely singing. Is it not true?" Was I too fierce, dear Reginald? "Who dares to deny it? Who among you will contradict *me*?"

Daniel Pegginton ventured to speak. "In this horrid wilderness, sir, some of the weaker brethren have indulged in wine or beer to preserve themselves."

"To maintain their spirits? Is that what you mean? Enough." I regained my calm. "This is no longer a wilderness. It is a commonwealth. I exhort you, therefore, all of you, to listen to me. The general end of every ordinance, be it ever so severe, is the good of man. In our present plight we cannot slacken the cords of intense thought and labor. We have a licentious enemy sporting and spawning at our very gates! There can be no more wine, and no more strong water. And no more beer." I felt their silence around me, and filled it with my own voice. "The political law must be employed to restrain all wrongdoing. If we allow this weed to grow up to any pleasurable or contented height, it will fasten upon the root of our polity. We cannot prune and dress vice as if it were some good plant. You do not wish for that, I trust?"

Good Seaborn Jervis was the first to speak. "Of course we approach our social duties with godly fear, sir, but to prohibit the brethren their morning beer—"

"Not all of us are brethren now, Mr. Jervis. I learn that

some merry men from Bristol have joined us. Carpenters, I believe."

"Not altogether merry, Mr. Milton. Not yet chosen, but not merry either. You know that they are being instructed."

"Destructed, more like, if they lift their flagons. New settlers must be trained in all good offices. There can be no delay. And beer is the beginning of these evils, Mr. Jervis. I am surprised by your remonstrance." I was pleased to think that the assembly was now thoroughly convinced by me. "We must banish all liquor forever, lest all good knowledge and learning should insensibly decay. Hold up your arms if you agree with me upon this." The boy murmured to me that all had assented. "The penalties for any disobedience are therefore to be fixed according to the severity of the offence. Shall we begin with the stocks? But oh, we must be more just. We must demand imprisonment and public whipping for those who flaunt our decrees. And what further but the cutting of the ear and nose?" They all joined with me then in the singing of "Zeal Abundant."

I was still exultant on my return from the assembly, and requested my fool to take down more words. "Goosequill, note down these instructions. No music must be heard, no song to be set or sung, but what is grave and Dorick."

"What is Dorick, sir? Is it a melody?"

Of course I ignored him. "No dancers at all, except for such as Plato once commended. All lutes, violins and guitars are to be placed under license."

"There are few guitars in this place, sir. And the only lute is my own."

"It must be examined. Our garments should also be

watched. The Indian women who work for us must wear less wanton garb.'' So great a weight had fallen upon me that I passed my hand across my poor darkened eyes. "But who shall regulate all the mixed conversation of our youth, male and female together? Who shall administer their discourse? How shall we forbid all evil company?"

"It is easy to see, sir, that you are tired after your long address. Will you not sleep? I have already prepared a healthful cordial."

"How can I ever sleep, Goosequill? I must guard and preserve you all. I cannot slacken the reins." Then, dear Reginald, so great was my grief and fear that I wept. I admit it. I wept.

F I V E

Voices around me like the swelling sea. He is walking down Cheapside, among all the trades, and hears them calling out in barter. No. I am hanging from a tree. Savage voices. Not trees around him now but men, whose eyes awaken him with their colors. You have the feathers of angels covered with billowing eyes. Your faces are brightly painted, as red as a butcher and as white as a baker. Ocher. Scarlet. *Anunama.* Help me. I am caught by my leg, and I cannot move. I am a white man from a dark world, but you are in the rainment of the peacocks of Solomon. Never was the world attired like this before. Help me. Yes. Take my hand. Smell my hand. I am no devil in a black cloak. I am a blind man who can see. *Anunama.*

He is being lifted down gently. The Indians are removing the rope which held him in their trap. I am being placed upon a coat of fur, and I see the trees rushing above me. I am an oak whose leaves have faded. I am a garden without water. Please. Water. He is given water. He is being carried away through the forest, where now a hand is stroking my cheek. What cheer? What cheer? He is lying within some enclosed space where an Indian, an aged man, is stroking his cheek. He is wearing a tall hat of beaver skin. Who, he says, who? I am John Milton from England, no longer blind. *Keen Milton?* Yes. Now I thirst. I point to my tongue. Thirst. He brings me some sweet-smelling liquid served in a gourd. He points at my leg, which is covered by leaves and animal skins. God, he says. God angry with you. But wherein have I offended? Tell me, sir, my sins. I feel nothing yet, even as the phantom of my limb appears before me straight and whole. Now the vision fades, and I am left with some memory of pain. God is angry. God has snapped my leg in two.

What was that word taught to me? *Npenowauntawaumen.* I cannot speak your language. The old man takes off his hat of beaver and knocks it against his chest. Me. Me. As old as Paul's steeple. Oh the young men dream and the old men see visions. How do you know of London? Trouser men come. English men. And the posts of the door moved at his voice, and the house is filled with smoke. Yes. I can see around me: the smoke comes from a fire in the center of this place. A kettle is upon it. A kettle of fish. A dog lies by the fire, and looks up through a hole in the middle of the roof. Let me see with my eyes, and convert and be healed. There is a pole in the center of the room, while around it are stretched the boughs of trees in a circle. They are draped with bark and deerskin and matting so that they form a covert from storm and rain. I am lying upon a pallet bed. The boughs still smell of the forest. I have been moved from one dark wood to another, and yet I still see. My heart is moved as the boughs of this tent are moved by the wind. *Meech.* He brings me fish from the kettle upon the fire. *Meech.*

Sleep after food is best. He wakes. He is taken on a stretcher of skins to be greeted by the sachem of the tribe. This I understand. *Winnaytue,* he calls me. *Winnaytue.* He bows to me.

His robe is embroidered with squares and circles of color. He sits upon rushes painted in all the glory of the daylight. He speaks to me. The sky is of the color azure, the tents are topaz and vermilion. There is a great mountain behind them, with striations of ice and ocher. He finishes his welcome, and bows to me. Thank you. Your words are blue, and your eyes are the color of the sun. Thank you.

I am carried into the shade of a spreading myrtle. I lie here and see wonders. A woman is pounding corn with a stone, and the steady rhythm of her work soothes me to sleep again. Awake. Other women are working in the fields, with the white mountain behind them. They wield hoes of wood and bone. A little girl sits by me. She is sewing the skins of animals. She shows me her thread of hemp, and her needle carved from a small bone. A splint bone, is it? Her hair is as lustrous as the ebony of the temple. Her teeth as white as any English girl's.

The children come to me then, offering their beads and their shells. A small boy is pointing to a round black stone. *Mowisucki.* He hands me a tiny white shell. *Wompesu.* He lays a blue bead in my palm. *Peshaui.* Thank you. We call it blue. A silk or a sky may be blue, you see. He holds out a green stone. *Askashi.* Yes, green. We have green pastures. Green hills. They laugh at me when I begin to cry. They run away, laughing and calling. I wipe my eyes. I watch them as they leap from the sun into the shadow, and then once more come into the light.

I have not yet seen myself. I have been so entranced by the world that I have not looked upon my own reflection. He gazes at his hand. Faint and faded in the light of this new world. Carry me to the river, please, so that I may see myself. What is their word for the ocean? What was the word taught to me?

Wechekum. Please. Carry me to the water so that I might see my own image. I am taken upon my pallet to the riverbank. I cannot move my leg, but I can raise myself upon my arm. Look down. Look down upon the surface of the moving river. My face. Pale as the water. My eyes, changing and stirring in the swift current. All the blindness of nine years still somewhere within them. Then he fainted away. I am taken back. Taken back. Taken. Back.

Oh Mr. Milton sir, it is very fine. The girl is struck by magic in the wood, is she? She is tempted, but she does not fall. You have read Ariosto on the perils of the forest, but you have quite changed the allegory. Very fine. It is all one. Alone. And you thought the wood began to move? Oh, good sir, only in our ancient stories. What is it Virgil tells us? Even gods have lived in the woods. Yet I have good cause to doubt it. In the thirteenth canto, does not Dante write that the trees contain the souls of suicides? Do you know the woods of Illyria? They are supposed to be enchanted. They are reputed to be full of noises, Mr. Milton. In a forest fast, you walk and weep. Have you by any chance glanced at Chapman's *The Tears of Peace*? ''And then did all the horrid wood appear. Where mortal dangers more than leaves did grow.'' Tell, if you saw, how came you thus? How here? How? Here. In the dark wood of this world I lost my way. John Milton opens his eyes, and sees the Indians around him.

SIX

The latest arrivals from Bristol had not attended the assembly in which Milton had forbidden all use of drink; on first hearing news of the interdiction, in fact, they had hidden their supplies of wine in a bound chest. There were six of them, for the moment sharing one large wooden cabin off the main thorough-fare; they had come to New Milton soon after their arrival from England, having heard of the fertility of its soil as well as the industriousness of its inhabitants. They were eager to work, too, and could see no better prospect. But they were not precise separatists; they were not part of the elect but had agreed, somewhat unwillingly, to be trained and catechized by Accepted Lister. Yet they could see no reason to pour away any wine; the eldest of them, Garbrand Peters and John Pethic, had devised the plan to conceal their bottles and bring one out each evening to accompany their food and tobacco. After they had eaten they would toast one another's health, and talk quietly of their times in the old country.

A week after the interdict against alcohol had been pro-nounced, Peter "Praise God" Pet—a great favorite with the ladies of the settlement, because of his forceful sermons on concupiscence—was passing the Bristol men's cabin. He heard laughter, and paused; he loved a godly cheerfulness, but this did not sound altogether pious. He crept towards a window—no more than an opening with a cloth across it—and sniffed. This was not the fruit of Christ's vine. There was wine somewhere within the room. The gross vapor assailed his nostrils, and he shuddered at these coarse men's malignancy; he cautiously parted the cloth against the window, and glimpsed three of them sitting together and drinking from wooden bowls. He was ready to admonish and rebuke them, according to the blessed rules of God's church, but, on reflection, he decided to run to the meetinghouse where Isaiah Fairehead was mending one of the benches. "Mr. Fairehead! Mr. Fairehead!"

"What is the matter?"

"Wild boars have broken into the vineyard."

"What vineyard? We have none."

"God's vineyard. I smelled their polluting breaths even as I passed them. Oh truly, Antichrist is Mammon's son!"

"Give me some plain stuff, Peter Pet. I am not one of your dangling females."

"I heard tankard drollery from the dwelling of the Bristol men. I peeped within, very charitably. Mr. Fairehead, they are stark drunk on unholy wine!"

"Are they indeed?" Isaiah Fairehead had not been pleased by the arrival of these new settlers: they were trained as carpenters or joiners, and he feared that they would take much of his work away. But his rage seemed pious enough. "Come with me, good Mr. Pet. I suppose our hard work is too tiresome for their soft bones."

"Serpents, sir. Serpents armed with mortal sting."

They marched across the road to the wooden cabin; there was laughter coming from within, and both men paused. "Do you think," Peter "Praise God" whispered, "that we may need more soldiers from the army of the Lord?"

So Isaiah Fairehead walked further down the street, and began knocking on various doors with the shout "The newcomers are drunken! The newcomers are drunken!" Six of the chosen came out, two of them in their night-shirts. "This hellish crew," Isaiah declared. "These so-called carpenters. They flout all our good laws and conventions!"

Preserved Cotton, the first to hear the call, was already approaching the cabin of the Bristol men. "I hear revels," he murmured. "I hear hellish noises." He waited for the others to join him; then he rushed up and pounded upon the door. "In the name of the Lord," he shouted, "come out!" There was a sudden silence, and then more laughter, from within. The door was off its latch: he pushed it open and, with the others behind him, marched forward.

Garbrand Peters was lounging in an elbow chair. "What is it that you want from us, Mr. Cotton?"

Preserved picked up the empty bottle. "This goes straight against our laws."

"What laws?" John Pethic was already angry at their violent entry. "In our own country you would have been hanged for murdering the King!"

At that Cotton ran at Pethic and, catching at his hair, pulled him from the table where he had been sitting. Pethic was holding a knife for his meat, and as he fell he accidentally gashed

Cotton's right arm; it was only a slight wound, but it bled freely. There was then general confusion as the brethren, screaming "Murder!" fell upon the Bristol men, who in turn defended themselves with their fists.

"Cease this savage clamor!" The stern, clear voice was that of John Milton. He stood upon the threshold, holding out one arm in admonition. They ceased. "What summer storm is this? What unseasonable riot?" He smelled the wine in the air. "Some here are guilty of trespass against our commandments. Speak out."

Peter Pet was eager to tell the story. "These Bristol men were drunk, sir. We came to plead with them, and they were very round with us." Cotton, slumped upon the floor, was still moaning. "Now Preserved Cotton has been foully stabbed."

"Which one of this fat and fleshy crew attacked that saintly skin?"

"The one named Pethic."

"Take the foul cudgeler to the watch-house. Let him cool there like some seething pot. His drink will congeal soon enough." The Bristol men, in the presence of Milton, put up no further resistance. They stood around, muttering to one another, as the brethren escorted John Pethic from the cabin. Milton looked towards the renegades, and smiled. "There will come a time," he said, "when we must winnow the wheat from the tares, the good fish from the other fry. We will not allow malignant men among us. Good night to you."

The next morning John Pethic was taken from his cell and whipped at the crossroads. The Bristol men continued to work in New Milton, under the articles of their agreement with the brethren, but they remained apart. Only Goosequill sought them out, and he was in turn welcomed by them. He had seen enough of the pious settlers to have grown bored and even distrustful of them; he preferred the company of these new men, even though his master continually directed his sarcasm against the "West Country sots." They took care not to drink now, but they still smoked their tobacco and talked. A principal topic of conversation had become, of course, the godly people of New Milton. "Let me put it to you this way," Goosequill was saying on their first evening together after the public whipping. "You cannot turn a fish into a flat-pan. Am I right?

"In this country, Goose, I believe anything may be possible." Garbrand Peters still enjoyed the wonders of the wilderness. "Did you see that creature with the head of a buck which strayed into the outer fields?"

"It is called a moose, Garbrand."

"*Moose?*" He pronounced the word as if it were a hunting call.

"You say 'Goose' to me, do you not? It is the same."

"I have never seen a goose with horns before. Please God it never happens to you."

Goosequill took the allusion with a good grace; he knew Katherine's nature very well. "May I plod down my old road, please? My fish and flat-iron are what Mr. Milton would call an allegory. You can no more become one of the precise brethren than, well, Beelzebub himself."

"Not even the devil could enjoy this place." John Pethic was still aching from his stripes. "I believe hell itself might be easier."

"How much longer are your articles?"

"Six endless months. It will be a weary time, but then we can move on."

"Well, John Pethic, I may be able to help you there. I may be able to perform a service. Have you heard of Mary Mount?"

"Rumors. Pieces of news." Another of the Bristol men, William Dauntsey, was suddenly interested. "It is a papist colony. Of priests. Some such stuff."

"I will tell you something else. It is magical!"

Garbrand Peters laughed out loud. "We have heard of sorcerers among the Indians. But I thought the men of Mary Mount to be English."

"As English as you or me. I know them well. And this is my point, you see. I can talk to them on your behalf." Goosequill had become excited by his own idea, and was twirling his hair in his fingers so that it stood up in clumps and twists.

"They say that papists are sodomites, Goose."

"No. Nonsensical. They have their own wives. Some of them arrived with Indian women." Suddenly he lowered his voice. "I mentioned it to Mr. Milton, when I should not, and I believe that he thinks of nothing else."

"Truly?"

"And they have children. As many children as the pigeons of St. Paul's. That is why they need skilled men to finish their houses and to furnish them. They need good Bristol men."

"If everything is so—"

"As God and Our Lady of Willesden are my witnesses."

Garbrand Peters looked around at the other men. "Shall we ask the Goose to plead for us? Shall he treat for us with the papists?"

"Oh yes." It was John Pethic who spoke out, but they were all anticipating an early departure from New Milton.

So Goosequill traveled to Mary Mount the following day; he said nothing to Milton about his journey, of course, and told the men of Bristol to be equally reticent. He found Ralph Kempis eating a dinner of fowl in the shade of some maple trees. "I am just eating you," Kempis shouted. "You are delicious!"

"I am always happy to provide you with a meal, Mr. Kempis."

"Hand me that squash, then. And sit down with me."

"Shall I say grace before I begin?"

"Be sure to keep it a secret from your master. He would like to reserve all the grace for himself."

They knew each other well enough to speak freely, and Goosequill explained to him the plight of the Bristol carpenters. "He was drunk, you say?" Kempis interrupted the story. "Why, he must come here at once!"

"They are willing to leave, Ralph, but if you will permit me to finish?" He explained that the settlers of Mary Mount would have to "buy out" the remaining six months of the Bristol men's agreement with New Milton, at which time they would be able to work honorably and profitably for their new employers. They might decide to settle there, too, and with their skills in carpentry and joinery they would bring great benefits to the new colony. They might build up families as well as houses.

Kempis approved the plan as soon as Goosequill had finished. "But," he said, "I cannot treat with Mr. Milton. You know him. You know how he would reply."

"You shallow man, you dunce!" Goosequill imitated the voice very well. "You presumptuous worm!"

"Oh surely not as cruel as that, Goose?"

"You cock-brained lozel!"

"That is why I will neither speak nor write to him. I cannot endure the impudence of the man."

"What is to be done, then?"

"I will send Bartholomew Gidney. He is a match for any madman."

Two days later a young Englishman rode into New Milton. He was wearing a blue silk shirt, green velvet breeches and a large hat with plumes of feathers fastened upon its brim. "What is this?" asked Preserved Cotton, who was the first to see him. "What is this walking maypole?"

Gidney reined in his horse. "Forgive me, dear sir. Could you possibly show me the house of the very reverend and learned Mr. Milton? I believe he resides here?" Preserved was too surprised to do anything but point in the right direction. "Very much obliged indeed. I shall be forever in your debt." He dismounted from his horse, and tied it to a post before strolling over to Milton's door. "Mr. Milton? Mr. Milton, dear sir?"

"Enter."

Bartholomew Gidney did enter, and saw John Milton sitting in a plain wooden chair by the window. "I am deeply sensitive to the honor—"

"I do not know your voice."

"Alas, not an overwhelming surprise. I—"

"From where do you come, sir?"

"Formerly Westminster Square, but currently residing in the picturesque spot of Mary Mount."

"Oh."

"Do you know it by any chance? A most delightful situation. Very rural. It sometimes reminds me of Chelsea in summer, where the bank turns just so." He made a serpentine movement with his hands, and did a little jump.

"I see that you may talk world without end, sir."

"I have been known to. Yes." He steadied himself. "But it is my nature to be highly amicable and confiding. My dear mother was the same. She had merely to pick up some sewing, and she gushed forth. Oh, how she reminisced! She could not be stopped."

"What is it that you want from me?"

"I am not sure that I want anything, dear sir. It is a question of what others may want. It is all marvelously delicate."

"I am not fowler good enough to catch you. Speak it out, Mr.—"

"Gidney. Bartholomew Gidney. Originally from the Gidneys of Cambridge, of course. Now intestate. I cannot begin to tell you how much land—"

"Do not begin, then. Tell me in plain words why you are here. Or leave."

"You are forceful, sir, but I am fond of forceful men. In plain words, then, I have come here at the request of Mr. Ralph Kempis. Do you know him? Always cheerful. Really delightful person." He saw the expression upon Milton's face, and hurried on. "You have some men from Bristol who are not—how may I put it?—who are not utterly and completely at their ease here."

"Those fools. What do they wish for? Ambrosial nectar and paradise fruit?"

"I am not sure if they have asked for those in particular, Mr. Milton, although I am sure that you would provide them."

"They are impudent rogues. I see your drift, Mr. Gidney, beneath your flourishes. They wish to be relieved of their articles, and move on to Babylon."

"Rather too far afield, I'm afraid. They were thinking of Mary Mount."

"It is all one to me. They wish to join the horn of the Roman beast. Crafty turncoats."

Bartholomew resented this allusion to his faith, and at once became more formal. "They intend to work, not to pray."

"But I presume, sir, that you know how to milk such easy kine. Will you give them the reins a little, Mr. Gidney? Let them play and nibble the bait for a while?"

"There will be no nibbling, I can assure you."

"Poor pitiful wretches. To be delivered up to papistical tyranny and superstition."

"I think not. There is no slavery with us. No tyranny. Only the perpetual benefit of liberty."

"License, you mean, not liberty. Well, well, go your own way to hell and take the men of Bristol with you. The silly fowl are caught in the net. Let them be plucked and eaten."

"How bountiful. How noble."

"The price of the articles is set. Ten pounds for each man."

"I know it. I have arranged payment with Mr. Goosequill. Do feel free to condemn me if I have anticipated you."

"Goosequill? What does he have to do with this?"

Gidney realized that he had said too much. "A charming young man, don't you think? Many lovely curls. And a curious Houndsditch wit." He did not wish to implicate him any further. "I met him by your delicious church. I was informed that he was your secretary. Is that not correct? Is he not, if I may mention the sad topic, your eyes?"

"I have an inward eye, sir, that sees through all flimflams, shows and devices."

"I am glad to hear it. It must prove invaluable here." He hesitated. "So I take it, then——"

"You take *them,* then, and you never return. No man can be an enemy of this settlement and remain a member of it. We do not need them."

So the Bristol men left New Milton and, singing and carousing all the way, rode to Mary Mount in the company of Bartholomew Gidney. Goosequill watched them go, and then returned sighing to Katherine. "Do you know," he said, as they sat together in the small arbor behind their cabin, "I long for us to join them." He patted her swollen belly. "The new one would thrive and flourish there."

"It is not to be thought of, Goose." Her niece, and adopted child, was playing beside them. "I promised Seaborn that I would take care of Jane faithfully. He would never permit her to live among papists." She leaned forward and whispered to him. "He would kill her first."

"No doubt. And he would always be able to find some biblical piece of learning to justify himself." He looked across at the wooden cabins and houses, scattered across the dry and dusty tracks of the settlement. "Do you think there will ever be a time, Kate, when we will all be at peace?"

She shook her head. "Seaborn says that light and darkness will always oppose each other."

"Oh, Seaborn is very righteous. No one talks more of righteousness than Seaborn. But I tell you this, Kate. Seaborn is a vain deceiving hypocrite." He lowered his voice, in case the child might hear. "I would willingly barter a thousand Seaborns for one Ralph Kempis." She looked across at him, and smiled.

SEVEN

The affair of the Bristol men was followed, three weeks later, by a more serious episode. A Roman Catholic missal was found in New Milton. It was discovered in the house of one of the newer families—John Venn was a cow keeper from North Devon, who had arrived a year after the settlement had been established. He was a quiet man who "recreated himself," as he put it, by collecting specimens of minerals; his wife, Sarah, was some years older but they lived together happily enough. She had been born, and educated, as a Catholic; they had agreed, at the time of their marriage during the "Commonwealth," that she should perform private devotions in order to satisfy her conscience. Venn himself was one of the brethren, and had attended the chapel in Barnstaple with them, but he was in no sense a zealous man. That is why he allowed his wife the comfort of private prayer, and why they had maintained this arrangement after their arrival in New Milton.

But her missal was found—or, rather, it was observed by Humility Tilly. She had seen Sarah Venn falling to her knees one morning and, curious, crept back to the window for another look; there, on a small table, was a Catholic missal. She knew it at once because of the fish and bishop's staff upon its black leather cover. She declared later that she had staggered back at the sight of the accursed thing, and would have promptly fainted away if a neighbor had not come to her rescue. It is true that she had whispered "Idolatry!" and then asked for a cup of water; but she had composed herself sufficiently to go at once to Milton's house at the other end of the settlement. She found him pacing up and down the narrow path of his garden. "Mr. Milton! Mr. Milton!"

"What is it, Humility?" He knew her voice well enough by now.

"Molten whores and abominations. That is what it is." In her excitement she confused her biblical allusions. "Pestilence and famine!"

"You are all in a pudder. Please calm yourself."

"I cannot be calm in the midst of desolation, good sir. Mistress Venn is infected."

"What? With what?" He stepped back from her; he was always fearful for his health.

"I saw her with a poisoned book."

"You are toying with me, Humility. Speak plain."

"I saw Mistress Vane cradling a papistical book of prayer. Do the demons call it a missal?"

"Is it so? You are sure?" She nodded. "Did you nod?"

"I did."

"Is Mistress Venn so brazen-faced?"

"She has always been brazen, sir. Ever since she came amongst us with her young husband."

"And she goes whoring after idols, does she?" He contemplated the matter for a moment, as Humility looked eagerly into his face. "Bring three members of the watch. If this is proved to be true, then we have godly work ahead of us."

Within the hour he and his watch were prepared. It was discovered that John Venn was working in the fields, some distance away, and so it was Sarah Venn who opened the door upon Milton's restless pounding. She was astonished to see him on the threshold and, without saying anything at all, allowed him to enter. Humility Tilly noticed with some satisfaction, however, that she was trembling. "Well, Mistress Venn," Milton began, "I hear that you carry a pope in your belly."

"Sir?"

"I hear that you have a book of scarecrow images. Some whorish volume out of Rome. Is it so?" She said nothing, but seemed to look to Humility Tilly for some assistance or explanation; the godly woman shook her head and smiled. "Search this place," Milton told the watch. "Smell out the running sore." The missal was found a short time later, hidden in the compartment of a stove; beside it, too, a rosary had been concealed. They placed the beads in his hand. "What baubles and trinkets are these, mistress?"

"It may not please you, sir, but it is my faith."

She seemed about to say something more, but he interrupted her. "Your faith is no better than a rush. Give me the book." One member of the watch placed the missal in his hand, and he fingered its pages as he talked to her. "Catholics are rarely to be found except where there are jewels and silver. Mistress Venn, why did you wander to our settlement?"

"I came with my husband."

"Ah. I feel the imprint of some scarlet letter." He was stroking the introit with which the mass itself opened. "This book is filled with all the names of blasphemy." He flung it to the floor. "Fit only to make winding sheets for pilchards."

She was so dismayed by Milton's rough handling of her missal and rosary that she became defiant. "It is the faith of my fathers. It is the communion of saints. It has been the truth these last sixteen hundred years—"

"Do not presume to teach me the history, mistress. I know it by heart." He was still rolling the beads in his hand. "Does your husband share your devotions?" She hesitated, and he sensed her indecision. "So he may be another cracked cymbal?"

"He is one of the brethren, sir. He is not a Catholic"

"Then more shame and horror upon his head, for fostering the serpent within our bosom."

She had endured enough of his ridicule. "You are the serpent, Mr. Milton, with all your blind orders and commands."

"Listen to her. Did you hear her saucy impudence?" Humility Tilly groaned. "Oh, my lady magnificence, I see that you cast off all shame. Does she even blush?"

"No, Mr. Milton." Humility was looking steadily at her pale, drawn face. "She would rather burst."

"Well, then, we may see the color of her blood another way. Take hold of her." Milton remained still. "Mistress Sarah Venn, against all the good laws and ordinances of this place, you have professed a heathenish superstition and worshiped false idols. Now carry her off."

Her trial began three days later in the meeting house. Her husband sat in the front-row of benches, tearful and trembling as the charges were read against her. She said nothing, until Milton in a terrible voice called out, "Do you profess the Romish faith?"

"Yes. I do. It is the holy faith."

"How she decks and magnifies her vice!" Seven brethren had been chosen to sit in judgment; they were separated from the rest of the court by a rope tied between two pillars, and now they began to murmur against her.

She ignored them, and spoke out again. "It is the ancient faith of our own dear country."

Milton laughed. "You are one with the Druids, then. You must consult the oak and myrtle. Enough of this tittle-tattle. Do you know, Mistress Venn, what you have just proclaimed? You have blown a trumpet and lit a fire-cross that would begin a perpetual civil war. It cannot be endured." She shook her head, but said nothing. "No civil society of good Protestants can admit you as a member. Do you understand that? You are a public enemy, Mistress Venn, and a plague sore to the commonwealth. Do you wish to say anything further?" Again she shook her head, and the elect shouted against her.

"Will you renounce your popish faith?"

"I will not." She was looking at her husband, who sat and wept.

"You will not abjure your false worship?"

"No, sir."

Milton turned to the seven brethren who were waiting to deliver their judgment. "How do you find her?"

"Unclean," declared William Hallelujah Deakin. "Her guilt blackens her."

"All are agreed?"

They raised their right hands, but then realized that Milton could not see them. "All assent!" shouted Job "Defiant in the Lord."

Milton walked over to them and asked anxiously, "Is it your wish that punishment should be determined and decreed by me?"

This strangely excited them, and Preserved Cotton whispered in reply, "That is our holy demand, good sir."

Milton was assisted back to the raised dais upon which he had been sitting, and faced Sarah Venn. "Well, mistress, it is meet and good that the punishment should follow the crime. Therefore"—and he smiled at this—"Therefore, I order you to be flogged with wax candles in some public resort. You will be expelled from your dwelling, and that place utterly burnt and destroyed so that it will no longer be a roof for such unclean birds to nest in. Then you will be banished from this settlement. No holy city can be built without the sweeping away of rubbish. Do you wish to speak?"

"No, Mr. Milton." She remained calm. "What is there to say against such brute violence and injustice?"

"Therefore are you driven from this hallowed ground. I pronounce perpetual banishment."

She was led away to the watch-house, her husband following in tears, while the brethren looked at one another in astonishment at the nature of the punishment. It was proper for her to be banished, of course, but was it wise to burn down one of the recently erected houses? And where were they to find Romish candles? Milton approached the brethren of the jury, and he was still smiling. "Your work was well done," he said.

"Mr. Milton, sir." It was Preserved Cotton who spoke for them all. "We have no wax candles. We have tallow for our lamps, of course, but those lights are no bigger than sticks. How could she be chastised?"

"Calm yourself, Preserved. Mr. Kempis has sent me two dozen of his votive candles. In part recompense for the men of Bristol, he said, except that he thought to laugh up his sleeve at me. He tried to make mock of me but I have turned the trick nicely, have I not?" They laughed.

"Are they thick and heavy enough for the whore's back?" Job asked him.

"Oh, yes. Her bones will be well thrashed by those fools' staffs. Come away now, and eat."

EIGHT

His leg is still broken from the Indian trap. My leg will not be healed. My bones will not be knit together, yet everything else congeals. My journey among the Indians begins with sickness. The sachem looks at the open wound and sniffs the air. A time for the spirits. A time for the powwow. No. No wizardry or conjuring. The skill of medicinal plants will please me. I pick up a golden flower and put it upon my mouth. But I cannot endure enchantment. I gesture towards the sky, and then place my hand against my head. No enchantment. Then they show him how the powwow placed the skin of a snake upon the body of an ailing woman, and how it changed into a live serpent which cured her. They mime to him how the powwow came from a mist in the shape of a flaming man, and how he caused the rocks to move and the trees to dance. Can it be so? In midwinter he took the ashes of a leaf and, putting them in a bowl of water, made a fresh green leaf to flourish. Truly? I know that in London there are some who are reputed to possess the gift of healing. Mother Shipton. The hollow boy, whose bowels sounded like a harp. Yet rare cures in this wilderness must surely be the work of the devil. *Squantum.* No no. The sachem shakes his head. *Mat enano.* Not true. There is a good devil. *Abbamocho.* The good devil heals. Then must I allow the visitation of this wizard? There is no help for it in my present plight. What is his name, this noble conjuror? *Wunettunik.* But am I to be cured or blasted?

He is clothed in a mantle of black fox skin. His face is daubed with soot or with charcoal, as if it is shadowed with wings. I am dismayed at the seeing of it. He strokes my face, and murmurs to me. *Kutchimmoke. Kutchimmoke.* Through his fingers he senses my fever. He calls for a bowl of water, and then puts his own face within it. He stands up with a piece of ice held between his teeth. He places the ice upon my forehead. *Kutchimmoke.* I am at peace.

Wizard, what now? He is gazing at the break in my leg. I hear him breathing deeply, yet he does not touch it. Surely this iniquity will not be purged from me, until I die? Well said, Isaiah. He opens a leathern pouch bound upon his waist, and takes out a bone. A fish bone. No. A splint bone. He snaps it into two pieces and, rubbing them within his palms, causes them to be one again. He bends towards me, singing softly all the while. He whispers in my ear. He begins to dance around me, violently turning and tossing. He shouts out, and his body glistens with sweat like a mist of dew. He foams at the mouth. He is kneeling down beside me, and putting his mouth upon my wound. Oh terrible. He stares at me, a wild look that lasts a moment, before he turns back to my wound. He spits something from his mouth into the bowl. It is a bone. My bone. There is a great shout from the others around us. He takes my arm, and helps me to my feet. I walk. My leg is healed.

He has been sleeping for two days and two nights. I am

asleep. The burden of the valley of vision. He awakes, as alert as a child, and he sees a white man sitting upon a blue mat. I am accustomed to wonders in this place, sir. Are you another? The white man seems astonished. What was that, Mr. Milton? So you are an Englishman and, by the sound of your voice, you are Mr. Eleazer Lusher. He rises from his mat and walks around me. Mr. Milton, you can see! So it seems. In the name of God, sir, this is an extraordinary thing. I know it. He claps his hands, and puts them up to his face. Overjoyed, sir. Thoroughly overjoyed.

Calm yourself, or you will make my head ache. Please be seated again. I have not seen an Englishman for many years, Mr. Lusher. I am a savage in that respect. I have not seen a white man since my blindness. He is wearing a canvas jacket and a broad-brimmed hat. This is no style of dress I have known before. He is like some figure from a dream. This is tremendous, Mr. Milton. This is like some dream, sir, to have your eyes again. I hope it is not a dream, otherwise I shall wake and see the night returned. Where did you get that hat, Mr. Lusher? My hat? Oh Lord, sir, it comes from the Seven Dials. My brother gave it to me before I crossed the ocean. Ocean. Seven Dials is notorious for its hats, Mr. Lusher.

Oh yes, the ocean. I had forgotten that. The ocean and all its dead. The ocean storm, when I fell beneath the waters. How did you regain your sight? Was it some native balm or cordial? Oh no. Indeed not. Ocean cries in the mist. I was hanging by my foot from an Indian trap. The blood rushed into my head, somehow reviving and refreshing my ocular nerves. I believe so, at least. Suddenly I saw. Saw colors without true form. Cages of light and brightness, as if the world were water rushing between a river's precious banks. And I spread forth my hands in the midst of them, as he that swims spreads forth his hands. A cathedral of gold and ocher with the painted images of eyes.

I heard about the trap, Mr. Milton. One of the Nipmucks came to me at once. They know me well. Milton rises from his pallet without pain. He walks easily. He shakes Eleazer Lusher's hand. These natives are remarkable people, Mr. Lusher, I grant you that. You walk without any stiffness, thank God. I have known a deer trap to tear the leg off a man. How did it heal so quickly? I cannot speak of wizards to an Englishman. I am spell-cast, but I cannot speak of spells to you. Well, sir, there was pain for a while but it is now gone. Quite gone. Thank God, sir. I do thank God. When will that be, said the bells of Stepney. I do not know, said the.

The brethren are surely concerned for you. Shall I send a message to them? No. No, Mr. Lusher. I shall rest here for a day or two, unknown and unclaimed, and then I shall return. But, sir, if it is possible you should stay a little longer. Oh, why so? And yet why should I not linger here beside the bright tents and the glowing mountain? In ten days' time they hold their festival of dreams and they long for you to see it. Indeed. Is it some carnival like our old Misrule? I have no knowledge of it, Mr. Milton, except that it is very ancient. Pillars. Arches under the ocean. The swimmer drowns in the evening.

It is evening, is it? So soon. I have not seen enough. He is taken down to the bank of the river. The canoe is fashioned from one piece of pine, and they carry it upon their shoulders to the water. He sits comfortably within it. I am below middle height and I fit nicely, do I not? On this clear night I see the moon and all the stars. When the evening stars sing together, the voices of all the peoples of the earth could not disturb them. Matchless. What is the fire flashing across the heavens? Now it is gone. The wolves howl. The world is an Indian dance.

The canoe drifts, moved by the current. The Indian boys stand up and watch the river. The boy behind me has a spear and hempen net. Guardian. The boy ahead holds a glowing torch fashioned from the branches of a birch tree. Oh see, it bursts into flame when he sweeps it above the surface of the water. Wizard. Spirit of the fire. The fish are seeking the light. They follow in its path. They sport and dance in the brightness. Wonderful. They are speared and taken as they jump, ecstatic, into the net. The finny tribe, he says to the Indians, are jocose at their peril. They do not understand his words, but they laugh.

Mr. Lusher, greetings. You are returned. I had thought you gone. Not at all, sir. You have your eyes again but, if I may be so bold, you have no tongue as yet. This morning I have come to translate your words to the Nipmucks, so that they may converse with you. And what is that they are saying now? They are asking if you might care to see the relics of their tribe. They are an ancient people, and hold their ancestors in reverence. It is very meet and fitting that they do so, Mr. Lusher. Tell them that I consider it an honor. No, sir, an honor for them. I have already explained to them that you are the historian of your own country.

Where are we going? *Wuttin.* Where? *Wuttin.* Brain. The sachem touches his own head, and then points towards the mountain. It is named Wachuset. The party of travellers, or pilgrims, sets off in single file. The path trod by generations. Their feet are bare, but I have great shoes of mooseskin. My cloak is woven from the fur of black wolves, to protect me from hostile spirits. The moss glows on the bark of the trees, and the webs spun between bushes gleam in the light. I am among Druids, seeking ancient temples. I am with the Trinobantes, on the tracks of Albion. They came to the foothills by dusk. I walk with more care and labor now, through rifts and gullies. But the ground glistens under my feet. Look, Mr. Lusher, this mountain shines with some kind of glossy scurf! Metallic ore, sir. But I also detect the savor of sulphur in the air. This might be a mountain out of hell itself!

The sachem hears them talking, and speaks out loud. What does he say, Mr. Lusher? He tells us that one of his tribe found a wondrous stone here. It was larger than an egg, and at night gave out a light by which you could find your way. The sachem speaks again. He says that there is a great fire somewhere beneath our feet. Indeed? Liquid ore in the veins of the earth? Such fiery bowels would form a true inferno. We walk on. They walk on, until it is decided that they should rest for the night in the shelter of a cave. Toilsome walking, yet I feel fresh and strong enough. I might merely have walked up Saffron Hill. Well tomorrow, sir, we begin the mountain itself. I shall be elevated enough, Mr. Lusher, to endure all.

Climbing upward at first light. Climbing through a gully made from the path of dissolved snow, grasping at the roots of bushes to make our way. Stepping stones. Two hours of the ascent, and we come to a level plain covered by moss. The sachem builds a fire, and with the moss and snow makes a most excellent soup. It restores me. So they advance across the plain to the next face of Wachuset. This will not be an arduous climb at all, Mr. Lusher, do you see how these stones are piled upon one another like some staircase? It winds around the mountain itself, and for six hours they climb. Among ice and snow. My breath freezes into a bright vapor. I am walking within clouds of my own being. Ah, a more soothing gradient. Level ground. They had reached another plateau, and had climbed so high that they could see all the territories of the region. Mountains. Lakes. Thick and innumerable forests. Infinite woods, Mr. Lusher. What is the sachem chanting?

They walked across the icebound plain, the Indians echoing the sachem's chant with their own low plaint. The area must be some three acres in extent, but what is this at its center? John Milton could see a lake of clear water. It is a lake of ice. Their chants grow louder, Mr. Lusher. Explain to me, please. Well, sir, look for yourself. He approaches the edge of the lake, and looks down. No. This cannot be. The bodies of native men lying at different depths and in different positions, suspended within the ice, perfectly preserved in their frozen attitudes. Oh no. I can see their faces as if they were yet alive. I can see the curious markings upon their skin. This one smiles. Can it be? Who are these people, Eleazer? Who are these terrible statues of ice?

Eleazer Lusher questions the sachem, as John Milton gazes into the open eyes of the dead. We have made a covenant with death, and with eternity we are at agreement. He that believes shall not make haste. What does he tell us? These figures are lost in antiquity, sir, and are perhaps many hundreds or even thousands of years old. They are worshiped as spirits. Oh, Eleazer, it is the strangest sight I have ever witnessed. The sachem speaks again. What does he say? They are immortal. But surely immortality must come in some other guise than this? To freeze for eternity, with no hope of thaw? It cannot be. Our friends must complete their ritual and prayer, of course, but then let us be gone. It is cold. Too cold. He walks further off. In his shoes of mooseskin, and his cloak of black fur, he might be some descendant of an ancient race.

NINE

Goosequill had witnessed the trial of Sarah Venn with dismay. He had known for some weeks that his master had changed since his return from the Indians. Milton seemed more anxious and uncertain, and yet at the same time he had become more demanding and aggressive. Now it had come to this. Sarah was to be whipped with candles in a public place, and her home burned to the ground, simply because he disapproved of her religion—perhaps he would even wield the candles himself, and hold the torch.

Once the proceedings were over, Goosequill took horse and rode hard towards Mary Mount. As soon as he reached the settlement he made his way to the house of Ralph Kempis, which stood in its own grounds along the principal street. The door was open and he could see him playing the harpsichord in the parlor. Kempis's Indian wife recognized Goosequill at once, and kissed him on both cheeks. "May I see him?"

"Of course."

Kempis stopped playing when Goosequill entered the parlor. He turned, and noticed the young man's expression.

"What is it, Goose? Have you seen some melancholy wandering spirit?"

"I believe that I am one." He proceeded to tell Kempis about the arrest, trial and punishment of Sarah Venn.

"So he will flog a woman, will he, for her religion? I thought him dreadful once. Now I see him as contemptible. And to use the candles—" Kempis had become very angry and, to calm himself, he sat down before the harpsichord again. But before he started to play, he rose from his stool and walked around the parlor. "You know, Goose, I must go to New Milton. I must go now."

Goosequill was alarmed at the prospect of some immediate and heated encounter, which might only provoke Milton to fresh wrath. "Perhaps you might first write in a friendly and neighborly way, Ralph, asking him to forbear?"

"Certainly not. I want to look that crafty Puritan in the face. I could spit upon him then."

"Or perhaps a letter in high terms, telling him to be better advised and more temperate?"

"I use speech, Goose, not writing. I will not play his own old games with him. Let us see how precise he is when I question him. Let us see if he dare give me any of his sanctimonious cant."

"Will you be fierce with him, Ralph?"

"Primitive. Terrible."

"Oh Lord. Can I absent myself awhile?"

"You can. I will not mention your name."

So the two of them rode back to New Milton but, as they approached the settlement, Goosequill went on ahead. He entered his own cabin, embraced Katherine, kissed the child and then hurried to Milton's house; he entered as if he had been nowhere in particular, and began dusting the books. His master was asleep in an elbow chair, but he was woken by Goosequill's low whistling. "Goose."

"Oh yes, sir?"

"That noise could wake the dead."

"Beg pardon. I forgot myself." He had wanted to rouse Milton, in any case, before the arrival of Ralph Kempis. "Do you know what I have been thinking, sir?"

"What have you been thinking, Goose?"

"Could we not use those candles to light the main street?"

"And have the whole town blaze with popery?"

He dusted the books for a few moments, and then spoke out again. "Your punishment of Sarah Venn may enrage our neighbors."

"What neighbors?"

"Mary Mount."

"That wandering race of Jacobites? Those grasshoppers? You are very funny, Goosequill."

"Thank you, sir. Let us hope we laugh last."

At that moment there was a loud rap upon the door, and Milton turned his face towards the sound. Without waiting for instruction, Goosequill let in Ralph Kempis. "Ah." Milton smiled. "The man comes himself. The door creaks, and the actor comes upon the stage." His nostrils were quivering. "I know your perfume, Mr. Kempis."

"Virginian oils."

"They are ripe. Sit down."

"I believe, sir, that the American sun ripens wits as well as oils."

"Sometimes it addles them, Mr. Kempis. Why have you come here?" Goosequill was pacing nervously behind him. "Goose, your shoes are not well shod. Spare them a little for my sake." Kempis had sat down upon a wooden stool, and was looking curiously at the blind man. "Some springwater, Mr. Kempis? We have none of your Mary Mount drink, but what we have is pure."

"No. I am content. I will be plain with you, Mr. Milton."

"What? No knotty Africanisms? No pampered metaphors? You are untrue to your faith, sir."

"You are guilty of a grave trespass."

"Oh, what will become of me!"

"You are prepared to flog a poor woman, burn down her dwelling and banish her, simply because she professes the Catholic religion. This is barbarously done."

"Goosequill, do you hear this most ridiculous orator?"

The young man was now standing by the window, listening to them and looking out into the garden. "He only speaks the truth as he knows it, sir."

"Have a care, boy, or you may become the mountebank's juggler."

"No. I also speak the truth as I know it."

"Come now. This is a conspiracy." Milton laughed. "I am undone." He bit his lower lip. "Tell me, Mr. Kempis, do you sodomize the poor goose? Is that your way to win allies?"

"You are reported to be a master of words. You sound like some old wife of Billingsgate."

The remark had annoyed or disturbed Milton; he shifted in his chair, and leaned forward. "I never mince the matter, Mr. Kempis. I am not some busy coxcomb with jangling periods. So I will tell you this. The whore Venn—"

"She is no whore, sir." Goosequill was still looking out of the window as he spoke. "That is unjust."

Milton ignored the interruption, and continued talking directly to Ralph Kempis. "The whore Venn is an abject slave of popery, and that superstition cannot be allowed to stay or grow within a well-founded commonwealth. That is why she is to be punished."

"I will not argue with you about faith."

"Will not? Cannot."

"I am told that Sarah Venn was a woman of blameless life, who prayed within her own house. Where is the harm?"

"Idolatry in private, Mr. Kempis, gives as much grievous and insufferable scandal as any open ceremony. I know you papists are not well read in Scripture, but may I quote you from Ezekiel? 'Son of Man, hast thou seen what the ancients of the house of Israel do in the dark?' There will be no darkness here. We have not taken our lessons from the first doctors of the Gospel, only to have the pope within our borders."

"It is a pity that your doctors have not given you good health. They do not cure. They kill."

"You do not offend me with your words, Mr. Kempis. You offend God. That is not a trifling thing."

"It is not a trifling thing to stripe the body of a woman and then to burn her house."

"It is a necessary thing. We want no Rome in this western

world. You cannot turn a scorpion into a fish, or a papist into a free subject."

"Be careful, Mr. Milton, or you will throttle yourself with your own similes. You forget that there are many Catholics in our own old country."

"You might as well tell me that there are some Londoners still addicted to paganism. I know it, and I lament it. Yet it serves only to prove what a miserable, credulous and deluded mind remains among the vulgar."

"Do you hear that, Goosequill? Are you one of the vulgar Londoners?"

"I expect so, Mr. Kempis. I have some very bad habits." Goosequill was intrigued by their conversation, in which the two men had come together like fencers.

"Do you see, then, Mr. Milton, how the vulgar are always with us? But those whom you denounce as credulous and deluded are, for me, true worshipers of the pious and the sacred."

"Oh yes. Let them grovel in the dust with the Indians."

"Why is it, then, that my heathen superstition, as you call it, has lasted time out of mind?"

"I would put no trust in mere antiquity, Mr. Kempis. All your old scrapings come from an empty barrel, since custom without truth is but agedness of error."

Ralph Kempis had become intent; he sat forward upon his stool, gazing at Milton as if he could see traces of his thought upon his features. The poet himself sat back in his elbow chair, apparently having regained his composure and cheerfulness, but a restless motion of his fingers betrayed his own nervous interest in the course of their conversation. "You forget also, Mr.

Milton, that our country was almost sixteen hundred years a Catholic nation.''

"Do not try to blind me with the darkness of obscure times. If England was once subjected to the laws of terror and fascination, in its extremity of bondage, then it were wise to render it free.''

"The English were a pious people once, sir. They were known for it across Europe.''

"I admit to you that they worshiped relics and beads. That they donned their superstitious copes and flaminical vestures. But what does it signify? The Babylonians worshiped stone dogs for a longer period.''

"Our faith was stolen from us by the crafty servants of false monarchs who sought to enrich themselves. The whole church was pillaged and plundered.''

"But in its place was elected a purer devotion, without the mumbled chants of impostor priests. We took Scripture, not the papal beast, to be our guide.''

"No. You destroyed the common worship of fifteen hundred years. I remember when the Cheapside Cross was taken down and hacked to make timber. The citizens looked on aghast. It was as if the axe had been taken to their own bodies.''

"That monstrous bedecked idol? You must make your god of wood because you are so far from the spirit. You make your god earthly because you cannot make yourselves heavenly.''

"Art and ceremony are the tokens of any universal faith.''

"Do you think that the Lord wishes for a material temple?''

"Our churches signify the communion of souls in the faith which Christ established.''

"And did Christ measure the size of the heathenish painted cross in Cheapside to see if it were worthy of Him?"

"We claim only that it represents on earth the passion of our Savior. You say that God is not earthly, but did He not come to earth? That is why in the mass—"

Milton put up his hand, and smiled. "How do you like this game, Goosequill? He shoots these relics of superstition at me, because his quiver is otherwise so thin."

"I would not entirely agree with you there, sir." The young man now felt himself to be caught up in the argument. "If the mass is for the people, where is the harm in it?"

"So you like these sugared pills, do you, Goose? You like their little drama upon a rotten stage?"

"You forget, Mr. Milton," Kempis replied for him, "you banished all our English drama in the years of your ascendancy."

"Do you mean the writings of those libidinous and ignorant poetasters, sold by the penny?"

"My charge, sir, is that your brethren destroyed a free and cheerful nation—"

"Go on. Go on. Empty the urinal of your thoughts over my head."

"You sought to undermine our faith, and to extirpate immemorial traditions."

"Good. Give up the whole inventory. Noise on till you are hoarse."

"Our nation was subject to your pious people. But it was the force of conquest, not of faith."

"It was the force of plain Scripture and right conscience. The individual soul sprang forth, once it was freed from the collected rubbish of stagnant custom, vainglorious luxury and prelatical pride.''

''You instilled your severity and malicious envy where there was once splendor and hopefulness. You tried utterly to destroy an ancient truth for some niggardly and beggarly set of doctrines.''

Milton was growing more heated. ''What schoolboy, what insignificant monk, could not make a more elegant speech than that? It is clear that you are miserably raw in divinity, and utterly unacquainted with the doctrines of the Gospel.''

''I may not possess your arrogance and overweening, sir. But at least I am not a hypocrite.''

Milton turned suddenly pale. Had this man heard reports of his time among the Indians? ''What do you mean by that, Mr. Kempis?''

''You pretend to a commonwealth, and yet you lord it over all. You are a tyrant, Mr. Milton.''

The poet breathed more easily. ''How hard it is when a man meets with a fool to keep his tongue from folly! Yet I will restrain myself for the sake of the poor boy with us.'' Goose-quill poked out his tongue, and then traced a halo around Milton's head. Milton felt the movement in the air, and touched his hair. ''You are a poor opponent, Mr. Kempis. You proffer against my supposed weakness, but you leave your own wide open. What are you in Mary Mount but the master of ceremonies? Or shall I say master of the revels? Or master of the perjuries, when you speak such words to me?''

''I do not beat the bones of innocent women. The Indians amongst us have more humanity than you.''

"Oh, you would wash an Ethiop, would you? Be careful lest their blackness sticks upon you."

"I tell you this, Mr. Milton. I believe the Indians to be more honest than many Christians."

"Hear this. The savages are civilized!"

"And wherefore are we civilized?"

Milton remained silent for a moment. "Civil liberties. Good laws. True religion. All of these matters weigh heavily with us."

"So it is in Mary Mount."

"Does he blush, Goosequill?"

"No, sir. He is ruddy in any case, but I see nothing crimson."

"He leaves the crimson for his priests' excremental vestments."

"I was going to add," Kempis went on, "that civil liberties and good laws pertain also to the Indians. They have their own discipline as well as their freedom."

"Oh, more. Listen, Goosequill. It is too good. His arrogance mounts so high."

"And true religion will follow."

"You mean that they will follow your hellish creed."

"I assure you of something else, Mr. Milton. I would rather remain in my hell than live in your heaven."

"Enough, I cannot dispute philosophy with a clown such as you."

"Now, sir, that is hardly fair. Mr. Kempis has come here in friendship."

Kempis laughed. "Never mind it, Goose. I shall not answer

the reviler in his own language, though never so much provoked.'' There was another silence between them, which Kempis eventually broke. ''So tell me this, Mr. Milton, as steadily and as calmly as you can. Will you allow this poor woman to leave your settlement? I am willing to take her and her husband with me.''

''No. It cannot be.''

''And what is the civilized man's reason?''

''Public judgment has been given. The die is cast, and there is no metal harder than the good purpose of our citizens.''

''You have no more to say than that?''

''Nothing at all.'' Milton sat back in his elbow chair, sighed heavily, and closed his eyes.

Ralph Kempis stood up, bowed, and waited for Goosequill to open the door. They went out into the street together, and walked a little way from the house. ''Where is she being kept?'' Kempis asked him quietly.

Goosequill immediately understood the purpose of the question. ''In the watch-house over the way.''

''Who guards her?''

''Saul Tinge is our jailer. There is also a woman there, Agatha Bradstreet, who stays and watches her in case of self-murder.''

''Do this precious pair keep the keys?''

''There is one only, as big as my hat. It hangs behind the door.''

''And you have a big head.''

''I know it.''

''Can a big head devise a small drama or interlude?''

"Do you mean—"

"Something to divert a godly audience. Perhaps a fire."

"Tinge and Bradstreet leaving the watch-house for a moment?"

"Exactly so."

"What if someone were to cry 'Thief! Thief!' into the night? Our watch would be obliged to march forth, would he not?"

"Goose."

"What?"

"You are a wonder."

So their plan was laid. Ralph Kempis rode back towards Mary Mount, singing very loudly. Just after midnight, Goosequill crept up to the house of Humility Tilly. She had oiled linen cloths for windows, as did the other settlers, and he carefully cut one of them open with a kitchen knife. Then he put his head through it, and let out a series of extraordinary yells before hastening away. Humility had woken at once, and was already hysterical by the time she leaped out of her bed. "A man!" she screamed to no one in particular. "There is a man by me! Thief! Oh, judgment!" In her hysteria she really did not know what she was saying; she rushed out of her house, in her heavy night-skirt, and began yelling "Satan! Thief! Oh, bondage!" The commotion had the effect desired by Ralph Kempis: Saul Tinge rushed out of the watch-house with his musket, and Agatha Bradstreet hurriedly followed in order to savor the excitement for herself. Humility Tilly had by now discovered that her window had been cut by a blade, and she fainted away. Alice Seacoal knelt down beside her, and started praying in a shrill voice. Other brethren now came out of their dwellings and, in the confusion, Kempis crept into the watch-house; he put a finger to his lips, unlocked the cell door, and led Sarah Venn away.

T E N

Within two days, dear Reginald, I was informed that the papist whore had been seen flaunting herself in Mary Mount. No more than Ezekiel, writhing in his dung, could I refrain from godly wrath. "That impudent liar! That jailbird! That abject Kempis! I would like to thrust a sharp iron into him. I would like to lance him as he sat upon the stool and strained."

"That is one place I would not guide you, sir." This boy, named Goosequill, was now a perpetual fret and gall to me. I surmised that he had been infected with the Roman sickness by that coxcomb Kempis, but I kept my counsel. I said nothing to him, even as I hardened my heart against him. I planned, and acted, alone.

I called a council soon after, to consider how the brethren might best proceed against our noisome and refractory neighbors. "We meet here for our common good and safety," I informed them. "We have a heathen settlement beside us which now plainly seeks to lessen our numbers, drain our estates and cow our free spirits. What are these papists, in truth? To our purses and goods they are a wasteful band of robbers, making perpetual havoc and rapine. To our state they will prove a continual hydra of mischief and molestation, a very forge of discord and rebellion. They threaten uproar and combustion. They shake the fearful burning brand of civil discord. They will go from craft to undermining, and perhaps even to violence. Who can tell?''

Accepted Lister stood up, moved by my words, and called upon the bowels of Christ. ''Purge out the old leaven,'' he cried.

''Mr. Lister is a godly man, and I am much refreshed by his quotation from Paul. It emboldens me to say to you, my Corinthians, what is in my own heart. I had thought, in the beginning, that civil intercourse with the papists was to be countenanced, even if there could never be true friendship and familiarity.''

''God forbid it!'' This was dear Humility Tilly, fully refreshed and cheerful after her ordeal on the night of the papist's escape.

''It will be forbid, Good Mistress Tilly. We understand now that we are supposed to bear indignities against our religion both in words and in deeds. We are to be wearied with seducements—'' I looked towards her, and she groaned aloud. ''We are to have idolatries and superstitions ever before our eyes. We are to be tormented with impure and profane deeds bruited to the world. Have we not seen already how rash, hypocritical and impious these Jesuitical settlers are become?''

''Our ivory gates have been torn asunder!''

''Indeed. You speak justly, Alice Seacoal. They are perpetually at our elbow, attempting to turn us from the true worship of God. This is all bondage to a Christian. You know that I am a man of mild nature, disinclined to arms or much commotion. But, truly, we cannot suffer such cruel hostility and such outrageous violence.'' I had not overshot my mark. There was a deep silence, pleasing to my blindness. "So we shall need forts and garrisons. We shall collect an armed guard. We can intermit no watch against our wakeful foe. Good brethren of New Milton, we must raise an army! We will have our own soldiers for the Lord Christ to lead!'' I heard a whispering among them, so I spoke ever more fiercely. "We are not yet called to battle. Not yet, I say. But we must train up soldiers and captains, chosen from among the sturdier and stronger of us, who will be duly exercised and drilled. We will keep our weapons in continual readiness, with all the muskets and swords, powder and bullets, which Christ can provide for us. And who can tell the result? It may be, godly people, that the Lord intends to achieve greater matters through us than the world is yet aware. Now will you sing with me from *The Covenant of Grace?*''

E L E V E N

Oh, here is Martha in your arms. Pretty Martha. Three-week Martha. What is going to happen to us now, little Martha? Shall I hold her, Kate? Kate, I believe this place to be in peril. Mr. Milton has persuaded the others to start up an army. He tells them that Ralph means to attack us. Either his mind wanders, or he has some scheme of his own devising. It is not right, Kate. It is not reasonable. He is as bitter as a Clerkenwell apple, but he may not be as green. I am away to Mary Mount, Kate, before that bitter apple poisons us all.

Goosequill! Whither have you wandered? In your lady's chamber?

No, Ralph. Upstairs and downstairs. Heaven and hell.

I suppose this is purgatory here?

Oh no. Mr. Milton does not allow me to believe in any such place.

Because he is a devil. Come and take some *uppowock*. Sit. Try this delicious cordial, made of wine and elderberries mixed. Have you seen the scaffold and the purple cloth? Have you seen

262

the painted battlements and the hall made of pasteboard? I am to be crowned tomorrow, you see. King of Mary Mount. You are familiar with all my courtiers, of course?

A regular Whitehall, is it?

Indeed. We have our own tennis court. We have our stairs to the river. And, as you can see, this is our banqueting house. Will you have some meat?

There is an old saying, Ralph, that it is best to speak before you eat. May I talk to you quietly and confidentially? You are determined to be crowned king, are you?

And why should I not be monarch? I have as good a right as Cromwell, who wore the royal purple.

I don't dispute it, but you know that our Puritan friends do not care for kings.

What of it? Am I bound to their pious wishes?

Listen, Ralph. This is why I have come here. John Milton is intent upon raising a standing army. He wishes to build garrisons and forts. He is a dangerous opponent, Ralph, and he will be on constant watch.

You have spent too long with the brethren, Goose. You are so full of nightbugs and terrors that I am surprised you ever sleep. Mr. Milton will not march against us, I promise you. Come outside for a moment. Look about you. Our colony has become great. We are too many for him now. Rest yourself tonight, and see the display tomorrow morning.

TWELVE

I was informed of this pageant, dear Reginald, this Miracle, this Mystery, this mummers' play, on the next day after. My praying Indian, Ezekiel Kuttowonck—which signifies in their tongue Ezekiel "who trumpets forth"—is my agent or secret eye in the gaudy mansion of the papists. He pretends their faith, but returns to me with news of their follies. So I heard at once of this coronation, this delightful blasphemy in a new world. Kempis, the king of ale and pastry, was carried upon a gilded pallet; he wore a garment of variously colored feathers sewn into a linen undercloth, and around his neck hung some great golden chain. The sodomitical Jesuits led his procession, chanting, while an Indian conjuror shook beans in a gourd to match their hollow voices. He was taken to some high stage by the holy pair, and led to a throne like a harlot's seat, while papists and savages sang to their Mary "All Generations Will Call Thee Blessed." I could no longer refrain from laughing out loud when I heard this, Reginald, and Ezekiel laughed with me. Then he told me that, in lewd pomp, a heathen crown of shells and mineral stones was placed upon the head of Kempis. Oh, magnificence!

"I see that the fool is like some bad stage-player," I said, "who is ambitious to be clapped. Well, I will clap him. I will clap him in some stinking jail. By nature the papist loves enthrallment more than liberty. But I will grant him no easy bondage. Not when I have him in my hands. And I tell you this, good Ezekiel. King Kempis will not be able to plead sanctuary within his bestial church!" I had spoken too deeply for an Indian, but then I commanded him in simple words. "Will you leave me now, while I speak to God?" Oh then I wept and moaned. I communed, and sighed, and lamented, so loud that the native returned to me in foreboding. He found me kneeling upon the floor, with tears blinding me who was already blind. "The Lord takes me by the hand and guides me, Ezekiel Kuttowonck. He whispers to me. He prompts me. I have been told now, in this simple parlor, that I must war with the wicked Kempis to the world's end. So be it." He helped me to my feet, even as I whispered to him. "And you must assist me."

I summoned an assembly, in front of which I rose in great fear and agitation. "You have heard," I said to them, "that the mountebank has been crowned king? Have we fled from the bondage of regal tyranny, to find it once again at our very door? We know these kings. We know how Kempis will try to bring the sum of things under one man, and reduce this land to slavery." They saw me rage, and knew that some great moment had come upon them. "What do we have beside us now but a strong and sequestered power, filled with evil and licentious men who are trained up and governed by papish counsels? Oh, never can it be. Never can it be." Ezekiel wiped my face with a linen cloth. "I am fearful for our commonwealth, good citizens. Who is to say that these inhuman papists will not secretly stir up and hire the mercenaries of some other armed nation? Who knows if they will swarm in at our casements? Why, they might bring a fleet to the harbors of New England and let out a filthy crew of Irish papists!'' It was sweet then to hear them sing snatches of the Twenty-eighth Psalm. ''And there is worse. They have other allies. They have the savages.'' Then did they chatter like swallows, and murmur like cranes. ''I heard it from the lips of that charlatan Kempis, who was so crazed in the brain that he once thought to debate with me. What a vain wretch is he! No beast is more void of sense! The sot confessed to me that the Jesuit hyenas have been traveling among the Indians, intilling their heathenish principles into them. They have taught them image worship, which even the savages once condemned as horrid. Such a snowball could be gathered, rolling through these cold and dark provinces of ignorance and lewdness, that might threaten us all. Well, masters, how do you like their game?'' Seaborn Jervis was moved to speak some verses of Revelation, in which I joined.

Then the question came from Preserved Cotton. ''You have spoken before of armies and garrisons, sir. Do you tell us now that we must truly levy war to subdue them?''

''What can be more noble and useful, good Preserved, than to contest the enemies of true-born Englishmen?''

''It is a grave choice, Mr. Milton.''

''Yet it will be justly done. Tyrants must be punished according to the intent and wrath of God. Our liberties must not be snatched away by an army of papists. Do you wish our righteousness to be trampled underfoot?'' I came to a sudden stop. ''And I tell you something beside, which must terrify us beyond all other cause. You all know Ezekiel, I trust? He found God among us and, since his deliverance from the devil, has worked unceasingly on our behalf. Now he has discovered such a secret in Mary Mount that it cries to heaven for vengeance! Speak out, Ezekiel Kuttowonck!''

My Indian took a step forward, folded his arms, and placed his hand upon my shoulder. "This is the man," he said, "that knows all and speaks truth."

"Thank you, good Ezekiel. He has brought to me certain intelligence of a vast and malignant treachery by the demon Kempis. That vile man is about to offer a universal league with all the Indians, to the intent that they might join in to extirpate the godly brethren from this region!" Never had there been such a roaring and groaning; for a moment it seemed that I heard the voices of Pandemonium. But I mastered my own fear, and commanded them, "Be still! Still!"

Accepted Lister, sitting close before me, shouted out, "Sir, these are locusts under our feet. They cannot be reasoned with. They must be trod upon!"

"I agree with you, Accepted. They are indeed vile vermin who endeavor to raise enemies against us. But be more cheerful. The high dispensations of God have given us a protection from the injuries of men, and I dare to say that His favor has rendered us almost sacred. But we must also act for ourselves. Kempis and his hellish crew are not to be repressed without a set war. Do we all assent?"

There were great cries of "Yes!" and "We do!" which were sweeter to me than all the myrrh of Hebron.

"Yet we are not so blind as to believe that even our women and boys would be able to rouse and chase them. I will go upon a journey, while there is yet time. I will travel to all the greatest towns of New England, and seek a confederacy with the other Churches of Christ. I will find the magistrates and tell them of their present danger. I will address the freemen, and the deputies who are in charge of their soldiers. I will raise an army of the Lord utterly to destroy these papists. Their arrows borrowed from the savages will lose their golden heads, their purple robes will untwine, their silken beads will slip their knots. God's people of New England will clean out that hole of Satan in our midst. The chosen race will be saved!''

Their words of ''War! War then!'' were like waves around me. One of the godly called out ''No submission!'' and another proclaimed for ''Open war!'' Thus had I prevailed.

On the following morning, upon my instruction, letters were sent by fast messenger to all the principal towns and settlements of our region. ''For the sake of the Christian world in New England,'' I wrote, ''we should all be united in a most strict and solemn confederacy.'' I suggested that we should name ourselves the United Colonies of New England, and that articles of association should be agreed and concluded within the space of one month. ''The Indian savages,'' I told the brethren of our region, ''may soon be converted by the papists into a warlike and subtle nation, and become like so many Irishmen loosed upon us. Act with all speed. Farewell.''

On the same evening, after the letters had been dispatched, it was reported to me that a comet or falling star was seen to cross the sky; it bent its blaze towards the west in the manner of a fiery pillar, and was taken as a sign portending much to the commonwealth. Certain other brethren, working to burn and clear part of the forest near New Milton, insisted to me that they heard all around them the sound of a great cannon and then the loud reports of short guns; a few moments later they heard drums in the air, passing westward, while invisible troops of horse rode among the trees and bushes of the dark wood. It is the beginning, dear Reginald, of a great change.

THIRTEEN

I took horse with Ezekiel Kuttowonck, and began our journey towards New Plymouth. It was an occasion for exhortation and good fellowship with the elder sister of all the united colonies, to raise arms and men against the horned beast of Revelation, and so I determined that the pious native should dress in English garb. It would have done your heart good, dear Reginald, to see him in plain jacket of cambric cloth, with a white band around his neck and a broad-brimmed hat upon his savage head.

My presence in these territories, my history and my reputation, were known well enough to the elders of New Plymouth. So they gathered and listened with due gravity when I spoke to them of King Ralph and his Indian army. "The Church of Christ," I told them, "was planted here eight years before any other in New England. So first I call upon you to serve under the standard of the Lord, and to muster up all your forces against the Antichrist." There was such zeal among them that I almost wept. They promised me a regiment of fifty men and sent an emissary south, to Connecticut, to implore military assistance in our common cause.

We then traveled further, to exhort the brethren of Hingham, on the seacoast; there are only eighty families worshiping here, but their town is being continually wasted by the sea, and they are therefore much regarded for their courage and endurance. There had been a dispute among them on the question of a militia election—even among the chosen are there divisions— but at my urging twelve young men agreed to serve under the Lord's banner. From Hingham we traveled a short distance to Weymouth; it was once known to Ezekiel as *Wessagusset,* he informed me, being the region where his own people were accustomed to dwell in previous times. I praised God that, where there had once been native swamps, the brethren had cultivated neat pasture and meadowland. Here, in a field nicely hedged and ditched, I exhorted the people to fight the good fight. From Weymouth we crossed the Fore River and rode into Braintree beside Mount Wollaston. "You have great store of land in tillage here," I told them. "Be sure, then, to guard yourself against the creatures which come in the night and waste it." Yet more volunteers flooded to the good old cause. We crossed the Neponset and journeyed on to Dedham, where Ezekiel described to me all of its well-watered fields and garden fruits. "You are given to husbandry here," I declared to them. "But now you must tend to the vine of Christ." After they had pledged themselves to my army, I turned to Ezekiel. "Come, good servant," I said aloud. "Now we must look to the young plants of Dorchester."

Yet as we approached it Ezekiel whispered to me that it seemed to take the form of a serpent. He observed that its main street wound its head northward towards Tompson's Island, while the houses of the brethren lay thickly in the middle like the body and wings of a beast. The tail of orchards and gardens was so long that the town could hardly have drawn it after herself. I ordered him to rein in the horses. "It cannot be," I said. "We cannot ride into the maw of the serpent's image." He understood me at once, and we changed our path towards Roxbury. I exhorted the senior brethren in that pious spot and, after very few words, persuaded them to lend me their company of soldiers. I conversed afterwards with their teaching elder, John Eliot, who is known as "the apostle of the Indians" because of his pastoral care. I sensed that he was too familiar with the savages, even as he spoke to me. "So you are sure of this conspiracy with the Indians, Mr. Milton?"

"You have experience of them, sir. You must know them to be a cruel and implacable people who would not scruple to slay us all in our beds."

"I have seen many of them come to Christ, sir."

"That is well done, Mr. Eliot, but the preponderance of them are still heathen."

"In time—"

"Time? We have no time. The danger is present and menacing."

"But where is your proof, sir?"

"Proof? My proof is my word." I bowed to him, but turned at once to Ezekiel Kuttowonck. "Come, faithful follower. We must ride on to doughty and undoubtful Boston."

I was greeted there by Outspoken Mather, who had already corresponded with me in godly and fulsome terms. We met outside the Church of Christ, and embraced with great tenderness. "You see before you, Mr. Milton, a town wonderfully changed under the Lord's guidance. Oh. Beg pardon."

"No apology, Mr. Mather. I see everything with inward sight, which is better far."

"Exquisitely spoken, if I may say so. No doubt your inward sight is like a mirror glass."

"As bright and strong as my heart, sir."

"Oh, aptly spoken again! Did you know that our great city is taken to be in the form of a heart, since it nestles between three hills?"

I reflected upon the shape of the serpent within Dorchester, together with the shape of the heart in this place, and for a moment, dear Reginald, the whole land of New England seemed to me as the painted body of an Indian. I shuddered, and shook off the devil's image. "But you have cleared away the native wilderness, I trust. You have removed any malignancy."

"Oh yes, indeed. On this paved street, where we are standing, there was once a great swamp. Where once the bears and the wolves nursed their young, now we have our pious children sporting up and down."

"All this to me, Mr. Mather, presages some sumptuous city. I thank God for it."

"That is a delightful reflection, which I shall share with the brethren next Sunday."

"But are you well defended against the savages who come in the night? Where are your garrisons and barricades?"

"Oh, Mr. Milton, as I informed you in my dispatch, we are fully prepared for feats of war. We have cannons and engines enough for any godly battle."

"You wrote to me, did you not, that you can rescue the Lord from the mouth of the lion and the paw of the bear?"

"I did indeed."

"It was well written. Woe to you, Antichrist! God guides every bullet that is shot at you!" Outspoken exuded a faint odor of faded linen which was not displeasing to me. "You know the nature of my mission, Mr. Mather?"

"Of course. The troop of Boston men, led by Captain George Hollies, is ready for your command. You know we have other regiments in this region, sir. I have arranged that bands should come from Cambridge, Sudbury, Concord, Woburn, Watertown, and other places hereabouts. They have been preparing for this moment, sir, ever since they were given arms."

"This pleases me."

"I mention Cambridge first, Mr. Milton, for you have an invitation there. You know of our college?"

"I have heard many good reports of its Christian learning."

"The men there are precious esteemed instruments, sir. Our former president became entangled in the snares of Anabaptism—"

"Oh! No more!"

"But now the college has returned to the Lord's work. The whole lump is holy."

"Well put, Mr. Mather."

"The fountains of learning have been unstopped—"

"—and the sweet waters of Shilo's streams flow forth." I knew the passage well and, if he had not spoken again, I would have ventured a commentary upon it.

"On Friday six young men proceed to be bachelors, and it was suggested that you might speak to them?" I assented, of course, and put my hands together as if in prayer. "Our college is less than thirty years old, but they have been trained in all good learning. A library has been bequeathed—''

''A library?'' It was the first reported to me in this land, and I could scarcely conceal my astonishment. ''Of what kind?''

''The founder, John Harvard, has left us two hundred and sixty volumes. Divinity, law and astronomy. We look within and without.''

''Harvard was a London man, was he not?''

Outspoken seemed to hesitate. ''His father was a butcher in Southwark.''

''Truly? Wolsey was also a butcher's son. There must be something in the meat.'' Yet my mind already wandered among books. ''This library must have grown since the time it was bequeathed to you?''

''A reverend minister, Theophilus Gale, left us a godly estate of treatises. But surely, sir, you will come?''

So it was, dear Reginald, that Ezekiel Kuttowonck lodged within a family of ''Praying Indians'' while Outspoken Mather and I took the ferry across the river to Charles Town. ''When I first came here,'' Mather informed me as we stood upon the deck, ''we used to cross in flatboats.''

I put my face to the breeze, and my heart lifted. ''The flatboats of contentment.''

''What was that, sir?''

''Nothing. I was dreaming of my youth beside the Thames.''

''Yes. Mr. Chauncy says he knew of you then.''

''How is this?''

''Oh, Mr. Milton, I was saving up this news. Charles Chauncy is the president of our college. He was once Professor of Hebrew at Cambridge University. He tells me that you were scholars there together."

"Chauncy? We will be well met, Mr. Mather, after such an interval!" This was great and welcome news for me—to meet a man of books, and an old companion, was so unexpected and delicious a surprise that I laughed aloud. "Not Hebrew alone, but Greek. How long is our journey now?"

It was not long. Soon enough I was walking upon a spacious and even green in New Town, or Cambridge as it is called now, when I savored the presence of learning. "Surely, Mr. Mather, my nose detects the library!"

"It does, sir. There is the hall of our college. There are the three houses for our fellows and students. Excuse me, I know you cannot—"

"Go on."

"Between them is our library. Oh, and here is Mr. Chauncy waiting to greet us."

"John Milton!"

"Is it you?"

We clasped hands, and then we embraced. "Well met by sunlight, John. Now you are returned to Cambridge!"

"But is it the old world or the new?"

"Both, John. It is both." Charles was ever a tall boy, and a tall man, and I sensed the familiar comfort of his companion-ship. "Come in now, and eat. You must eat!"

And so, Reginald, we sat together after our meat and talked of earlier times. He had been a blue coat of the Christ's Hospi-tal, while I had been a pigeon of Paul's, before we ever jour-neyed to Cambridge. "Do you remember the game, John? *Salve tu quoque, placet tibi mecum disputare?*"

"*Placet.*" Oh those London days, when we disputed among the wagons and the porters. "We used to meet in Cornhill."

"No, you forget. It was Bucklesbury. Where the barges were."

"Where Tom Jennings fell. Do you recall if he was drowned?"

"Unfortunately not. He became one of the King's Bench, and hanged a great many." Chauncy grew silent, and I could hear him swallowing the water from his cup. "So you come with terrible news, John. I have heard of Kempis and his crew." I had been contemplating the days of my youth, when I walked the City walls and dreamed of great deeds; at that name, I was startled into wakefulness. "Is there to be a war?"

"It cannot be averted." I was more harsh with him than I had intended. "He means to destroy or enslave us all."

"But we have our bands of soldiers. We have so many cannon he could not think of taking us."

"I tell you, Charles, he has the savages with him. He intends to raise them all in armed rebellion against us."

"It is not possible—"

"Yes!" I rose in righteous anger, and then resumed my seat. "It can be done. I have seen them. Your scholars are exempt by statute. They need not serve."

"I fear a conflagration, John, which will envelop scholars and all."

"The poisoned air of Mary Mount will be purged by burning."

"When we were young, we always spoke of peace. Do you recall how we read *Utopia*?"

"Thomas More was a papist. We must put away childish things now—"

"But to start a war in this new land!"

"I seek to start nothing. I wish merely to protect that which we have all gained. Liberty. Faith."

"I cannot believe that there is anyone in this vast land who truly intends to destroy such things."

"It is human nature, Charles. Fallen nature." I could endure this talk no more. "May I see the library now?"

"Of course. Do you know we have the first part of *Poly-Olbion,* annotated by Selden?"

"Truly? How did it make its journey across the ocean?"

"I carried it with me." He laughed. "Come." So we walked across the green from Charles Chauncy's house and, as soon as I entered the library, I sensed the presence of the books around me. It seemed to me that the words were flying about the room. I could almost hear them, dear Reginald, as they whispered to me of truth, presence and consanguinity. "John, take this."

He gave me a book, and I passed my hand across its binding before caressing its frontispiece. "I know it. *De Antiquitate Britannicae Ecclesiae.* It is Matthew Parker's work."

"Excellent."

"It was the first book to be privately printed in our realm. Where do you keep it?"

"In a cabinet filled with other rarities."

I put it to my nostrils. "Beware the beetle, Charles. I sense something strange within the leather. What else do you have for me here?" I was introduced then to many of my old and good friends, among them the *De Nuptiis et Concupiscentia* of Augustine, Cicero his *De Fato,* and the *Metamorphoses* of Ovid. There was a scholar working at a desk near to us, and I approached him. "I hear your pen upon the page, good sir. What is it? Some worthy treatise?"

"No, sir. A poem."

"A poem?"

"Young Mr. Thornton is our epic poet, John. He celebrates his country according to the sweet rules of Aristotle."

This interested me strangely. "Do you deck out its title in classical dress?"

"It is called *America,* sir. Or *Paradise Regained.* I am following the model of *The Faerie Queen.*"

"In rhyming iambics?"

"No, sir. In six books. I am using heroic verse without any rhyme."

"Very good. It is the old measure of Homer and of Virgil. May I hear a little of it?" He recited to me the opening passages of his *America;* I listened carefully, and pronounced it good.

On the following morning I spoke to those six scholars who were proceeding to their bachelorship. At the end of my oration, of course, I alluded to the occasion of my journey to them. *"Populum nostrum tyrannicide pressum, miserati (quod humanitas gratia faciunt), suis viribus Tyranni iugo et servitute liberent."* Charles Chauncy coughed, with some contagion of the throat, while the scholars of Harvard naturally remained grave and silent.

FOURTEEN

So Milton persuaded the settlers of New England to join his
great cause; within two weeks of his mission, bands of soldiers
from Salem, Boston, Ipswich, Roxbury and the other towns
were encamped in the fields beyond New Milton. From the
beginning Ralph Kempis had known of the blind man's plans; as
soon as Goosequill had heard the declaration of war in the
hurriedly gathered assembly, he had ridden secretly to Mary
Mount. Kempis could scarcely believe the news. "He suspects
me of plotting with the Indians against the other settlers? It is
madness. Nothing but madness. Why should I kill my own
kind?"

"He says that you wish to be king over all."

"Oh yes. And no doubt make all bow before horrid idols?"

"That seems to be the general plan."

"Lies and folly, Goose. Farted wind and fury." But he had
become more agitated, and started walking nervously around
the parlor of his house.

Goosequill noticed a small volume on a side-table; it was
bound in black leather, and had a metal clasp, like some bible or
missal. He walked over and took it. "Do you see this, Ralph?"

"Of course I do."

"Will you swear upon it?"

"If you wish. Why?"

"Swear an oath, Ralph Kempis, that there is not one jot or tittle of truth in any of these reports."

Kempis solemnly placed his hand upon the book. "I do so swear."

"Solemnly?"

"Very."

"Will you kiss the book, please, Ralph Kempis?" So he bent over, and touched the volume with his lips. Then he started laughing. "This is not solemn at all, Ralph."

"But it is indeed a sacred book, Goose. Look." He unlocked the metal clasp, and revealed to the young man a manual on the cure of venereal diseases. "We could do nothing without it."

That evening Kempis and his closest associates met in one of the taverns of Mary Mount. Goosequill had already alerted them that Milton planned to gather military reinforcements from the towns and villages of New England, and the tone of the discussion was accordingly somber. Goosequill was also sure that the brethren of New Milton intended to attack the papists as soon as they had sufficient numbers of soldiers. What, then, could be done? Theophilus Skelton, a pastry maker, suggested that they should leave the settlement and return to Virginia. But Kempis was vehemently opposed to any such action; he would not be oppressed by tyranny, he said, or flee like some trembling colt from these Puritan tormentors. No, they should build a fortification around Mary Mount while there was yet time. There were seven hundred men among them, including the Indians;

they had their guns and mortar pieces, while the Indians still had their deadly bows and hatchets. "It is Milton," he said, "who has disturbed our blessed peace and brought misery into these territories. He has instilled malice into thousands, but it will redound upon his own head. We may not be equal to them in number but, with Christ and His Holy Mother beside us, we will drive them away!" The matter was to be decided by general assent, English and Indian voting alike with ivory tokens, and it was eventually agreed that Mary Mount would be fortified and guarded.

Two weeks later, only a few miles away, John Milton addressed the brethren. There had been accusations that the soldiers of New England, encamped on neighboring fields, had been eating the corn and other staples of the community; the price of commodities had been driven up, and the settlers were understandably aggrieved. It was the first occasion when Milton felt obliged to assert his authority after the general call to arms, and he took it willingly. He spoke of their common pagan enemies, and of the devastation and desolation which would surely follow if Ralph Kempis were allowed "to wallow up and down." "I understand that there are some just causes for your complaints," he went on. "But do *you* understand the impious malice that transports our adversaries? Down with them! Down with them! Even to the ground!" This shamed the brethren into fresh fervor, and they began singing snatches of "The Cobbler's Silver Trumpet." "In my imagination," Milton continued, calming them with a motion of his hand, "I see a forest huge of spears, and serried shield in thick array of depth immeasurable. This is the army of Christ's soldiers marching towards its destiny!"

In the course of that day Milton declared that the settlement should be encompassed by earthworks as well as a broad trench; every point of access was then guarded by heaps of stone and by a permanent band of soldiers. Ralph Kempis had taken his own precautions. Along the bank of the river which ran close to Mary Mount he placed sharp stakes, and he protected the settlement itself with trenches and fortifications. He had also decided that the women and children would flee to the safety of the swamps at the time of any confrontation. In this interval before battle, however, he decreed that high mass should be celebrated each morning. In the same period, Milton ordained a day of solemn humiliation.

All of these preparations were soon completed and, in the final weeks of 1662 there followed some sporadic and inconclusive activity. If one party set out to forage, the other party set upon the foragers and beat them back. At dawn one morning the barns just beyond the fortifications of New Milton were discovered in flames—with the evidence that the soldiers of Ralph Kempis had caroused there all night. In retaliation the Puritan soldiers, under cover of darkness, drove spikes into the bed of the river to catch the horses of the enemy. Neither side set out in great hordes, or in close order, but in small divisions; they also made their various assaults with secrecy and speed so that, for the time being, they remained quite safe. There were skirmishes among the woods, when bullets were fired among the rocks and trees without inflicting serious injury, and on one occasion a band of Kempis's soldiers was confronted in a pea field by men from Salem and Dorchester. But there seemed a reluctance on both sides to begin hostilities, and a truce was negotiated

which allowed all of them to march away without a shot being exchanged.

Then, a week after this last encounter, the situation became
more dangerous. The "Praying Indians," and those natives who
worked as laborers in New Milton, escaped from the settlement
and made their way across the fortifications to Mary Mount.
Once they arrived in the presence of Ralph Kempis they fell
upon their knees and asked for sanctuary; they proclaimed their
hatred for the elect, and described in vivid terms their life of
labor and privation. Now they wanted vengeance upon their
former employers. *"Nickqueentouoog,"* one cried out. *"Nippau-
quanauog."* Which was to say, I will make war upon them and I
will destroy them. The others took up the refrain, *"Niss-
nissoke!"* Kill, kill them!

The clandestine departure of the Indians seemed to confirm
all of Milton's warnings, and it became generally agreed among
the brethren of New England that Ralph Kempis was indeed
planning to mount a vast insurrection against them. Military
maneuvers were intensified, while bands of troops now made
regular forays into the area around Mary Mount as if daring the
Catholics and the Indians to advance against them. A regiment
from Roxbury were the first to suffer from this strategy. At first
light they had glimpsed a party of Indians apparently fleeing
from them into the forest; the soldiers, some thirty in all,
pursued them and traveled a little distance into the forest before
realizing that they had become lost among the trees. In fact they
were in a worse predicament. They found themselves suddenly
surrounded by the natives who, taking advantage of the under-
growth, shot and killed several of the men. The soldiers fired
back among the trees without noticeable success, and so they

took up a square formation as the best possible form of defense; then they charged through the forest, shouting, and were fortunate enough to find a trail that took them back into open country. They assumed that the Indians were pursuing them, and their commander decided that they should make their way to a barn just visible on the horizon; here, at least, they could keep watch and defend themselves against further attack. The barn had once been used to store corn, and seemed solid enough to withstand assault. So they hastened towards it, and took cover.

Within an hour the Indians had once more surrounded them. The men of Roxbury fired, but drew no response. Then, a few minutes later, flaming arrows were shot through the openings in the side of the barn; the soldiers took off their shirts, and managed to extinguish the flames before any serious damage could be done. For two hours there was silence; but then, through the same openings, wooden poles were hurled; rags, dipped in burning brimstone, had been tied to them and began to smolder on the floor of the barn. They could scarcely breathe in the heat and acrid smoke, but they knew that escape would expose them to the arrows and hatchets of the enemy. They fell to their knees and began to pray out loud for the salvation of their souls; they had only just intoned "Amen" when they heard a volley of shots. It came from outside, and within seconds the sound of horses and Englishmen was all around them. These were soldiers from Lynn who, on routine patrol, had seen the smoke and flame issuing from the barn—they had ridden up quickly, firing all the time, but the Indians had retreated to the forest.

When John Milton heard of this skirmish, and of the death of six Roxbury men, he stood very still. He bowed his head and, within the hearing of those around him, murmured, "Some different blood must be drawn before this commonwealth is healthy once again." His demand was met a few days later, when two spies from the camp of Ralph Kempis were seen crossing the river in a shallow-bottomed boat. They had been noticed by a young recruit from New Plymouth who had gone hunting for squirrel—he took the precaution of hiding himself within a bush, and then ordered the men to halt when they had reached the bank. They took out their weapons and so he fired, nervously, at them; one of them dropped dead upon the ground, but the other escaped into the trees. The recruit did not try to pursue him; he was so dismayed at the sight of the body by the riverbank that he sat down beside it and wept.

Two days later one of the "Praying Indians," who had absconded from New Milton, returned. He was arrested immediately, and taken to Milton himself. "What is it, reprobate, that you can say to me now?"

"*Neenkuttannumous.*"

"Speak English. You know our tongue well enough."

"I will guide you."

"Guide me? I have no need of guides."

"To the Englishmen." He pointed in the direction of Mary Mount. "*Matwauog.* Soldiers." His meaning was clear enough and, on being questioned further, he revealed that he knew of an undefended path from which the fortifications of Mary Mount could be breached. Asked why he was willing to assist them, he affirmed his respect for his old employers as well as his love for the English god; he had left with the other Indians only after threats of punishment and torture. He was a true Christian. But this was not enough for John Milton. He took his Bible from a private drawer, and placed it in the native's hand. "You know this book well enough, I believe?"

"*Weekan.*" By which he meant "It is sweet to my taste."

"Then swear the truth of what you have said."

"I swear. True."

This satisfied the blind man, and a few days later the Indian led a party of twelve soldiers on a reconnaissance of the area around Mary Mount. He first guided them two miles downriver where, as he had reported, there was a stone footpath across the water which led to an undefended and unfortified track. They soon came in sight of the wide trench built around the settlement itself, and the guide motioned them to their position behind an outcrop of rocks in case they were observed. They did so, willingly enough, but they had just stretched out upon the ground when they were disturbed and astonished by the sound of loud laughter. Ralph Kempis was standing on the rock above them, his hands upon his hips. "So these are the soldiers of Christ! Boys, come and see." At once they were surrounded by a party of fifty or sixty men, dressed in a bewildering variety of hunting outfits, colored breeches and plumed hats. "Where do you hail from, soldiers?" The leader of the party, Ozalius Spencer, gave no reply. "Let me take a guess. Boston? Watertown? Or are you New Plymouth brethren, perhaps?"

"We are the soldiers of New England."

"Yet it is not new at all. We are at war with one another in the good old fashion."

"It was not begun by us."

"Oh, no games for boys, please. No apportioning blame. You know the truth of it."

"Our consciences are good."

"I do not ask you to look into your own conscience. I ask you to look into that of John Milton." They were all silent. "Enough. Escort them away, and keep them closely tied."

Ralph Kempis rode off alone, while they were bound in thick ropes and taken into Mary Mount. In fact he returned to that part of the river where the Indian guide (who had been working on his behalf) had led the unfortunate soldiers. He dismounted by the path, and strode over to the small footbridge of stone; he whistled softly, and waited for a reply. It came a few moments later, and two huddled figures walked up to the bridge. "Halloo ahead," Kempis whispered.

"Halloo. All well?"

"All well."

Then Goosequill and Katherine, holding the two children in their arms, crossed the bridge to the other side. Their journey had been planned for some days. As soon as Milton had declared war on Mary Mount, and begun the work of fortification, Goosequill had determined to leave New Milton. He discussed it with Katherine through the night, and finally agreed that they would stop briefly in Mary Mount for horses and provisions—before traveling westward towards new lands or new settlements. They would strike out for the interior! So on this evening, at a prearranged time, Goosequill and his family walked across the bridge into the territory of Mary Mount. It was the first day of the new year.

Milton guessed at once where they had gone. He had already learned of the Indian guide's trickery and of the capture of his soldiers; when he was told of Goosequill's disappearance, he immediately suspected his former secretary of also having some part in the ambush. Then he raged. "Consider," he said to

Seaborn Jervis, "how this filthy groom, this pot of piss, has taken your sister and your daughter."

"As well as my lovely niece, sir."

"Was it well done? Was it justly done? Oh no! By God and God's Mother I shall have him back here."

"What then, sir? What will you do to him?"

"I shall whip him so that he limps through life with no more wholesome skin than a leper."

"Not burned, sir? Or hanged?"

"You speak more piously, Mr. Jervis, and remind me of my duties. I will, of course, hang him." And, even as he spoke, he determined that the moment had come to launch his long-prepared assault against Mary Mount itself.

"The papists will be cut to pieces," he told Preserved Cotton that day. "I shall have them scorched and rolling in their own fire like the devils they are."

"They will burn in hell, too, sir."

"Oh, Preserved, they must also be burned on the earth. Do you not see it? From godly fire to everlasting flame. We cannot allow their slaughtered carcasses to pollute our good land."

On the following morning he addressed the captains of the various New England troops. "You know well," he said, "that soldiers generally conduct themselves in the manner of their commanders. So consider your righteousness before the struggle as much as your demeanor in the field itself. We know already that these savages and Jesuits fight without due order, and that they do not willingly give battle except by stealth and ambush. When we come against them, no doubt they will disperse themselves into several rambling and raging parcels like so many unkenneled wolves or mad bears. So we must circumvent them.

Come.'' They followed him to his house, where they proceeded to draw up their plans.

Three days later, at the dawn of a cold January morning, a regiment of New England soldiers marched to the river. They dragged two cannon with them, on sleds, and after due preparation they fired upon the wooden stockade that Ralph Kempis had erected. It was an easy task, but it cheered them to see fall the first of the enemy's defenses. Then they crossed the river and, chanting hymns, began their march upon Mary Mount itself. They were soon within sight of it, but there was no sound at all from the beleaguered settlement. So they continued singing ''Christ the Redeemer,'' and marched up to the edge of the wide trench which had been cut around the town. There was still no sound, and no sign of movement. Milton already knew of this ''defensive ditch,'' as he described it, and had consulted his captains in advance. If the soldiers entered the trench they would at least be safe from the muskets of Mary Mount, and from that position could then mount an effective siege. Yet this tactic would cause further delay. And Milton, who could hardly wait to begin a proper assault upon the papists, had persuaded the captains to take more direct action. So they had brought with them a large wagon filled with the trunks of felled trees; these they placed over the trench and, tying them together with stout ropes, created a makeshift but serviceable bridge. The soldiers crossed the trench in single file, expecting at every moment that shot would be fired upon them from Mary Mount. Yet there was still no noise, even as they reached its outskirts— except for the barking of a dog. The town seemed quite deserted. Captain Hollies from Boston, who led the march, now halted it at the beginning of the main street. ''Kempis!'' he called out, "Kempis!" He knew the trickery of the papists, and believed that they might be concealed in the houses and taverns. "What is it to be, Kempis? Surrender or a quick death?" There was no reply, and so he decided to taunt the enemy in hope of a response. "Do you know what they say of your popes? When the dog is dead, all his malice dies with him. Do you wish to die like a dog?"

No answer came from Mary Mount and, in his anger and frustration, Hollies ordered a general conflagration of the town to flush out any of the enemy waiting in ambush. Flaming arrows were fired into the windows of the nearby dwellings, although the main body of soldiers stayed back in case of counterattack. Half the street was soon alight. "If any remain," Hollies told his subordinates, "they will be broiled to death. But we should go amongst them, and skewer them, too." So on his order the regiment moved slowly down the burning street, putting to the torch any building that had not yet been touched by the flames; they were retching and coughing among the heat and smoke, but they continued their advance. A torch of birch wood was thrown into one of the taverns, and then a few moments later there erupted such an explosion that many soldiers were thrown upon the ground. Hollies knew at once what had happened: a store of gunpowder had been left within, waiting for the fire of New Milton. A few of his men were killed, while some were burned and bruised by the force of the blast; others were suffocating in the acrid air. Those who could still walk now ran, and made for the open fields beyond the settlement. They rushed down the main street, their uniforms singed or on fire, when again there was a loud report. But this was no explosion; the ground had given way beneath their hurrying feet, and many of them fell, screaming, into a deep hole. A trap had been set for them; a pit had been dug in the road, and then covered with canvas and dirt to conceal its position. Ralph Kempis had done his work well; he had placed a barrel of gunpowder where it would wreak most havoc, and then caught the enemy as they fled from it.

Captain Hollies looked on, bewildered. Many of the remaining soldiers tried to help their colleagues climb from the pit, but the smoke was so thick and the flames so close that they could not stay to rescue them. So they perished, screaming, as the fire covered them. Other soldiers lay dead from the explosion. The tattered remnant of the New England regiment, weak and dazed, fled from the chaos. Seventeen had been killed, and twenty wounded. So ended the first operation of this war.

There was a day of general mourning and lamentation among the brethren, but Milton refused to countenance any delay in the prosecution of the struggle. That would be interpreted as weakness or, worse, loss of belief in their righteous cause. Before he and his captains could proceed, however, they had to resolve one question. Where had Kempis and his cohorts gone? It was believed by some that they had all returned to Virginia rather than risk extermination in battle, but Milton was not of this opinion. "No," he said. "We have not lost their scent. They will have gone into the swamps with their Indian guides." His nostrils quivered. "Yes. Even the swamps are being polluted with their unclean ways."

His assumption was the right one. Ralph Kempis and his followers had retreated into the forest and marshland two miles from Mary Mount. Here, in a clearing, he entered a solemn treaty with Cutshausha, the chief of the tribe that had come into

New Milton, pleading for food, two years before. An embassy of four Indians and two Jesuits was then sent to the principal sachem of the Nipmucks in the adjacent territory, where Milton himself had once wandered; he needed no persuasion, of course, to enter a compact against the Puritan settlers. So Ralph Kempis laid plans with his native allies; he knew that the moment of true battle was approaching.

FIFTEEN

Those icebound figures that we saw upon the mountain, Mr. Lusher, brought to mind the old stories. The son of King Lud, Androgeus, is supposed to be buried within Primrose Hill. Carried one summer's day upon the shoulders of the chieftains. Cassibelan's tomb is to be discovered in a mound by Rochester Cathedral. Shall we be a fisher of men, Mr. Lusher, and dig deep down into the earth? Will we find them saved in their mortal shape, too? No. It cannot be. Remember the words of the prophet. Thy speech shall whisper out of the dust. What is that clamor outside? I am reminded of the king who, on approaching his end, had himself completely weaponed so that he might fight with death. Whence comes that weeping?

It is the beginning of the festival. The festival of dreams. Known to them as *Ononhara,* Mr. Milton. How curious that its name resembles the Greek verb "to dream," *oneirein.* Perhaps they have some common origin? Indeed not, Mr. Lusher. A thing impossible, that civilized and savage races should be so joined. What is that horrid clamor? They are beating metal dishes, and imitating the cries of wild beasts. I believe, sir, that they are expressing all the forms of madness. But what have

dreams to do with madness? Or with weeping? I laugh. Say
nothing, Mr. Lusher, our good English poets have already ventured upon that theme. I shall see with my own eyes. A young
man is writhing upon the ground before me, sighing and groaning, crying and wringing his hands. Can you writhe and wring
your hands? It seems so. His body is painted black, entire, and
the drops of ebony color are scattered across the earth. This is
hellish, Mr. Lusher. Do you see him? Yet now, listen, the man is
laughing and singing.

The noises cease at midday. Quiet. But then questions and
pleadings. What can this be, Mr. Lusher? They are moving from
dwelling to dwelling, sir, demanding the satisfaction of any secret wish that has been vouchsafed to them in their wild dreams.
Tobacco. Beads. Copper bowls. The young man with the black
paint streaked across his body like pain approaches. He lifts the
mat of my entrance. Then, humbly and graciously, he asks me
for my wooden pipe. I give it to you willingly. Here is the pipe
of your dreams. Its fumes are more light and various than the
feathers you wear. I surrender it to you in honor of Morpheus.
My dream.

SIXTEEN

Lead forth my armed saints," John Milton declared. "Lead forth my inviolable warriors against this godless enemy." Three weeks after his treaty with the Indians, Ralph Kempis had marched out of the forest at the head of his army. He knew that the commanders of the Puritan forces had discovered the location of his camp, and were likely to harass and ambush his men before mounting some general assault. In any case he was confident enough of his Indian allies, and of the quality of his own troops, to be ready for proper confrontation with the enemy. So the Catholics and natives broke their cover, marched over open country and then crossed the river that divided the two settlements. The army of New England was quickly assembled, and was even now preparing for battle on a large plain just beyond Mary Mount. "Our men fight in the cause of God," Milton was saying, "and their heroic ardor will lead to many adventurous deeds. I believe, Seaborn, that this day will prove remarkable in my life." He and Seaborn Jervis stood upon a wagon as the soldiers marched past in formation, while the Catholic forces were being marshaled in the distance.

"These papists look a barbarous and lunatic rout, Mr. Milton. I see their jewels and rosaries glittering in the sun."

"A winter sun. A token of their unnatural brightness." As he spoke, the horse and the foot, the slingers and the archers, passed them to the beat of drums.

"Oh, sir, I wish you might be able to observe our cannon. They are glorious."

"I do see them, Seaborn. In my mind's eye I see our soldiers and all our instruments of war. I see the ordered shields, I see the upright beams of rigid spears. Oh, what harmony these drums make!"

Ralph Kempis and Goosequill were talking quietly together as they rode at the front of the army from Mary Mount. Goosequill had intended to move on, further westward, but how could he abandon his friend at such a time? "I tell you this, Goose." Kempis was grave, now that a true confrontation was about to begin. "I did not seek this quarrel. It is John Milton who has disturbed the peace of our new land and brought misery to us."

"I know it. He has turned himself into a devil."

"A devil who talks piously of heaven. He grew too proud."

"No, Ralph. It was not pride." He could not find the word to express Milton's strangeness after his return from the Indians. "He grew apart. Something happened."

At this moment, Milton was execrating Kempis. "Go hence, foul thing." He had turned his face to the opposing army, and shouted into the cold wind. "Go back to your place of evil with your offspring. You cannot hope to chase us from this soil!" Of course he had not been heard, but with a smile of triumph he raised his arms in the air.

There were prayers and hymns on both sides before the commencement of the battle. Milton led his troops in a spirited version of "Christ Hath Decreed" while the priests of Mary Mount celebrated benediction in front of their own soldiers. The Indian troops fighting for Kempis remained silent during these devotions but, at the end, they spoke briefly to one another and clasped hands.

Both armies now faced each other in silence. Kempis raised his sword and shouted out, "Await the command!" Milton stood in the wagon and said, almost to himself, "They await my word to begin the slaughter. Well, it is given." He bellowed to his captains, "Go forth!" At the same moment Kempis lowered his sword and called out, "Advance!" So both armies marched towards each other with yells and oaths and cries. As soon as they were within distance they began to shoot, wildly at first. The darts and arrows were barbed with fire, but they overshot their mark with a sound like that of rain departing. Then the soldiers used their muskets, and the first to fall were the men of New England.

"I hear sweet sounds," Milton shouted to Seaborn Jervis. "Are our artillery bent against them?"

Jervis dissembled. "The papist flanks are impaled, sir. It is a mighty spectacle."

"It is always mighty when heaven and hell meet in combat."

The two armies now stood close together. There was only a narrow space between the front lines, and at once they hurled themselves against each other in a bitter engagement with neither side giving ground. Arms clashed upon arms, muskets firing, darts hissing in the air above the struggle, horses falling beneath their riders, the whole field engulfed in smoke and flame. The New England army had changed its formation in the first shock of battle; the main phalanx had been in the shape of a great square, which advanced in unison while being protected by weapons at the front and sides. Milton had earlier advised them to retain their freedom of movement, so that they could fly out, as he put it, "in rhombs, in wedges, half-moons and wings"; but inevitably the central formation had become impacted under the assault of the enemy. But they kept their ground and, as the battle raged, both sides at first swayed back and forth upon an even scale.

It seemed to Milton, standing in the wagon some way off, that the whole air was filled with fire and with cries. All seemed confusion, and darkness, and death. But in fact a pattern soon began to emerge. The back of the New England army had remained open, and Kempis suddenly ordered his horsemen to attack from the rear and break up the formation. Many of their horses were killed underneath them as they executed this movement, and some of Kempis's soldiers themselves were maimed or killed as they became part of the raging mass of men and arms. The troops of Mary Mount did indeed penetrate the phalanx, but Milton had anticipated their strategy; at a shout of command from their captains, the soldiers of New England split up into smaller squares and went on the attack. The regiments of Lynn and Plymouth were dispatched towards the Indians, who were fighting on Kempis's left flank, while the men of Boston had been instructed to ride down upon Kempis himself. In their frenzy they dashed towards him, screaming abuse, and Milton plainly heard them. "Now," he said. "Now is the time."

He raised his hand high, and waved a white linen handkerchief. His troops had been waiting for the sign—now they rolled forth their cannon, lit them, and fired. The smoke and noise terrified the Indian warriors, who were indeed the principal target; some of them were dashed to pieces in the first assault, while others fled back to the shelter of the river and forests behind. The Boston men pursuing Kempis kept on firing. He was hit in the leg, and fell, bleeding, to the side of his horse; the path of the animal could have been traced in his blood. Then his horse was killed beneath him and he rolled upon the ground but, in some extraordinary feat of will, he stood up brandishing his sword and musket. He swung wildly at the horsemen as they rode down upon him, but he was stabbed several times and fell back to the earth. Goosequill had been fighting close by and, seeing his distress, rode towards him, screaming. One soldier turned his fire upon him: he was hit in the shoulder, but still he galloped forward with his drawn sword in his other hand. His fury and self-possession were such that he alarmed the New England men; four other soldiers from Mary Mount were alerted by his actions and, together, they kept the enemy at bay while he took up Kempis upon his horse. The news soon came that Kempis had fallen, even as the battle continued, and Milton clapped his hands. "Tell me that they cry out to the Virgin in doleful prayer."

"They do, sir. But many are expired."

"Fill up a great ditch with their carcasses. It will be a sweet sacrifice."

Seaborn Jervis had already been told that one of the dead from Mary Mount had been found with a leather pouch about his neck. The soldiers thought that it might contain some great jewel but, when they ripped it from him and cut it open, they found a printed paper of indulgences. Jervis told Milton of this, and he laughed out loud. "Oh, Mr. Jervis, butcher them. They deserve no less."

The soldiers of New England had begun a second concerted assault; but, with Kempis down and gone, most of the regiments of Mary Mount seemed to lose appetite for any further battle. So the brethren put them to flight and, in particular, pursued the remaining Indian warriors, burning and laying waste to their fallen bodies on the field. The battle degenerated into small frays and fights, with some of the men from Mary Mount putting up resistance while others fled to the woods and swamps. The New England troops did not to pursue them, since they knew the dangers of ambush in that terrain; instead they turned back and made their way slowly between the wounded and the dying on the battlefield. They killed the Indians with their swords or muskets, but three barber-surgeons tended the wounds of the Englishmen from Mary Mount. Milton himself was exultant. "They are fallen!" he cried out. "They are all fallen!"

Ralph Kempis was carried in mourning through the darkest part of the forest to a secret encampment which the Indians had built. His corpse was covered by deer hides and bark; he was borne upon a stretcher of bear skin, to the sound of continual lamentation. Goosequill, wounded by the bullet in his left shoulder, was assisted by two young Indians who carried him gently between them; he swayed from side to side, and sometimes fainted in their arms. So the warriors of Mary Mount made their retreat.

Katherine had been waiting with the other wives and children. They had heard the sounds of the battle, the firing and the shrieking, but none of them had spoken. They simply looked at each other, and soothed the children. But as soon as Katherine caught sight of Goosequill being carried back, she screamed out loud and ran over to him. He said nothing, and seemed scarcely to recognize her.

The body of Ralph Kempis was laid with great ceremony upon a mat woven with green and purple thread. The Indians from Virginia, who had been with him for so many years, wished to bury him in the manner of their *weroans,* or great lords, but the surviving Jesuit priest (his colleague had died in the battle) insisted upon the Catholic ceremony of the dead. The requiem mass was held beneath the trees with the remaining soldiers, some of them still dressed in their military gear, acting as altar servers. The Indians sat upon the ground and lamented; they had taken the dish from which Kempis had eaten his last meal, and the coat of skin he had used as a bedcover, and hung them upon a tree close to the site chosen for his grave. When the body was lowered into the earth, they set up a second great lamentation which lasted until nightfall.

Goosequill heard them as he lay in a fever. He had been carried to a small covered enclosure, made out of deerskins and branches, where Katherine sat beside him throughout that day and night. His wound was deep, and had not begun to heal despite the attentions of the powwow; there were some men, the wizard said in his native dialect to those around him, who had no choice but to die. Katherine had not understood this, but there was one word that she recognized—*chachewunnea,* which is to say, dying. In his delirium Goosequill had begun to talk wildly. "Any to spare?" he whispered. "Not even a little piece of that cheese, good sir?" Then he said that he was walking among wide streets, and bright buildings which reached up to the roof of the sky. "I am a poor boy indeed." Katherine sat beside him, using a fan of leaves to cool him and occasionally putting a bowl of water to his lips; she tried to comfort him in his wanderings, but she knew that he had traveled too far from her to be called back. He died on the following morning. She had slept for a while next to his pallet, but was woken by the powwow who pointed to him and said gently, *michemeshawi*. He is gone forever.

SEVENTEEN

It is time for the feast. The feast of dreams. Where am I to be seated at this banquet, Mr. Lusher? Here, sir, within the row of Indian men. The women sit on the side opposite to us, do they? Kettles of sea fish and dishes of berries are placed between. Corn and beans. A mash of fish and flesh. The drink, sir, is known as *isquout*. It is a distilled spirit mixed with certain herbs. It is very powerful. It is very fragrant also, Mr. Lusher. It has a sweet taste, and is nothing like our strong water. I drink it down, and ask for more. My bowl is filled and filled again. I am merry, mistress, now that I can see again.

Falling to the ground. Oh, can it be? I rise to my feet and sit again, drinking off the rest of the bowl. So delightful. Well, mistress, are you smiling? She is wearing a small red cap upon her head, and an apron of deerskin covers her from navel to thighs. Bare breasts. Lustrous and sweet. You exhale a heady odor, my dear. It is as if all the incense of Araby were burning. What shining hair. You put up your hand to hide your gay laughter, do you? I am laughing. Oh you fair defect of nature, may I sit beside you? May I converse with you upon the Song of Solomon? There. I need only to steady myself. Where is my bowl of sweet water? Bring my sweet water. More like some goddess than a mortal creature. You are some virgin majesty, no doubt. May I rest my head upon your shoulder? Only for a moment. What white teeth. I wager that you draw hearts into your net, you sorceress. May I touch your leg? How coy you are.

The red cap upon her head, Mr. Milton, is an emblem of her virginity. On the feast of dreams she gives herself in marriage to the first man who proposes to her. Have a care, sir. Come away. Oh you touch me, do you? And then point towards yourself? What is this motion of your fingers, entwining two of them? Oh, lewd gesture. May I kiss your neck? You are a lustful strumpet, mistress. Now may I kiss your lips? Mix sweet water for me. Do you also care to mix soul with soul, or flesh with flesh? Mr. Milton, sir, you may go too far. Take care. Leave her. Give me unchaste looks and foul talk, do. I beg of you. Sir, this is a part of their marriage ceremony. Marriage? Who is to be married? It is their custom here, Mr. Milton. Well, dear Eleazer, they say that marriage and hanging come by destiny. Better to be hanged for a spring lamb than a shire horse. Is that not so, my dearest? My concubine. Go back and sleep, sir. Sleep? What has night to do with sleep?

John Milton is dreaming. Eden. Paradise. He is reaching out to touch the fruit that is the cause of all his woe. He awakes. My head aches terribly. He flings out his arm in distress, and he touches someone beside him. Who is here? A woman is lying with him. What is this? What horror is this? The young Indian woman smiles at him tenderly. I awake, and my soul is empty. I have some memory of your face. No. Oh no. This cannot be. You are naked. Why are you naked? She puts her hand upon his thigh, and he realizes that he is naked also. He turns away, and vomits upon the floor. It has a sweet odor. He vomits again. She is whispering to me in her language. No. Evil. You are evil. She wishes to console him, and strokes his back. No. Foul concupiscence. Go. Leave me. He knocks her to the floor. Hyena! She rises, trembling, from the rush mat they had shared that night. He is hunched over, whispering to himself. Heat. Motions. Cattle. Venom. Wailing, she leaves him. Excrement. Incubus.

He is alone now, but he dare not move from the mat. There is someone watching me. Their eyes are upon me. There is a movement behind me. Where shall I run? Where can I hide from this wrath? Mr. Milton. Be still. Compose yourself. You are trembling, sir. Here. Cover yourself with this cloak. Oh Eleazer, Eleazer. I am a swamp. I am a maze. He is crying. Trembling still. I am a tainted thing. No, sir. Sick. You are unwell from the drink they gave to you. Poison? Poison to you, at least. You drank too much of it. Drugs, Eleazer, some Indian concoction. I have been the victim of some magician's hellish arts. Otherwise, how could it be possible? He looks down upon the mat of rushes, and sees the virgin's blood spilled upon it. Evil. Evil done. I am undone.

Who is calling to me? *Kukkita!* It is the sachem, his voice rising in anger. Go out to him, Eleazer. Plead for me. *Kukkakittous.* Lusher will listen very humbly. The man *keen* Milton has committed an act of dishonor. He must marry this woman, or leave us at once. He could have been killed, but he will be spared because of his age and learning. *Kunnanaumpasummish.* Thank you. I apologize on his behalf. I will lead him from you. Mr. Milton, sir, we must leave this place. Oh God, I go willingly enough. Where are my shirt and breeches? No. No cloak of fur. English garb only. I had a carbon pencil, did I not? Ah there, on the ground. He bends down to retrieve it, when he feels a sudden lightness in his head. He passes his hand across his eyes. What is it, Mr. Milton? Nothing. Nothing at all. Unless it be the poison they made me drink. Lead on, Eleazer. I am prepared.

The sachem waits, his arms folded, as Milton comes out. *Cumusquauna mick qun manit!* What does he say to me? God is angry with you. I know it. I feel it. I am in hell even as I live. He bows his head. He does not look up until he reaches the margin of the forest. He looks back then at the brightly colored tents, and the great mountain, and he sighs. He goes among the shadows of the trees with Eleazer Lusher.

This is an old track, sir. We will find our way safely. Eleazer, Eleazer. Nothing can be told of this. Nothing must be told of this. On my oath, sir. I will be silent always. Eleazer, I have fallen.

Fallen. He has tripped against the roots of a tree, and has fallen heavily to the ground. He lies still, among the earth and leaves, and then raises his head. He looks around. No. It cannot be. In the name of God, no! Mr. Milton, what is it? Why are you weeping? It has returned. I am returned. Sir? I am plunged in night and darkness. God in heaven, what is this? Eleazer, I am stark blind again. I cannot see. Oh God, sir, please, no. Let me help you to your feet. Dark. Dark. Dark. Dark still.

This is the end. The is the beginning of all our woe. The blind man wandered ahead and, weeping, through the dark wood took his solitary way.